Returned

DELTA FAMILY ROMANCES #9

CAMI CHECKETTS

Birch River
PUBLISHING

Free Book

Receive a free copy of *Seeking Mr. Debonair: The Jane Austen Pact* at https://dl.bookfunnel.com/38lc5oht7r and signing up for Cami's newsletter.

Chapter One

Six Weeks Previous

Kelsey James held her son Mo tightly in her arms as they waited for the beautiful mid-August wedding of Thor Delta and Shelly Vance to begin. Part of the reason she clutched him so tight was because Mo was itching to run around and bouncing impatiently on her lap. The instant he saw Shelly and her brother Klein walk down the aisle, he would want to throw himself at them. Kelsey was one of the in-home nurses for Klein and Shelly's Granny Vance. Klein, Shelly, Thor, and Granny were so loving, Mo assumed he was part of the family. Thor didn't know Mo was his nephew. Unless she was mistaken, the people who knew the truth about Mo's father was a very short list.

The other reason she held her boy tightly was to calm her own nerves. Mo's father was standing less than twenty feet in front of them. Kelsey's stomach flip-flopped, and her palms were sweating.

She wished she could blame the tachycardia and diaphoresis on the stress of hoping nobody connected the dots of who Mo's dad really was. She'd been hiding that truth for four years now and she wasn't about to spill it at this huge and beautiful wedding and ruin the day for all the Deltas.

Though she wouldn't mind ruining Hudson Delta's day. It ticked her off that she still wasn't immune to the charming, funny, heartbreaking daredevil. She was terrified that she never would be. The daily reminders of Hudson with her adorable, impetuous son who shared his father's blue eyes, delightful personality, and no-fear attitude made it impossible to forget how much she'd once loved Hudson. Her "Brave." She hadn't said that nickname aloud in a long time. Tried not to even think about how he'd rescued her from the rattlesnake she'd almost stepped on, plucking her off the ground and swinging her to safety and then springing into a tree like Tarzan as he barely missed being struck by the rattler.

She'd called him Brave after that. Her Brave Hero. Not anymore. Now his nickname on social media was Death Wish Delta. Fitting, she supposed, as he risked his life every day with his stunts. She tried to be strong and avoid looking at anything about him on social media—the women, the over-confident eyebrow pump he had once claimed he only did for her, the crazy stunts that might kill him. She hated all of it. Unfortunately, she worked for Klein and Shelly, who were both marrying Deltas and occasionally proudly showed her something Hudson was doing.

Why did he have to be so handsome and appealing? He stood next to his brothers and cousin in a dark gray suit and pale blue tie. His dark hair was perfectly mussed. His blue eyes sparkled like he had a funny secret he wanted to share with everyone; he used to share them all with her. Not anymore. His far-too-delicious lips were turned up in his patented smirk. A shadow of a dark beard covered his cheeks and jawline and made him look older and even more handsome than the last time she'd seen him in person. Four years ago.

She tried to focus on the beautiful scenery—the green sweep of grass down to the gorgeous, calm blue lake, the thick trees and mountains surrounding them. The sun was sinking in the west, streaking the clouds with pink and orange. It was beautiful.

Her gaze dragged back to Hudson without her permission. She sighed. Nothing was as beautiful as Hudson's face.

She occasionally let herself Google him, but it hurt. Not only seeing him with a variety of other women, but how she ached to be the one he was laughing with, holding tight, and whispering his funny comments to.

They'd loved each other desperately in high school, but they'd mutually decided to go their separate ways to pursue their dreams. Of course, they would weather a long-distance relationship and have their happily ever after. They adored each other. He swore he would come back for her when he got himself established and she was through school. He'd be an extreme athlete sensation by then and she'd be a registered nurse. They'd travel the world together. She would doctor up his injuries and help people wherever they went.

It had sounded like the perfect plan, but it would have been a long time coming. She'd thought it would break her heart to be apart from him, and it had. They'd kept in touch with Zoom calls and Snapchats and they were both busy, so somehow she had made it through each day.

Shortly after he'd started his extreme sports career and was getting more followers and attention, she'd seen a picture of him on social media kissing a beautiful redhead. Of course it had made her sick, and she'd called him immediately. He'd promised the girl had planted one on him and he'd pushed her away, but someone had captured the brief contact on camera and posted it. He begged her to trust him and not to look at social media as things were often skewed, only a piece of the real story.

She'd trusted him. She hadn't looked.

The summer after her sophomore year, she was home helping her mom in the ice cream shop and he'd surprised her and his family with a visit. She could still picture the scene, better than any movie, of seeing him outside the glass windows of the ice cream shop, screaming and running to him, him sweeping her off her feet, swinging her around, and giving her the kiss to end all kisses. She'd been crazy in love.

That first night back together had felt like a dream. It had been incredible. Each touch had been magical and intense and ... they'd both let any self-control slip.

She had made things right with her Savior, but she could never find it in her to regret the enchanted, powerful moments together and the perfect result—Mo.

Hudson had been remorseful the moment they separated. He'd taken her home very early in the morning with one last, lingering kiss, and then he'd disappeared. She'd received a short text explaining that he blamed himself, prayed she could someday forgive him, and he'd come back when he learned perfect self-control. She texted back that she didn't blame him, that she loved him and she was just as much to blame for not stopping as he was. He claimed it was all on him and he was going to become stronger than ever and be the man she deserved.

It was so like him to take the high road and also to be so passionate and unwavering about it. He would fix this; he would be the one to learn the self-control of Buddha; he would be the one to keep her safe and happy. She admired that about him.

Until she didn't hear from him for months. He paused his career and went off the grid searching for self-control. Her texts got a heart emoji and her phone calls a quick, *I'm almost there* text back. It was frustrating. She needed *him*, not Superman. She hated the distance between them, and she was an emotional mess. She lost weight, was often sick to her stomach, and her mom fretted over her every time she went home for a weekend.

Kelsey had never had regular periods, so when she realized she was expecting more than three months after that night with Hudson, it had been a shock. At least it explained her nausea and out or control emotions. She was in a panic and at school in Boulder when the test she had taken out of curiosity came back positive.

Her mom drove the three hours to be with her, let her cry, and try to talk it out. She had no idea what she should do. How to go forward with her life. She had her CNA and a decent job at a nursing home, but she couldn't provide for herself and her baby and somehow get through the RN program.

Would all her dreams disappear? Her mom would help all she could, but she didn't have much extra money running the ice cream shop.

At least she'd had Hudson, and no reason to doubt she could trust in him. He would come for her, and their baby would be amazing. They'd be a family. No matter how it changed their life plan. Those few months had been weird with the self-control passion and never hearing from him, but she'd never doubted he loved her and knew he was finding self-control mastery to be the man he thought she deserved. She knew how deeply honorable and good he was.

Her Brave would somehow make it all right, and their life together with the incredible human she was carrying inside her could begin. She already loved her baby, and she adored his father. She always teased Hudson about his charmed life and his magical powers, but he'd always used both to take care of her, protect her from snakes and anything else that threatened her, and treat her like a princess. With Hudson by her side, she could make it through school and being a twenty-year-old mom. Of course he'd come home and marry her. There was no other option. Even with him not calling or texting for months, she knew he still loved her. A Delta man would never ditch her or their child.

She tried to call a few times. Finally, some girl had answered his phone, sounding very annoyed. She said he wasn't there and she didn't know when he'd be back. That was confusing and hurtful. He'd claimed he wasn't calling her so he could become the strong man she deserved, but some girl had his phone?

When she heard that girl's voice on his phone, she had to wonder ... was it the redhead or some other in-love-with-him groupie? If he was off the grid learning self mastery, why would some girl have his phone? She'd kept her promise of not looking at social media, but since he'd gone off the grid, there'd been no reason to look as he wouldn't have been posting anything new.

When she heard that girl's voice on his phone, she knew she had to look. She let herself Google him. It was a complete shock, and worse than she'd imagined. Lots of women cheering on his every stunt and even some of beautiful girls posing with him in lots of different locations throughout the world.

Self-mastery? Off the grid? What a liar! Her Hudson ... a liar. She would never have believed it possible, but maybe a life of fame had changed him.

Her heart broke in two, but even then, she couldn't give up on him. She sent him an abrupt text that she was pregnant and she needed to see him as soon as he could break away from his busy schedule.

He never texted back, and she hadn't seen him since. It was still shocking sometimes that her Brave had ditched her. She'd wake up in the night thinking they were still together, then it would hit her like a sledgehammer.

She thought she'd been heartbroken initially. It had grown into a hollow ball in her chest, filled alternately with pain, confusion, sadness, and anger. Four long, lonely, heartbreaking years. But she had Mo, and that was all that mattered. Their son was a delight to everyone around him, but especially to her. He kept her laughing and happy.

It was Hudson who was missing out. She had to harden her heart and not care about him. Maybe someday she'd be able to feel compassion for him with his shallow lifestyle, death wishes, and not knowing and loving Mo. Even after four years without him, the anger and pain were still too strong to feel any sort of pity or compassion.

"Mama, too tight," Mo whispered loudly.

A few people turned to smile at her three-and-a-half-year-old son. He was a crowd favorite wherever he went. Big surprise that he was irresistible, just like his father. She was sometimes stunned that no one besides Hudson's sweetheart of a mom, Myrna, had ever directly confronted her about who Mo's father was. Before Kelsey would answer Myrna's inquiry, she'd asked if Hudson had claimed he was Mo's dad. Myrna had admitted that no, he hadn't. Kelsey's heart had broken a little more and she'd lied to the angelic woman. She wasn't proud of it, but if Hudson didn't want her and Mo and if he wouldn't come to her on her own, she refused to use his mom to force him into being responsible. She didn't want to be his responsibility. She wanted his love. For her and for their incredible son.

Myrna was adorable with Mo. Her eyes lit up whenever she saw him, and she took every opportunity to talk to him and give him hugs. Kelsey had found gifts for Mo and cash hidden in her piece of junk car on various occasions. Myrna either still believed Hudson was the dad, or she was just that sweet and kind. The rest of the Delta family was just as friendly and welcoming with her and Mo. She had no clue what they believed about Mo's father, but she would not be the one to tell them the truth. That was on the famous, death-defying, jerk-bait Hudson.

Death Wish Delta.

She hated that name. The only thing worse than him being absentee would be him killing himself for fame. The stupid slight chance she hid in her heart of him knowing Mo would forever be extinguished.

"Sorry." She relaxed her hold on her boy slightly.

The bridesmaids were sauntering down the aisle. Delta women and future in-laws, all looking beautiful in fitted, silky pale blue dresses.

She shouldn't have done it, but she let her gaze slide to Hudson while everyone else focused on the line of women walking up the aisle.

He must've sensed her stare, because his blue eyes swiveled to hers and stopped. His eyes filled with warmth and longing. Kelsey couldn't catch a full breath as she was caught in his gaze like a gazelle being focused in on by a lion. The lion seemed playful and powerful and enticing, but in reality, he was deadly and dangerous and sneaky. Hudson could rip her apart faster than any predator, but he didn't seem to want to track her down. He'd never come after her in the four years since she'd told him she was pregnant. If someone would've claimed her beloved, fun-loving, yet honorable Brave, the indisputable love of her life, would ditch her and his own son four years ago, she would've ranted, raved, and probably hit something.

But here she was. A single mom deserted by the man she'd loved and who she'd thought loved her back.

The wedding march started and Kelsey stood, cradling Mo in her arms. He was almost forty pounds and off the charts in height for his age. He would be tall and strong like his daddy. Her son would definitely prefer standing on his own, but she could hold him for long enough to prevent him from running to the bride for hugs, begging the groom to "throw him," and effectively interrupting the gorgeous ceremony. She knew Shelly and Thor would roll with it, but Kelsey wouldn't mess up her friends' day. No matter what.

The problem was, with Hudson looking at her with such longing, she wanted to hand Mo to her mom, push the happy couple out of the way, and fling herself into Hudson's arms. It had been so long since she'd felt the excitement and safety of those strong arms.

Hudson's gaze shifted to their son. His face tightened, his brow furrowed, and his blue eyes filled with ... concern. Anger made her neck hot, and any thoughts of forgiveness and reconnecting disappeared. How dare he look at their son like that? Like he was worried about him. *If* he actually cared and was worried about Mo and how she was raising their son, he should've gotten his backside home and stepped up to take care of him and be part of Mo's life.

She was doing just fine on her own. Mo was charming, hilarious, smart, cute, and everybody loved him. Everybody except the one person who should. What a jerk.

Obviously, the Hudson she'd known and loved no longer existed. The Hudson standing in that line of perfect Delta men didn't deserve his spot there or his surname. The Delta family was honorable and incredible and she admired them as much as any family she knew. She wanted to scream to the entire crowd of family and friends that Mo was Hudson's son and the selfish playboy had deserted his own flesh and blood to pursue his extreme-sports career and have a different woman in his arms every night. Her stomach rolled at the thought of him with other women, but she couldn't deny the truth.

Pastor Sam asked everyone to be seated. Kelsey was seeing red and hoped she could get through today without making a scene. She cradled Mo close, love and protection for her boy surging through her. She'd make sure Mo never knew who his traitor of a father was. She'd raise her son up right and give him all the love of a mother and a father. Maybe someday Kelsey could meet someone she could love and who could be an example to Mo and adore him, his cute antics, and his innocent and fun personality, like his own father should have.

She made the mistake of glancing at Hudson again. His eyes were focused on her. She glared at him as fiercely as she could before focusing her attention on the bride and groom. How dare he not love Mo? She guessed the concerned look in his eyes made sense; he was worried about how his son was doing. But he had no right to worry when he'd been the one to desert them. Besides, his blue eyes should sparkle when he saw their boy. He should be the one making a scene, pushing people out of the way to get to her and their son and make up for all the time he had missed. Her heart was pounding so hard she feared her mom would notice, and her anger multiplied with every passing moment.

Kelsey, and most people who knew her, would claim she was even-tempered and wouldn't squash a spider. It was a pillar of her life to use her meager nursing skills to heal and do no harm. However, if Hudson Delta dared approach her tonight ... Ooh! She'd do all she could to squash him emotionally and maybe she'd even punch him too. Yeah, that sounded good. She'd slug him in those perfect abs that he seemed to like to show off to the world. She'd hit him hard and try to hurt him. It wouldn't make up for the pain and neglect of the past four years and he deserved much worse, but what else could she do? Write a negative review on his YouTube page? Tell beautiful women to steer clear of him? She wondered how many other children he'd fathered around the world. She wanted to puke. She could do nothing to warn other women away. Hudson was irresistible. None of his adoring female fans would listen to her. They'd look at her as the jealous ex that he'd dumped. Nothing she did would matter to him, or hurt him like he'd hurt her.

She prayed inside to somehow let the pain and anger go. She'd been down that road far too many times and it only made her bitter and not able to be the fun and involved mom, and the example of God's love she wanted to be for Mo. But couldn't she just hit Hudson? Just once? It sounded fabulous, but heaven obviously wouldn't approve.

The good Lord would have to get her through this wedding and the dinner without resorting to violence. Even if she punched Hudson, he was so strong-looking it probably wouldn't hurt him. She focused on not looking at him. It took all her self-control. If she could only get through the ceremony and the dinner, she could slip away before the dancing started. Mo would need to get into bed. He'd prefer to stay and become the center of attention like his dad used to be. Hudson and Mo both had dance moves the likes of which she could never copy. Hudson could take the entertainer role tonight like he'd done at every dance and party they'd ever been to together. She used to love watching him and of course he'd always made her part of the show and made her shine.

She didn't want to be around to see him shine, probably with some other woman. Ugh!

The one guarantee she had was that Hudson would disappear

by morning. Then she and Mo could go back to their settled, happy life.

There were only a few things she could count on with Hudson Delta. He was an expert at extreme stunts, and he could easily charm every woman he set his blue eyes on. But he was even more reliable at disappearing quick and never looking back to see what he was missing.

Chapter Two

Hudson was sweating in the monkey suit Thor had forced him to wear for his wedding. He didn't blame Thor. If the woman Hudson had loved his entire life, like Thor had loved Shelly, agreed to marry him, he'd jump over any obstacle and force his brothers to strut in front of the wedding party in Speedos if that's what his bride wanted.

He discreetly dabbed at his forehead. Even though it was August, it wasn't hot outside. The temperature was at least twenty degrees cooler than his last filming location in the Dominican Republic and there was practically zero humidity in Colorado. The reason he was sweating was the gorgeous, out-of-reach love of *his* life sitting less than twenty feet away.

Kelsey looked more beautiful than even his visions of her. She was wearing an off-white fitted dress that set off her tanned skin and her beautiful shape. Her facial features were a little more defined and her curves a little more generous than the last time he'd seen her. Almost four years ago, to be exact. Motherhood looked incredible on her. If only it wasn't the reason they were apart.

He snuck another look and his stomach did a happy flip flop. Meeting Kelsey's gaze was more exciting than swooping through a twisted and dangerous mountain forest in a wingsuit. It seemed like every time he glanced her way, she was staring at him. He kept lying to himself and thinking the looks were full of longing, remembrance, and love.

Then her little boy would squirm around and luckily that would break Hudson's concentration on her and throw him back to the stark reality that Kelsey didn't love him, had gotten pregnant with another man's baby while Hudson was living like a monk trying to learn self-control and be worthy of her, and Hudson had no right to be staring longingly at her.

Where was Jason, anyway? Hudson gritted his teeth just thinking about his backstabbing friend. He assumed Jason and Kelsey would be happily married with another baby on the way by now. He didn't ask for news from home and luckily his family had slowly learned not to spew that information to him when they chatted. When they tried to talk about anything besides his family, he changed the subject quick.

But was she married or not? Had she not ended up with Jason?

Jason Spackman had been one of Hudson's close friends in high school. The guy had always teased and flirted with Kelsey. Hudson had tried to be chill about it. After all, Kelsey loved Hudson desperately. Or so he thought.

He focused on Thor and Shelly. They were both beaming—

the perfect cowboy couple. Shelly even had cowboy boots on with her wedding dress. Hudson was ecstatic for them. He missed his family with an ache that was almost as bad as how much he missed Kelsey. None of them knew or understood why he rarely came home and when he did, he only stayed for a short time and never went anywhere near church or town where he might run into Jason or ... her. Just his luck, Kelsey was Shelly's Granny's in-home nurse and had been invited to the wedding. He glanced around at the huge crowd, realizing it wouldn't have mattered if there was any connection. The entire population of Summit Valley, and he was guessing some surrounding areas as well, had been invited.

He tugged at his sleeves and tried to focus. He didn't want to miss out on any of his short-lived family time. It wasn't right to let *her* distract him and not enjoy the few hours he'd be here. His mom would happily spend that time hugging him. He let her, knowing how much she missed him and how she probably stayed up at nights wondering why he'd distanced himself from all of them and worrying he was going to kill himself with one of his stunts. He tried to keep in touch, but his career was insane. He traveled nonstop, and it was easier to avoid any mention of Kelsey and break his heart over and over again if he didn't call or Face-Time very often. His Sunshine, who wasn't his at all. Not anymore.

He'd loved Kelsey for as long as he could remember noticing there was a difference between boys and girls. It had been torture to go their separate ways after they graduated, but it had been a mutual decision. He'd been young, impulsive, and driven enough to think his dream of being an extreme sports sensation was the most important goal of the moment. He'd reasoned that once he was successful and Kelsey was through college, destined to be the smartest and most caring nurse ever, they'd get married and travel together. She could bandage up all his wounds and provide health care to locals in the different impoverished areas he visited. It would be ideal.

If only he hadn't lost all control that one night when he'd come home to visit over four years ago. It had been too long since he'd held her, touched her, and kissed her. Every touch had always felt like heaven with Kelsey. That night, each touch had been a heat and happiness he couldn't get enough of. He'd sped past the boundaries they'd set for themselves. As a God-fearing Christian who believed in moral cleanliness, he never should've let himself ignore those hard and fast rules.

It was conflicting to regret the most beautiful moments of his life, but he blamed himself for taking Kelsey's innocence and not waiting for marriage like he'd vowed to himself, God, his parents, and most importantly, her.

Rather than face the heart-wrenching fact that he'd stolen his Sunshine's innocence and cheapened their love, he'd taken off, begged Kelsey's forgiveness through text, and told her he'd come back when he gained perfect self-control.

Luckily, he'd made it a habit to record extra videos and scenes with fans every chance he got, so he was able to put a close friend in charge of posting regularly and responding to comments for him. It was a lot less frequent than normal, but he didn't lose too much momentum as he went on a three-month-long quest to control his passions and become the man Kelsey deserved.

He'd spent the time praying and studying the good word in some of the most picturesque and serene spots on earth. He'd talked to pastors, preachers, teachers, and holy men. He'd learned to be an expert at meditation and had also improved the fighting skills taught to him from youth on up with tai chi, kickboxing, capoeira, and judo, which all focused on mind and body being in control. He spent his last two weeks without his phone or any kind of outside interference, praying and only partaking of bread and water at some retreat in the mountains of Peru.

After more than three months, he remembered feeling confident and ready to see Kelsey again. He believed he could be moral and respectful of her. He flew to the friend who had his phone in Kauai and was shocked by the fateful, week-old text.

I'm pregnant. I need you to come as soon as you can fit it into your busy schedule.

It was a punch in the gut and the most excited he'd ever been. He'd jumped on a shuttle plane to the closest international airport in Honolulu and traveled to Colorado as fast as he could.

He was going to be a father. It was so surreal, so exciting. It was going to turn his world upside down and he was stoked about it. He wanted to call or text her, but that felt hollow and anticlimactic. He had to see her in person, swing her around in ecstatic happiness, tell her how he loved her and their future child, and then make plans for their wedding. Everything would work out with their careers and their plans. Somehow. With all his mind-body studying, he should've been more worried about the details, but his impetuousness took over and he let his excitement grow.

Throughout the long hours of travel, weird doubts occasionally popped into his frenzied brain as he studied her text. *I'm pregnant.* Why hadn't she said ... *with our baby?* He'd shove those thoughts away and think how insane it was of him to doubt his angelic beauty. The only Sunshine he would ever need or want. Though they were apart, they didn't date other people. She trusted him no matter what women posted on social media and he trusted her no matter how he knew men would chase her because of her sweet, fun personality and gorgeous face and body. No way would she hook up with some guy. Not possible.

Yet what if after they'd had been intimate and he'd left to get his head on straight, she'd turned to other men? He hadn't let himself talk to her as penance, and to make sure he was worthy of her. What if the separation had been too hard on her? What if she'd found solace in another man's arms in his absence? What if …

All the sneaky thoughts accumulated, pushed out the excitement, and pounded through his head until he was ready to explode from the stress and the unanswered questions.

It seemed three months of mind-body connection had failed him because he couldn't calm down for a second. If any of his worries were a reality, it would be on him for not just picking up the phone when he got her texts or phone calls, or reaching out to her over the past few months. He should've at least filled her apartment with flowers, candy, and presents every week of the induced separation so she knew how much he still adored her.

He got to her off-campus apartment in Boulder a little before ten p.m. There was a balcony and her apartment was on the second story. As he jogged through the parking lot, he saw a couple out front of her apartment door, embracing. He paused, not wanting to run up the steps and embarrass one of her roommates and the woman's date or boyfriend.

The woman was clinging to the man, her head buried in his chest. It looked like she was crying. Ah, that was too bad. He wasn't trying to openly stare, but he was impatient for them to move so he could get into that apartment and hold his own love. As he kept looking back at them, he saw the guy's face under the porch light. Jason Spackman. His old high school buddy. He knew Jason was at school at the University of Colorado in Boulder like Kelsey, but hadn't known they'd stayed in touch. Was Jason dating one of Kelsey's roommates?

As he'd waited, the woman raised her head for the first time. Hudson could only stare at her beautiful, tear-stained face. Kelsey. Sunshine. Jason was holding his Kelsey. Despite the months of mind-body mastery, Hudson was still impulsive and often acted before he thought, but at that moment he'd felt frozen. He'd wanted to storm up those steps, hit Jason, rip Kelsey from his arms, and hold her close for a long, long time. He should be the one comforting his girl. Helping her through the tears and anything life threw her way.

But maybe not.

His mind pinged different directions, and that text was at the forefront. *I'm pregnant.* Why wouldn't she have said *with our child*? Or *We're pregnant*? Or *We're gonna have a baby*? What if Jason had stepped in while Hudson was gone and Jason was the father?

It had been three and a half months since their impassioned and incredible night together. How long did it take a woman to know she was pregnant? His sister Esther was more private, but his cousin Maddie used to complain about her monthly cramps loudly. Most women had their cycle every month, so Kelsey should have known a lot quicker than three and a half months if she was expecting his child.

So it wasn't his child?

No, no, no! This couldn't be happening.

Hudson had to turn away so he wouldn't pulverize the father of his girlfriend's baby. How twisted was that? How could Kelsey do this to him? Yet he could easily pin this on himself. He was the one who'd been off traveling the world. He was the one who'd stolen Kelsey's innocence in the first place. He was the one who'd turned inward to learn self-mastery when maybe he should've forgotten self-control and asked her to marry him that night.

Another horrific thought hit him. What if that night hadn't been Kelsey's first time? It had been insanely perfect for him. Had she known how to ... make it amazing? Oh, man. Hudson was so sick he hid behind some cars and spewed all over somebody's tire.

The most disturbing questions of his life were pinging around in his brain, begging for answers but there were none.

He straightened and wiped his mouth. He was sweating and tasting vomit and he was in a dark, cold place, shut off from his Sunshine and every hope and dream he'd had for the two of them.

A blonde walked past him. She smiled and lifted her eyebrows. "Hey, handsome."

He swallowed, not able to even respond. He stepped closer to her, and her smile grew. He pointed up at the balcony. "Are those two together?" he demanded.

Her smile disappeared. She looked up at Kelsey and Jason and then back at him. She nodded. "All the time. Why?"

He shook his head and turned away from her—his tongue thick, his throat dry, his mouth tasting of vomit.

She gave a disgusted grunt and walked off, opening and then slamming the door to her car, starting the engine and roaring out of the parking lot.

He wished he would've treated her nicer, but he could hardly hold his head up and he wanted to vomit again.

All the time.

Jason and Kelsey were together all the time.

The picture was clear, and right in front of him. He turned his back so he wouldn't look at them together again.

Not the father. Not the father.

Could that really be true?

All the facts were stacking up, but he had to know for certain if the love of his life had betrayed him and all of his dreams were now smashed under car tires in this parking lot and then spewed on. His stomach churned again.

He heard footsteps coming through the parking lot. He walked from behind the cars and came face to face with Jason.

His old friend reared back in surprise and then grinned widely at him. "Hudson Delta! What's going on, brother?" He held out his hand to clasp.

Hudson could only stare at him. It was all he could do to stop himself from giving the man a dental bill he'd have to pay monthly payments and accumulating interest on for years.

Jason's smile slipped, and he lowered his hand. "Everything okay?"

"No," Hudson burst out with. He turned and paced away from the man and then back. He made sure not to get too close so he didn't tackle him and show him exactly how well-trained the Deltas were in hand-to-hand combat. Skills learned since he was a boy to protect an important family secret. Hudson had perfected his fighting execution throughout the past three months.

"Just tell me the truth," he demanded, wishing he could grab the guy's shirt to shake it out of him. He chanced a glance at the balcony, but Kelsey was gone. "Are you the father of Kelsey's baby?"

Jason's smile blossomed on his face again, and his blue eyes lit up. "Yeah, I am."

Hudson stared at him. He took one slow breath in and one out. *Calm. Don't react. Mind over body. Breathe in. Breathe out. You are powerful and in control.*

Another breath and on the exhale ... he tackled the backstabbing jerk.

Jason cried out in surprise as they hit the asphalt. Hudson slammed his fists into his former friend's face. To heck with being in control.

Jason threw his hands up to protect himself. Hudson ripped the guy's hands away, but then it hit him—he had accomplished nothing but ruining his own life the past three months. He was more out of control right now than when he'd gone too far with Kelsey. He'd loved Kelsey and hadn't been able to stop, and he was going to kill Jason if he didn't stop.

All those beautiful memories of him and his Sunshine were now tarnished. She was with Jason. Jason was the father. Not Hudson. Never Hudson. Every dream of him and Kelsey's happily ever after had been slammed into the asphalt that night.

Hudson had said a prayer for some kind of strength, then he grabbed Jason's shirt, shook him hard enough his head bounced off the asphalt, and leaned in close. He growled in the guy's face,

"You take care of her. You marry her, spoil her, and love her, and don't you ever let me hear she isn't the happiest wife and mother on the planet, or I'll come back and I'll destroy you. I'll take you apart piece by piece, and I won't even care how you beg for mercy. Do you understand me?"

Jason stared up at him. His mouth flopped open and closed, but he said nothing. Hudson was shaking with rage and he was going to puke again. He'd just told another man to marry, spoil, and love the only woman he had ever loved and the only woman he would ever want to spoil, love, and marry. But it was the right thing to do. Jason was the father of her baby. He was the one who would get to marry and take care of her and their child.

If Hudson hadn't been so furious, he would've been sobbing hysterically.

"Do you understand me?" he asked louder.

"Yes." Jason nodded.

Hudson leaped off of him, strode to his rental car, puked one more time, climbed into the car, rinsed with a water bottle and spit out the window as he spun out of that parking lot. He didn't let himself look back.

His life had shattered that night. He'd gone back to his world of stunts and extreme sports and reviewers and media had claimed Hudson Delta wasn't just ultra-talented and strong—he thought he was invincible. For years now, the hashtag #deathwishdelta had trended. His producers had even named his cologne line Death Wish Delta.

Maybe he did have a death wish. What was life without Kelsey? He'd never heard from her or Jason again. And every time his family tried to bring her up, the call mysteriously dropped or some other huge interruption prevented further details. Eventually they caught on to what was triggering the end of nearly every conversation and they stopped bringing her up.

Now she was right here. Right in front of him. Holding Jason's baby. The little man was adorable. Where was his father? If Jason hadn't taken care of her and their baby, Hudson would follow through with his threats. Gladly. He wouldn't even worry about lacking self-control because it would be a completely premeditated assault. Was that the right legal term? He'd have to ask his older sister Esther.

Suddenly everybody was cheering and Thor and Shelly were kissing. Hudson whooped and clapped and acted as happy as everybody else. Kelsey had already taken so much from him. He couldn't let her take this brief time with his family. Because as soon as they ate, danced, celebrated, threw the rice, and Thor and Shelly ran for Thor's decorated truck, Hudson was out of here.

He'd take any kind of physical pain from punishing his body with his stunts or to be ultra-fit. He could *not* handle the emotional pain of being close to Kelsey James and never being able to hold and love her again.

Chapter Three

Kelsey congratulated herself. She had made it through the wedding and the delicious dinner. Well, everybody else said it was delicious. All she could do was methodically chew and swallow a few bites. Nothing tasted right with her stomach churning.

Most of the evening she'd been able to keep her focus on her son, her mom, and the kind people they sat by at dinner. Tom and Annalea ... somebody. They had tragically lost their only daughter and given Shelly their daughter Alexa's renowned barrel-racing horse. They'd had a part in Thor and Shelly's happily ever after. It was a touching story and Kelsey thought she held up her end of the conversation, kept Mo eating and for the most part in his seat, and didn't let her gaze stray to Hudson too often.

Until Annalea said in her sweet Southern accent, "I think our little angel mama has a crush on one of those hot Delta men. Whoo-ee! If I was twenty years younger and not head over heels for this stud," she patted her husband's cheek, who just smiled at her, "I'd be chasing a Delta boy myself."

Kelsey's cheeks and the back of her neck got hot. "I ..."

"Mama, you look funny," Mo said, giggling as he pointed at her.

"Your mama is a beauty, sweet boy," Annalea said.

"I knows that." Mo nodded. "But she's all red."

"Sorry, darlin'," Tom said in a too-loud voice to Kelsey. "My girl calls it how it is."

Kelsey tried to laugh, but she was just miserable. What did it matter if she had a crush, or worse, was still in love with Hudson Delta? She'd never trust him with her heart again, and she'd never let him break Mo's heart as well. She could only imagine how Hudson and Mo would take to each other. She'd often wished she could see that, but it wasn't worth Mo loving his father and then being deserted by him.

"Why don't you go talk to him?" Kelsey's mom, Lori, asked softly. "Dinner's finished, and he's been sneaking glances at you, too."

Kelsey felt the stab of betrayal deep down. Her mom knew exactly what Hudson had done to her. In fact, her mom was the only one besides a couple college roommates she struggled to keep in touch with and her friend Jason who knew that Hudson was Mo's father and had deserted her when she needed him most. She'd had to quit school and move home. Luckily, she'd been hired by home health care and loved working with Granny Klein, but she didn't make near the money she could've as an RN and it stunk to still live with your mother at twenty-four.

Her mom shrugged, but her dark eyes looked repentant. "It

might give you some closure. I could take Mo home and get him into bed."

This had gone much too far. Kelsey set her napkin on her plate, swooped Mo off his chair, and said, "It was lovely to meet you both and eat dinner with you. I've got to get this little cutie home to bed."

"No," Mo groaned. "No bed!"

Kelsey kept her smile on. "Yes, bed."

Annalea sprung from her chair and gave Mo a hug, then turned to Kelsey. Tugging her close, she said, "I'm right sorry if I embarrassed you."

"You're fine," Kelsey lied. "It's just a lot of history that I am not ready to face."

She probably shouldn't have said that last part.

"I understand. I pray you'll figure it out because that boy ..." Annalea pointed at Hudson, who was at the head table with his family.

Of course he glanced their way at that moment and that irresistible, beautiful grin grew on his handsome face. He even had the audacity to lift his eyebrows and give her the signature Hudson Delta smoldering look that he used to claim he only did for her. Yeah right. Women the world over swooned at that look as Hudson kissed and loved every one of them.

"See, I was right," Annalea crowed, somewhat quietly. "He is head over heels for you, darlin'."

"Doesn't matter." He wasn't, but she wasn't about to argue about Hudson's lack of commitment to her and their son with this strong-willed woman. "That ship has slammed into the iceberg that is Hudson Delta's heart and sunk, leaving no survivors," Kelsey said. "I hope I see you again sometime."

She meant it. Annalea was delightful, sassy, and yet kind. Kelsey only hoped the next meeting wouldn't be with Hudson in the same state.

"You too." Annalea thankfully backed down, surprising for the amount of Southern sass she had in her.

"Bye," Kelsey said to Tom, and then spun and threaded her way through the wedding crowd. Some other people mingled, making their way to the dance floor where the beautiful couple was headed for their first dance as husband and wife. Kelsey would've liked to watch that, but she needed distance from Hudson to somehow tamp down all the desires for him that arose from being in the same location. Too many memories. Too many unfulfilled dreams. She had to leave. Now.

She smiled and said goodnight and let Mo claim the attention as she steadily progressed through the crowd. Everyone was happy to see her, and even more happy to see Mo. He got lots of notice and she had to pause for some hugs. Her son grinned and laughed and seemed to forget she was taking him home to bed.

They made it out of the crowd and into the parking area where at least a hundred cars were parked. Hopefully their car wasn't pinned in. Could she even find her compact car in the midst of all these huge trucks and SUVs?

"Kels ... wait."

Kelsey pushed out a breath, but stopped and spun around.

Her mom hurried up to her. "Why don't you let me take Mo home and you stay for the dancing? It'd be fun for you to act like a young person once in a while."

"Let's dance, Mama," Mo crowed.

Shaking her head, Kelsey started walking toward the car again. She hoped she was going the right direction. Her mom fell into step with them. "Thanks, Mom. That's nice of you, but I'm tired."

"Me not tired," Mo piped up.

She smiled at him and kissed his soft cheek. "You're never tired."

"Nope. 'Cause I'm a tough guy!"

"So true."

"And I like to dance!"

Kelsey's throat felt thick and she could only smile at him. Like father, like son. She and Mo danced a lot. They could dance at home tomorrow. When Hudson was gone from the state and her heart wasn't so tender and her emotions so close to the surface.

Kelsey spotted her old Honda Accord. It used to be red, but the orange rust spots were taking over. They should've driven her mom's nicer Cherokee, but Kelsey hadn't wanted to move the car seat.

She hurried to the car and her mom swung the door open for her and then went and sat in the passenger seat, not trying to force her to stay, which she appreciated. Kelsey sat Mo in his car seat and lifted her purse onto the console between the seats. She could hear the music from the dancing floating to them, soft but enough to make her wish she could go dance and be carefree and fun.

"Love you, Mama," Mo said in his darling little voice.

Ah, her boy. Who cared if she missed out on dancing? Hudson Delta may have deserted her, but first he'd given her the most beautiful gift in the world. This precious boy.

"Love you, cutest boy." Strapping Mo into his car seat wasn't easy wearing a fitted dress, but she managed and then gave him a kiss on his soft, sweet cheek. She inhaled the perfect scent of baby lotion and little boy.

She was easing out of the backseat when she heard footsteps. She straightened, shut the door, and turned to see none other than the famous Hudson Delta—aka Death Wish Delta, no longer her Brave—jogging through the parking area toward them. Her heart tried to pound its way out of her sternum.

"Hudson," her mom called out, springing out of the passenger seat and hurrying around.

"Hey." He raised his hand in greeting, slowing as he approached.

Her mom sprang at him and hugged him. Hudson returned the embrace, grinning over her shoulder at Kelsey. What was he grinning about and why was her mom acting like he was her long-lost son? Ridiculous. Her mom knew Hudson needed a slug in the gut and usually she was Kelsey's biggest support. What was she playing at? Had she been talking to Myrna Delta and scheming? Her mom would never betray her secret, but she might plot with a friend. No!

Her mom pulled back and patted his cheek. "Just as handsome as ever, aren't you?"

"I try." Hudson shrugged and looked adorably innocent and manly and perfect at the same time. Women the world over agreed. A lot of people claimed he looked like Chris Pratt. Kelsey thought he was even more good-looking, talented, and fun.

Ooh, he made her spitting mad.

"And world famous?" Her mom shook her head. "So impressive, Hudson. So impressive."

"Thank you." He beamed and looked over at Kelsey, as if she would join in this ridiculous circus and praise him, too. He could wait until the Second Coming for that to happen.

When Kelsey said nothing, he looked back to her mom. "You look beautiful as ever, Mrs. James." Kelsey's dad had died when she was only one, but Chandler was a Delta, so respect was important and he would never call her mom Lori like a lot of young adults would.

"Ah, thank you, handsome. Now you be good to my girl or I'll rip out your nose hairs," her mom said in a sweet voice. Kelsey couldn't help but smile at that. For some reason, her mom wanted her to reconnect with Hudson, maybe even to get some closure like she'd said, but she wouldn't let Hudson hurt her again. Kelsey understood; she'd never let him worm his way into Mo's heart then desert her boy. Not on her watch.

Hudson turned the force of those blue eyes on her. The parking area wasn't lit as well as the dance floor, but she couldn't miss seeing the longing and warmth in those dang blue eyes. "Unfortunately for me, anything Kelsey asks I would do for her," he said.

Kelsey tried to puzzle out that response. Unfortunately for him? She'd give him "unfortunately." He was the one who'd deserted her. And she wouldn't ask anything of him, so it was a pretty safe bet for him. Why would she ever ask something of the guy who'd failed her when she needed him most and who would be gone before morning? Again.

"Get her home at a decent time." Her mom yanked open the driver's door and plopped inside.

Hudson shut the door for her, and her mom hit the lock button, grinning up at Kelsey through the glass. She pulled the keys out of Kelsey's purse and started the car.

Kelsey's mouth was half open. What was her mother doing?

"Stop," she finally managed, starting forward as her mom put it in gear and backed up quickly.

Hudson reached out and pulled her back so she didn't run into the side of a moving car. Kelsey gasped as he stepped closer while tugging her to him. He somehow pivoted her and wrapped her up in his nicely built arms, cuddled against his too-perfect chest.

As her devious mother drove off with their son.

She stared up at him. So perfect. So close. Ah, Brave. He wore a different cologne, definitely expensive, definitely mouth-watering, but his base scent was still the same and somehow filled with the pheromones that made Kelsey want to arch up and kiss him and stir up all the old memories of long, delicious kisses.

No! She was a responsible mother now. She wouldn't fall for Hudson's tricks. He was the king of tricks. He'd tricked her into kissing him the first time, telling her if he could do a double back-flip off the dock at his family's lake, she had to kiss him. She'd known he was a talented athlete, but who could really do a double backflip with so little spring or space between the surface of the water? He'd done it, and then he'd yanked her into the cold water and he'd kissed her. Wow, had he kissed her! She hadn't even felt the chilly temperature; everything had been hot from Hudson's kisses.

She blinked to break the spell he always had on her and yanked out of his arms. His smile and warm look turned cooler and almost broody. That wasn't like her Brave Hudson. Maybe he needed his Sunshine to light up his day.

Her Brave Hudson? His Sunshine? Grr. She had to stop this. She couldn't believe her mom had ditched her with him. Somebody else from town would be headed home soon. She could easily get a ride with any of the hundreds of wonderful people who'd come from the main Summit Valley to the Deltas higher and smaller mountain valley.

"Where's Jason?" Hudson demanded in a hard voice.

"Jason?" She blinked up at him.

"Spackman," he said with derision and unbelief. As if she should've immediately thought of their old high school buddy. Hudson had always been annoyed with Jason hitting on her and teasing with her. When she was at college, Jason had lived in the same apartment complex. They had remained friends until she left school to come home. The day she finally gave up on Hudson ever coming for her and all her dreams.

Jason had been a good friend, often taking her to dinner or hugging her when she needed a strong shoulder to cry on, especially after she'd sent that text to Hudson that he'd never responded to. Jason had pressed her quite a few times to marry him, promising to take care of her and the baby. She always told him no. Ironically, as soon as her baby bump and her rear had gotten larger, he'd stopped asking for anything more than friendship.

"Well, he's not here," she snapped back at him.

Hudson's eyes lit up, and he stepped closer again. That delicious cologne messed with her head, and his handsome face right there in front of her, scrambled her brain. "You aren't with Jason?"

"Obviously not." She'd never been with Jason. What was this nonsense?

"So what you're saying, Sunshine, is ... there's a chance?" Hudson asked, his voice pitching up in excitement. It reminded her of all the times he'd get excited about some new stunt he'd mastered on a bike, wakeboard, or wingsuit, or even better, the times he'd get excited about being closer to her.

A chance? A chance for what? How dare he call her Sunshine? She wasn't his Sunshine. Never again.

Before she could muddle out why Jason not being here had made Hudson so happy and made him think there was "a chance," Hudson slid his hands around her hips, tugged her to him, bent down, and captured her lips with his.

Kelsey gasped in surprise, but her body took over instinctively. She went on tiptoes, wrapped her arms around the back of his neck, tried to pull him even closer, and devoured his mouth with hers. She should've been embarrassed by her enthusiastic response to his longed-for kiss, but all she could feel was intense pleasure and happiness. She was back in Hudson's arms. The world would find peace and joy.

Kissing him was even better than she'd remembered. How was that possible? Their kisses had always been off the charts. But somehow, it was. Longing for him, no matter how she'd fought against it, had made him taste more delicious than anything in this universe.

They kissed desperately, clinging to each other, exchanging love and devotion and so many beautiful emotions.

Until someone walked past, laughing and whistling loudly at them.

Kelsey forced herself to release him from the kiss and pull in long breaths of air. She stared into his beautiful blue eyes, glinting happily at her, and then he said, "We've still got that incredible spark, Sunshine. Remember how you wouldn't kiss me until I tricked you into it and from then on you could never get enough of me?"

Couldn't get enough of him? That was for sure. And it had been her downfall. She would never trade Mo for the world, but being a single mom and dropping out of college hadn't been anywhere on the possibility list of her life's plan. If this man that she "couldn't get enough of" had only come for her, they could've raised their adorable son together. Instead, Hudson had pursued his own selfish dreams and become a multi-millionaire with his own cologne line—Death Wish Delta cologne. She'd let herself sniff it in Macey's once. It had been a great smell, almost as tantalizing as he smelled right now. Oh my! He was wearing his own cologne. Some chemist had probably designed his cologne to match him perfectly. Why not make the perfect Hudson Delta even more irresistible to his throngs of female fans?

Couldn't get enough of him? Oh, she could definitely get enough of him.

She stepped back just far enough to get a full swing, then slapped his handsome face as hard as she could. Her hand stung, and the slap reverberated through the semi-quiet parking lot.

He didn't even flinch. He stared at her for far too long, and then he said quietly, "I guess this means there isn't a chance?"

"No, there isn't a chance! How dare you? You ... jerk! You ditch me and—"

Her tirade was only getting started when a loud alert of some sort sounded on Hudson's phone, buzzing over her voice.

The Hudson she'd known and loved would've never looked at his phone, especially when she was around. This new Hudson, who could kiss better than ever, didn't have the courtesy to focus on her. He ripped his phone from his suit pocket and his eyes widened.

"Excuse me," he murmured, taking off at a full-on sprint through the parking lot and toward his grandfather's large home. No explanation. No apology. No goodbye.

Kelsey stared at his rapidly disappearing backside in shock. She let out a disgusted grunt and threw her hands in the air. "Isn't that par for the course?" she demanded of thin air. "Hudson Delta, ditching me once again. He's not brave. He's a spineless wimp! Ugh! I hate him!"

She finished her private tirade, relieved that no one was nearby. Then she stomped off toward the road leading away from the Deltas and back home to Summit Valley. It would be miserable and probably give her plantar fasciitis to walk the distance in this dress and heels, but it might help her anger at that infuriating man to cool off. Somebody would come along and pick her up. She knew her people, and they were good people. Still, she marched off, not willing to wait for the ride Hudson was supposed to give her. What was so important anyway? A summons from one of his many bimbos?

What a deserter. What a heartbreaker. What a jerk.

The stupid fantasies she'd let herself indulge in of Hudson coming back for her and Mo needed to disappear for good. Yes, he could still kiss like a fairy tale dream, but that was probably because of the long list of women he'd kissed since he'd last kissed Kelsey. He'd probably given her mononucleosis from swapping spit with so many women.

Ugh! He disgusted her. She was washing her hands of Hudson Delta for good, using a bottle of hand sanitizer for extra precaution to make sure the alcohol killed everything she'd ever felt for him.

She hated that Mo would never know his father, but it was for the best. The charming, fun Hudson she knew and loved was dead and in his place was a spoiled, cocky jerk. Good riddance. She and Mo didn't need him. They'd done fine on their own in the past and they'd do even better in the future. She'd make sure of it.

If only she could eradicate the memories of hers and Hudson's kisses from her brain. She touched her lips and stumbled on the dark road. Falling to her knees, she caught herself with her palms.

Her palms stung, but luckily no rocks had serrated the flesh. She stood shakily and looked down at her dress. Her favorite dress. There was a tear and smudges of dirt embedded in the off-white lace. Tears stung her eyes. It was probably ruined. Just like her relationship with Hudson was ruined. She supposed the dress could be replaced if she was careful and saved for it. Hudson couldn't be replaced. No amount of careful saving and patience would bring him into hers and Mo's lives. She believed firmly in prayer and heaven's help, and both had gotten her through some hard times these past four years, but not even heaven could bring Hudson to her.

Walking more slowly down the road, she let the tears fall. She'd tried to talk herself out of loving Hudson for years, but she hadn't succeeded. How was she going to eradicate him from her heart? She had to let him go. It was too hard to keep going like this.

Chapter Four

Six weeks had passed since Hudson had held Kelsey in his arms and kissed her like she was still his Sunshine and the sun wouldn't shine tomorrow.

It almost hadn't for Melene Collier or the rest of the country. The alert that had pulled him from Kelsey cussing him out, after that impressive and dream-shattering slap, had been a Delta Protection alert. Hudson had raced for Papa's house, just like he'd been trained, and carried as many A.R.s as he could straight to Aiden's location in the trees. Some family members had helped carry weapons as well, others had made excuses to the wedding guests about a volatile ex-boyfriend trying to hurt Melene. They laid down the cover story quick so no one suspected what the Deltas were really about, and had rushed to converge on Aiden's location.

They'd helped Aiden rescue Melene from the evil dictator King Frederick's right-hand man, General Carl Phillip. Aiden had shot and killed Phillip, and the rest of them had made certain his men didn't try anything. That threat had passed, but the danger for the Delta family and the secret his grandfather and family members had dedicated their lives to protecting continued to escalate. Apparently King Frederick was on a quest to secure the "Delta weapon" and as soon as he got it, he would bomb the U.S. with nuclear weapons.

Terrifying. And Hudson needed to get home and help protect the secret. He knew he did. Everybody was gathering and Aiden was after him to book a flight—today.

He stared blankly at the Caribbean ocean, sitting in a beach chair at a small resort on the island of Cozumel. It was the twenty-first of September. He and his friends, who doubled as camera man, videographer, and stunt support, had come here to do the drift dive and had even seen some whale sharks. His producers would be happy that he had gotten some good footage. He always recorded extra stunts, but lately he'd pushed for more so they would have unpublished film saved to use when he went to help full-time with Delta Protection. He knew it was coming. Still, he dragged his feet.

The warm tropical sun couldn't be to blame for Hudson not wanting to move. Did he have the flu or was the lethargy stress-induced? He always wanted to move. He never slowed down. His friends were all inside filling up at the buffet. He wasn't even hungry.

Six weeks. He should've stayed around and forced Kelsey to talk to him. He'd been so excited that she wasn't with Jason. Though he'd threatened the man pretty violently if he didn't take care of Kelsey, the past four years thinking of them together had been brutal. If Kelsey's son's dad wasn't in the picture, Hudson would've happily stepped in and loved that little guy. But instead of talking about it after that incredible kiss, Kelsey had slapped him and then started screaming at him about there being no chance and him ditching her. He supposed he had ditched her after they'd been intimate. It was stupid of him to have focused on self-mastery when he should've just focused on Kelsey.

People claimed he was brave. That used to be Kelsey's nickname for him, actually, but he was a wimp when it came to her. If only he was brave like any of his impressive brothers, he would've chased her down after the threat to the Deltas and Melene was contained. He would've begged her to talk it out, to give him a chance. But at the same time, it ticked him off that she'd cheated on him and now he was the one getting slapped and yelled at and he'd even convinced himself that *he* needed to beg. Maybe his Sunshine should ask *his* forgiveness. He'd give it in a heartbeat. Then could he hold her again and get to know her son?

He rolled his eyes, pushed to his feet, and felt sharp, cold steel press against his neck.

"Do not move," a male voice said. He was shorter than Hudson, but the knife was in perfect position to slice his neck open and have him bleed out. The guy stood behind him, so Hudson couldn't see his face.

"What do you want?" he asked. The moniker and hashtag Death Wish Delta had surged in trending since Kelsey had devastated him again. If only he could get the vision of her in that off-white dress out of his head, the feel of her in his arms, the taste of her on his lips. He didn't really want to die at this moment, but he wasn't afraid of death, either. He'd faced it far too many times doing insane stunts to let the fear of death hamper him. The next world sounded incredible, and Granny Delta and his Pops and Grams Hendry were there waiting for him.

"I want you to quietly fly home to Colorado," the man said with a slight Spanish accent. "You will meet my man at a location that will be texted to you, and you will take him to the Delta weapon."

"Why would I do that?" Papa had instructed that Hudson come home as soon as possible. He wanted to, but facing Kelsey again was terrifying. Maybe he wouldn't have a choice but to go home, help the family, and see her again. If they could just sit down and talk reasonably, could she explain why she'd cheated on him? He could forgive her, and they could make a path forward together. Could he be a dad to that cute little man she'd held on her lap during the wedding? He was concerned about her son not having a dad. That loser Jason had a lot to answer for.

"If you don't, I slice you open."

Hudson chuckled. "If you slice me open, I can't go home and lead your people to some mythical legend, now can I?"

"You claim it's a myth?"

"Yep. I've heard the stories all my life, just like the Holy Grail. But if you want to play Indiana Jones, I say let's do it. Do you mind if I bring my film crew? Sounds like a great adventure."

"No film!"

The knife pressed a little harder, and Hudson instinctively flinched. "All right, no film. So I just fly home and you text me where to meet your buddies?"

"You do it?"

"I was supposed to go home anyway." Might as well humor the guy with the knife to his throat. "Do they have my number?"

"You give it to me. I memorize."

Hudson rattled off his number.

"You have to get them weapon."

"There is no weapon, dude."

"If you don't get them weapon, they kill your girl and your son," the man said.

"My son?" Hudson should've kept the confusion from his voice.

"Don't play stupid," the man said fiercely. "Kelsey and Mo. Your girl and your son."

Hudson's gut tightened. They thought Kelsey's son was his? Why? These guys had done their research to know he'd loved Kelsey. But maybe it wasn't too hard. There were social media posts of the two of them back in high school. Innocent, fun times and pictures they'd shared with the world.

It shouldn't surprise him that some mercenary was after him now. Others in his family had been kidnapped, threatened, or attacked to get the secret. Every other Delta was now in the valley, working to protect the cave from King Frederick's lackeys, or more misguided military forces, penetrating the secret's sanctuary. These guys must've thought it would be easier to go after the loose cannon.

He wasn't sure what the guy's plan was, claiming Mo was his son, but he'd have to riddle that out later. It was past time Hudson had the upper hand. He elbowed the guy, ripped the knife from his hand, tossed it into the sand, flipped the guy over onto his back, and brought his elbow down on his chest, a few notches below lethal force.

The smaller Spanish-descent man gasped for air and couldn't get it. He clutched at his chest and stared wide-eyed at Hudson.

"Now here's what will really happen," Hudson told him. "You're going to tell me everything you know about your friends who are supposed to meet me in Colorado, and I will go take them out. If any of you *dare* go near Kelsey or her son, I will gut you like a fish. Understood?"

Hudson heard some shouts from his friends, who must've seen him from the restaurant's windows. "It's all right," he called. "Stay back." He held up a hand to wave them off.

The man finally gasped for air, panted through a few more breaths, and then managed, "They will ... kill your girl and son if you don't go." A pause for more oxygen. "They already have them in their possession."

"You didn't think it would be a good idea to lead with that?" Hudson's comment had been flippant, but he felt anything but. His stomach did a double back flip, and every muscle tightened.

Kelsey and Mo had been kidnapped? When? Why hadn't somebody called him? What could he do?

Praying desperately for help, Hudson felt every ache of missing Kelsey over the years multiplied by a million. Kidnapped. No!

His mind spun. He had to find them. He had to get them free. He'd give anything to protect them. But sadly, it wasn't in his power to get the Delta Weapon. Not only would that result in nuclear winter rained down on America, but he wasn't the Secret Keeper. Only Papa or whoever he'd named Secret Keeper could get into that cave. No way would Papa ever remove the weapon from the cave. Not until he or the Secret Keeper was inspired to use it to protect the free world.

Kelsey and Mo were all that mattered to Hudson, but what if it wasn't in his power to save them?

Chapter Five

Kelsey and Mo were playing checkers with Granny Vance. She and Granny had put together a chicken and veggie casserole, salad, and mixed up and rolled out dinner rolls while Mo had colored at the counter. The casserole was in the oven, the rolls were rising, and the salad was in the fridge. Kelsey loved her time here with Granny, and the sweet lady doted on Mo.

Granny suffered from dementia. It was progressing, and that was hard for Kelsey to watch. She loved the elderly lady. She couldn't imagine what Shelly and Klein were going through.

As far as home health care jobs went, this one was an ideal situation for Kelsey and so easy that sometimes she felt guilty they paid her so well. Granny could use the bathroom herself, only required minimal help getting ready for the day or for bed, and took her oral medications every time they were given to her. It was more glorified babysitting, so definitely not the challenge to her nursing skills she used to long for, but a perfect fit where she could have Mo with her while she worked. Not to mention the home and environment were incredible.

There had been a little awkwardness a few months ago when her mom and Granny had both been convinced that Kelsey should make a play for Klein Vance. He was an impressive and appealing man, but he wasn't Hudson. She'd given it a valiant effort, but Klein was already in love with Alivia Delta, Hudson's tough cousin who owned her own construction business. It was fine with Kelsey, but it was also embarrassing, and it had taken a few weeks for Klein to be comfortable around her again.

A rap sounded on the front door. Kelsey stood to go answer it. Mo followed her, curious and cute as ever. He reached up his hand and she wrapped her palm around his perfect, squishy little fingers. He grinned up at her, those Delta blue eyes sparkling. How she loved her boy. Far too often, he made her ache for his escapee of a father.

She swung the door wide and looked out. Her jaw slackened, and she tried to compute what she was seeing.

Two blond men were pointing pistols at her.

Kelsey grabbed Mo and yanked him behind her. Her heart raced and her palms were instantly slick.

"Whoa!" Mo cried out, trying to break her hold and peer around her legs. "You guys got guns. Can I see?"

The one smirked at the innocent question and stared at Kelsey. "Hi, pretty lady." He had a slight accent, but she couldn't place it. "You and your son are coming with us. Right now."

Her eyes widened, and her stomach churned. "I can get you money," she lied.

They exchanged a look. "*Geld*," the spokesman explained to

the other guy. They both chuckled. The spokesman's gaze raked over her. "We don't want your money."

Horror filled her. The only thing worse than what he was intoning was they wanted Mo to come with her. Human trafficking was despicable, but she'd never imagined it could reach them here in their safe little valley.

Her sweet Mo! How could she protect her boy?

"Kelsey?" Granny Vance's voice floated toward them and shuffling footsteps. Oh, no!

"Stay back, Granny," Kelsey yelled. "It's just a salesman." She begged the men with her eyes. "I can't leave Granny alone. She's got dementia."

The one guy grabbed her arm roughly and yanked her to him.

"Hey," Mo called. "Don't you hurt my mama!"

"You're lucky Granny's not getting a bullet between the eyes," the man growled.

The silent guy ripped Mo from her. Mo cried out, and the guy clasped his hand over his mouth and easily secured her squirming little boy in his arms, rushing down the steps and toward a white Suburban.

"No!" Kelsey screamed, running after her son.

The guy holding her arm kept up but didn't release her. There was another guy in the driver's seat. The man holding Mo climbed into the front passenger seat with her son in his arms. Kelsey only got a glimpse of Mo's blue eyes wide with fear before the door slammed. She'd never seen her son terrified like that. She had to stop these monsters!

She yanked at the door handle, but the man next to her wrapped her up tight and shoved her toward the back door. The driver rushed around and helped him manhandle her into the seat behind Mo.

"Stop," she screamed. "Let him go!"

They got her into the backseat and the spokesman wrapped her in his arms and held her tight against him. She thrashed and tried to claw at him, but she couldn't get a hand free. She leaned down and bit his shoulder. He yelped and squeezed her tighter.

"Stop fighting or we'll shoot your son."

"No," she screamed in horror as the driver climbed back into his seat.

"*Sheiben*," the man holding Kelsey said.

The driver pulled a pistol out and pointed it at Mo's head.

"No! I'll stop. Please! Don't hurt him." She stopped moving completely, frozen with terror and worrying any movement would set them off. The only thing moving was her stomach rolling, panic and shock overwhelming her.

"Better. *Fahrt!*" he commanded.

Fart? What?

The driver set the gun in the cup holder and put the vehicle into gear. Kelsey wondered what language that was, but what did it matter? These horrible men had kidnapped her and Mo and would threaten and hurt her son if she didn't obey their every command.

Tears streaked down her face as they pulled away from Granny's house. She saw the older woman at the open door, watching the Suburban with confusion. Could Granny possibly call the police? Kelsey doubted she could reason that response. At least these men hadn't killed her, which she could sense they wouldn't mind doing. Chills filled her. These men were an evil she'd never experienced in her life.

The only thing she could think to do was pray. She did. Desperately.

No peace or rescue came.

Oh, Mo. He wasn't even in his car seat. What if these idiots got in a wreck and killed her boy? What if they were truly monstrous enough to hurt Mo? She could see his little body trembling in the man's arms. Her baby boy. How was she going to comfort and protect her son?

Chapter Six

Hudson kneeled over the man, trying to think what he could do to ensure Kelsey and Mo were safe. His gut churned, but he channeled all his former meditation and self-control training to not let his distress overtake him like his younger self would have. He was a natural hothead and showoff who had learned to control himself. He used to kid himself that he was a master, but for him, master level meant not thumping someone who challenged him, not chasing after Kelsey every day like he wanted to, and not letting himself get overly dramatic about everything.

Focus mattered. Especially when the woman you loved and her innocent son were in mortal danger.

"Give me your phone," he demanded.

The man slid his phone out and handed it over.

"Password?"

"2244."

He stood and punched in the code on the phone.

"Hudson?" His cameraman and friend Giles approached. "Everything okay?"

"Get the police to arrest this man. He tried to kill me. Make sure they lock him up without bail, or whatever they call it in Mexico."

"Okay." He nodded. "You all right?"

"I have to go home. Brad? Can you come with me to the airport in case I need some help?"

"Sure."

Brad was his close friend and the guy who made sure his stunts were somewhat safe and that they worked as planned. He could fix almost anything, and Hudson trusted him with his life daily. He wanted him with him.

"What about Panama?" Noah, the videographer and worrier of the group, asked.

"Sorry. It's a matter of life and death. You have all the extra footage and stunts we've prerecorded." Hudson waved at all of them, but he was focused on the phone in his hand as he rushed through the resort and toward his room to grab his stuff. Brad trailed behind him. Luckily, Brad just figured junk out. He wasn't the type to ask questions.

The text messages were in Spanish. Dang. He knew some Spanish, but not enough to decipher which messages might be from this guy's partners and what they said.

He stopped and grabbed the closest employee. "*Habla inglés?*" he asked.

"*Sí, señor.*"

"Can you read through these text messages for me and see which ones might be about a woman and her son being kidnapped?"

The man's eyes widened, and Hudson could feel Brad easing closer. The employee took the phone and scanned through. He clicked on the third message down and read back through. Hudson stared at the words and saw Hudson and Delta in some of the messages.

"This is the one about a woman and boy taken."

"Can you translate it for me?"

"*Si*. It says he is to inform Hudson Delta that they kidnap his woman and son."

Hudson felt like someone had slugged him. "They're planning to kidnap them, or they already have?"

The man's brow squiggled. "Already have, *señor*."

"No!" Hudson shook his head as icy panic raced down his spine. Despite what the man had said, he'd held out hope. They couldn't already have Kelsey and her son. No! "Walk with me, please."

"*Si*." The man carried the phone as Hudson raced through the resort toward his room and pushed on Papa's phone contact. Brad stayed close behind them.

"What's your name?" Hudson asked.

"Carlos, sir."

"*Gracias*," Hudson said.

"My pleasure."

"There you are," Papa called out, welcoming and loving as always.

"Papa, I need you, Sheriff Reed, Aiden, those new Navy SEAL guys, anybody you think can help. Get to Kelsey James's house, make sure she and her son are all right, and then relocate them to one of your houses. Protect them, Papa." He knew the new four-man elite SEAL team and their EOD were already staying with Papa to help protect the secret, but his family had plenty of nice, big houses. His family was well-trained and the houses and valley were wired with sensors and cameras. Any of them would be happy to host Kelsey and her cute little boy. If only they weren't already kidnapped. Please say the translator had understood that wrong.

"Get Reed on the phone," Papa told somebody, then to Hudson, "What's happened?"

"A man pulled a knife on me, demanded I lead him to the Delta weapon or his associates would kidnap my girl and child ... I mean Kelsey and her son. I took the guy out and got into his phone. The man translating says the messages claim they've already got them." He reached his room and used his bracelet key card on the door, then pushed it open.

He gestured the other two men in and started grabbing things and shoving them in his suitcase.

"Hold on," Papa said. There was a pause.

Hudson zipped up his suitcase and threw his backpack on. He gestured to the men to go out the door and whispered to Carlos as they walked, "What does the last text from that number say?"

The man looked at the phone and said, "Passcode?"

"2244."

He typed it in and then read and translated, "Secure Hudson Delta and force him to come meet us and lead us to the Delta weapon. We are in Colorado with the woman and child."

Oh, man. He was at least a four- or five-hour flight to Denver, then he had to drive to the valley. That was if he could get a chartered flight secured. He should've bought his own plane long before this, but the charters worked well. When planned in advance.

"Brad, get on the phone and charter a jet to Colorado as soon as possible. Please," he added lamely. Hudson wasn't one to order his friends around, but he was desperate and a mess right now.

"On it."

"Thanks."

Papa came back on. "Reed and a couple of his guys are racing to Kelsey's house. We didn't know we should be watching out for them."

He was probing. If only Hudson had answers. "Neither did I." Hudson hurried down the hallway, hauling his suitcase so it didn't slow him down. "Should I try to text these guys on the phone I took?"

"You could try. See what info you can get out of them."

"Okay." Hudson tried to think what to say. They made it to the lobby, and a few employees hustled over as his translator friend gestured frantically. "Taxi to the airport," Hudson told them.

"*Si, señor*. This way."

The group of three hurried over to a taxicab. "Can you come with us to the airport?" he asked Carlos. "I'll pay you a thousand dollars and smooth it over with your boss."

Carlos's eyes widened. "Is too much. A small tip is fine."

Hudson always forgot how little money the employees at all-inclusive resorts made. On average, twelve to eighteen dollars per day, and their tips were a huge bonus for them.

They all slid into the backseat.

"This is a matter of life and death," Hudson told Carlos to

explain the large money offer. "Your translation skills could save two people who mean everything to me." It was odd that he'd included Kelsey's son in that. He didn't know the boy. Though he'd always resented Jason, he didn't blame the innocent boy. He would love that little guy if he was around him, because no matter who his father was, Mo was part-Kelsey. She might be ticked at him for reasons known only to her, but he still loved her and he wouldn't let anything happen to her.

"Hudson?" Papa said in his ear.

"Sorry. Just getting in a taxi." He put the phone on speaker and held it out. "We'll try to send a text now. How's this sound, Papa ..." He looked at Carlos. "Please type in a text, Hudson Delta is a dead end. He said there is no weapon. It's a myth like the Holy Grail. We are to release the woman and child or he will send the police and a team of American special ops soldiers after us." He paused. "Yes or no?" he asked his grandfather into the phone. Hudson hadn't asked Papa for advice in years, but he trusted him explicitly and this was his field of expertise.

"Yeah, it's a great idea. Send it."

Hudson nodded to Carlos.

Carlos finished typing and read it back to Hudson to make sure he had it right, and then hit send. Time seemed to freeze. Brad was talking to someone about getting a charter to Cozumel. That wasn't good. It sounded like the plane was in Cancun, which was only about fifty miles away, but he'd never been so impatient in his life. He closed his eyes and prayed desperately for Kelsey and Mo's protection and for them to not be afraid or hurt. If those men injured them ...

He gripped the phone tighter as his pulse sped up. He should try some of his meditation techniques or breathing, but he couldn't even focus on something like that.

Why weren't the kidnappers texting back?

"Reed didn't find anybody at Kelsey's mom's house," Papa said.

No! Hudson's stomach dropped. "You think they already have them?" His voice shook. He didn't care how weak he looked. This was Kelsey.

"Aiden called Thor and he says that Kelsey and Mo should be with Granny Klein until six or seven on a weeknight. It's only five our time. Let me send some people that way."

"Okay." He settled back against the taxi seat, staring out the front window, praying for a text from the kidnappers saying they would let them go, or better yet, Reed or somebody finding Kelsey and Mo and preventing them from getting kidnapped. His dad, grandpa, and all his family would keep her safe until Hudson could get there and take over the job he should've had his entire adult life—protecting and loving Kelsey and her son. If only she'd let him.

The phone in Carlos's hand beeped and Hudson leaned toward him eagerly.

"They say 'Hudson Delta is lying. Either he promises to come for the woman and child or we shoot the boy now and the woman will be dead as well if he's not here by morning."

Hudson's heart took off and his stomach twisted. "Tell them I'm coming. Tell them if they touch or harm the woman or the boy in any way, Hudson Delta will send an elite special ops team after them and his highly trained family will hire mercenaries. They will never escape." He didn't ask for Papa's approval.

"That's all right," Papa said. "Threatening them isn't out of line."

Carlos typed the message in Spanish and then asked, "Send?"

"Yes, please."

Carlos hit the button.

They pulled up to the airport. Brad paid for the taxi, and they all climbed out. Carlos stayed with them as they walked into the waiting area.

"The plane will be here in about thirty minutes," Brad told him.

"Thank you." He pushed a hand through his hair, mussing it up. "Papa, what's happening on your end?"

He meant what Sheriff Reed was finding, but Papa said, "Another team of mercenaries made an attempt two days ago."

Hudson immediately hit the speaker button off and put the phone to his ear. Even someone as close to him as Brad didn't need to have any more information than necessary.

"We intercepted and Reed has them locked up," Papa continued. "Trying to figure out what to do with them. My contacts with the FBI have helped too much already and there are a lot of questions coming up. Thankfully, no more special ops teams have showed up since our new SEAL friends brought Maddie's Braden here last week. Admiral Gusbane and Admiral Seamons have both contacted me, pledging their loyalty and fishing for information about the secret. I don't know who to trust anymore, but King Frederick has to be behind this. It's been manageable for us so far, but if they're resorting to kidnapping your high school girlfriend, they must've realized they needed to up the stakes or they'll never get the weapon."

He had no idea what to say. Kelsey wasn't just his high school girlfriend, and he knew Papa wasn't trying to be flippant about the kidnapping. He was only saying Frederick was grasping and going to get more desperate in his attempts to get the secret weapon. So far the Deltas had kept everything under control, but it was going to end badly for somebody. Hudson just prayed it wasn't Kelsey and Mo.

He should've headed home last week when Aiden had started bugging him. He'd told his brother he needed a week to finish some stunts that were lined up and do more extra recordings so his fans wouldn't feel neglected in his time off, but it really had been because he wasn't ready to face Kelsey and make a fool of himself by begging her to love him. He kept stewing about what had happened with her and Jason, but he'd also been so relieved that Mo's dad was out of the picture. None of that really mattered at the moment. He should've been there. He'd take any slap to the face to somehow have prevented this.

Did these mercenaries have Kelsey and her little boy? He couldn't even stand to think about it. What if they hurt them? His free hand clenched, and he paced in front of the chairs that Brad and Carlos had settled into, clinging to his phone and studying the one in Carlos's hand like it was a creepy spider waiting to bite him.

It beeped, and he stopped moving and edged closer. He pushed the speaker button on his phone so Papa could listen in again as Carlos translated the text, "Hudson Delta can make any threats he wants. We are the ones holding his woman and child. What is his phone number to send the location of the meeting and how soon can he get here?"

Hudson was so sick. He wanted to puke like he had that night he'd found out Jason was with Kelsey. Somehow Jason was out of the picture now, but that hardly seemed to matter when Kelsey and Mo had been kidnapped. He held on to hope that the mercenaries were bluffing, but it was pretty slim.

"They think Mo is your son?" Papa asked.

"Apparently."

"Your mom has mentioned that possibility to me before."

The pain stabbed at him as if he was seeing her with Jason all over again. "He's not mine," Hudson said shortly.

Papa luckily didn't follow up and make the ache dig even deeper.

Hudson rattled off his number, which Carlos typed quickly. Then he looked at Brad.

"At least seven hours. Five on the chartered jet, a bit slower than commercial, and then if I remember right, it's a two-hour drive to your valley?"

Hudson nodded. Carlos typed that information in.

"Can you set me up a rental car to be waiting at the Centennial Airport?" he asked Brad.

"For sure, man." Brad got back on the phone.

Hudson's phone beeped a text. He clicked on that app. From an unknown number, it simply read, "Text us when you drive into Summit Valley. We will be waiting with your family."

His family. Hudson's heart beat heavy in his chest. Kelsey and Mo weren't his family, but he'd still protect them and do anything to ensure they weren't harmed.

He texted back quickly. *If they are harmed in any way, I will tear you apart. There's no place you can run, no place on earth you can hide.*

The incoming text beeped back quickly. A laughing emoji. Then, *Get here.*

Anger boiled inside him. They had better not hurt them. He didn't know what else to threaten. Could he bribe them? That might be the ticket. They were probably mercenaries, after all. His mind scrambled with ideas and possibilities. He could have Brad get in touch with his financial people while he traveled and get money into easily accessible accounts.

"Ah, no," Papa's voice came from the phone's speaker.

"What?" Hudson demanded.

"Reed found Granny Vance wandering around the yard outside, frantically searching for Kelsey and Mo, muttering about mean men. He can't find them anywhere in the house, but Kelsey's phone and Mo's coloring books are on the counter and dinner is in the oven. Klein had security cameras and sensors set up, but they must've disabled them."

Somehow, the picture of Mo coloring while Kelsey made dinner wrenched his heart. How would it have been to walk into his and Kelsey's home and see that beautiful scene after a long day? He shoved his hand through his hair. This was a long day, and he needed to focus.

"You okay?" Papa asked.

"No. But I'll get there as fast as I can, and we'll rescue Kelsey and Mo and nail these guys. Right, Papa?"

He couldn't think of the last time he'd begged reassurance from his beloved Papa, but he needed it now.

"Yes, son. We will."

Hudson felt reassured. For a brief moment.

Papa started giving him instructions, needing the number the texts had come from. Telling him they'd be waiting at the canyon entrance that led to Summit Valley with pants made with weapons and tracking devices hidden in them so Hudson could go directly to the meeting place without the men knowing he was prepared.

Reassuring them Kelsey and Mo would be okay, Papa reminded him they were well-equipped and well-prepared to rescue and protect them, and God was on their side. Papa and the entire family would be praying. Hudson knew they would. He knew God was there for them, had been there for him many, many times, but awful things happened to good people.

Please, not Kelsey and Mo.

Chapter Seven

Kelsey alternated between prayer and despair as the men drove them toward the canyon leading out of Summit Valley. They pulled off onto a side road, yanked them out of the Suburban and into a high-end off-road camper van. It had dark-gray leather couches wrapped around the back with a built-in kitchen. Somebody she never saw drove off with the Suburban.

The man holding Kelsey, who she assumed was the only one who spoke English, shoved her onto the couch and said, "Sit still and we'll let you hold your boy."

She nodded quickly. She'd do anything to have Mo in her arms. The man holding Mo stepped into the van, still with his hand clamped over Mo's mouth and covering most of his face. Only Mo's innocent and scared blue eyes stared at her.

The man walked over and dropped Mo onto her lap.

"Mama!"

Mo cuddled into her as she wrapped him up tight, cradling

him and rocking slightly as the tears she couldn't stop wet his soft hair.

"It's okay, love. It's okay," she soothed, lying through her teeth, but what was a mom to do?

"I'm scared, Mama."

"I'll keep you safe, love. You're okay." She kissed his soft cheek. Having him in her arms helped, but she was still so scared and had no clue how to keep her word and keep him safe. "Have you been praying?"

He nodded and pointed at his head. "In there."

"Perfect." She smiled at him, but it was wobbly. "Keep praying 'in there', love. He'll help us."

Oh, please help us.

The doors shut. The other two men sat up front, and the spokesman sat across from her, smirking. The van moved away from the Suburban.

Kelsey had so many questions, but she wasn't certain she wanted the answers. She kept softly rocking Mo and praying inside, looking at her son and refusing to look at the man seated across from them.

"I'm Stefan," the guy said. "It's nice to meet you, Kelsey and Mo."

She ignored him. She didn't want to know his name or anything about him.

"Aren't you wondering what we want with you?"

She glared at him. "I'm sure scum like you have reasons I'll never understand for kidnapping a mother and her innocent boy."

He laughed outright at that and rubbed his thumb and finger

together, his blue eyes glinting. "Millions of reasons, beautiful. Millions."

A new horror traced through her. Nobody would pay millions of dollars to ransom her and Mo, so that flimsy hope went out the window. She didn't know anyone besides Hudson who was a millionaire. She'd heard the horror stories of human trafficking and any mother was petrified of that happening to her child, but would they really pay millions for a mom and her son? That seemed a steep price.

"You're a bad guy," Mo shot at the man, glaring at him impertinently.

Kelsey sheltered her boy, praying the man wouldn't retaliate.

Stefan only laughed. "I am a bad guy." His laughter stopped and he gave them a cold stare. "So don't make me mad or you'll see how *bad* I am."

Kelsey's stomach flipped and her heart raced.

He spread his hands and smiled. "I am a highly educated, highly trained machine," he bragged. "I am from Germany but am fluent in Russian, Spanish, and English. I am also fluent in fighting, torture, and killing."

Her eyes widened and his creepy grin grew. The van turned abruptly, and she slid down the bench a foot. She put out a hand to stop herself. The van started up a bumpy road, thick trees scraping against the side.

She looked out the window and then back at Stefan. "Where are you taking us?"

"We're going to camp for the night, but don't worry. Your man will be here in the morning to rescue you." He was back to smirking at her.

"My man?" There was only one man Kelsey could think of, the one she rarely stopped thinking of. Them targeting Hudson could explain the millions of dollars comment, but would he really come for them? Kelsey counted on Hudson to follow through about as much as she believed Mo would brush his teeth if she didn't remind him.

"Hudson Delta." The guy smiled broadly.

A dart of relief and happiness rushed through her. Would he really come? For her? For Mo? The Brave of her teenage years would come for his Sunshine. She could only imagine Hudson swooping in, grinning and teasing as he defeated Stefan with grace and athletic ease.

Fear and uncertainty followed the brief respite of her silly dream. She and Mo were in desperate trouble. The adult Hudson was not the same man she'd fallen in love with. He wouldn't interrupt his famous life for her or his son. There was a possibility he'd send one of his capable family members with the ransom money. Yes. Hudson would at least do that for her and his child. She prayed even more fervently, clinging to that tiny flicker of hope.

"Your daddy is going to come," the guy told Mo.

Why was he so confident Hudson would come?

Mo looked at him, wrinkling up his nose and brow. "I ain't got no daddy."

"You haven't told him who his daddy is?" The guy studied her as if he thought she was an odd woman. He probably assumed that most women would want to lay claim to a man like Hudson Delta as their son's father.

She tilted her chin up and said coldly, "Mo's father is not in the picture."

"But it is Hudson Delta."

She shook her head, not willing to give him anything. "No, it's not."

He studied her, looking for any sign of weakness. "Are you telling me our intel was wrong?"

She shrugged. "I don't know what your intel claimed." Her stomach pitched, and she bounced on the seat as they hit a bump.

Mo looked up at her. "What's intel, Mama?" He seemed to be a lot calmer now that he was in her arms. That was a relief, at least. She prayed they'd put her and Mo into a tent and leave them alone until Hudson, or whoever he sent, came. Would they truly let them go after the ransom was paid? What if Hudson wasn't willing to give up his broken-neck-risking-earned money for them? She couldn't think like that, or she would panic even more.

"Information, love," she said.

"Oh." He shrugged and looked at Stefan. "Why are you a bad man?"

Stefan laughed. "Cute kid."

At least the question didn't tick him off.

"I'm a bad man because I'm good at it and it makes me a lot of money," Stefan said to Mo.

Mo's mouth twisted. "You can't go to heaven if you're bad."

The guy laughed harder. Then he got distracted by his phone beeping. While he replied to the text, Kelsey pulled Mo closer and whispered, "Don't make him mad, love."

"Sorry," Mo said. He looked up at the man. "But if you're nice, then you can go to heaven. My mama can show you."

"There is no heaven, buddy. And your mama here is telling me that there is no daddy either." His blue eyes twinkled at her and he said, "Which would be very bad for the two of you. Very bad. You know what I'd do with you if Hudson Delta doesn't come for you?"

A shiver went down her spine.

"What?" Mo asked innocently. He loved being part of adult conversations and had never been close to an adult who wasn't kind to him. Even if he thought this guy was a bad guy and he'd been terrified earlier, he was in his mom's arms and no one had ever hurt him.

"I'll kill one of you slowly and painfully, and then we'll see if the famous Death Wish Delta is willing to show up for the other one." His blue eyes were deadly serious.

Kelsey recoiled in horror and pulled Mo closer. Mo stared up at her and whispered, "He's really, really bad, Mama. Let's go home."

Stefan laughed, hard. Kelsey hated his laugh, and she hated him. He started texting again.

"Just focus on Mama, love," she whispered in her son's ear.

He kept his face turned up to hers and nodded bravely. "Okay, Mama."

"So you claim Hudson Delta is not the father, but is he your lover?"

Kelsey wanted to just ignore him, but she was horrified by him saying he'd kill one of them. He'd meant it.

"He's not," she said, still looking at Mo.

"Is Hudson my Thor's brother?" Mo asked.

She nodded at her boy.

"Thor should come kick the bad guy's bum," Mo said. "He's way tough."

Kelsey would love for anybody to come kick this bad guy's butt. Thinking of Thor and all of Hudson's impressive family gave her hope. The least Hudson could do was contact his family. They all loved Mo and were great to her. They'd come for her. Somebody would. She didn't know how they'd stack up against trained killers, but some of Hudson's family had been in the military and his brother Aiden was a Navy SEAL. All the Deltas were tough and with it. They'd rescued Alivia and Klein from kidnappers, Greer's wife Emery from a depraved lunatic, and the night of Thor and Shelly's wedding they'd saved Melene Collier from a jealous ex with armed men on his side. They could rescue her and Mo.

Please send the Deltas. Please.

She kissed Mo's forehead. "Shh, love. Let's not make him mad."

"Okay," he whispered back. Even though he was impetuous and precocious, Mo would usually listen if she asked him to be quiet. In church, most of the time. How many times had she wished away the hours on the hard bench trying to keep Mo distracted and quiet? What she wouldn't give to be safe in church right now.

"Oh, by all means, make me mad," Stefan said. "One of you is expendable."

Kelsey was going to throw up. She tried to shelter Mo with her arms. She couldn't look at Stefan.

The van stopped and the driver and passenger got out. They opened the back door and Stefan said something in what she assumed was German. The men responded, then opened compartments, lifted out tents and other camping equipment and then closed the van doors again.

"They'll get us set up and then you and Mo can quiver in your tent, waiting to see what happens."

"Stop it, please," Kelsey begged him. She just wanted to get away from him. Could she escape from the tent? Running blindly through the woods wouldn't be as terrifying as being in this man's power.

"So you claim that Hudson Delta isn't head over heels for you and this isn't his son? Those blue eyes aren't straight from his daddy, huh?"

Tears traced down her cheeks, and she hated that she was crying. She didn't want to let this guy get to her. But she couldn't let him hurt Mo and she was so, so scared.

"So interesting. Let me read you my recent text stream with the famed Hudson Delta. I'm a big fan of his, by the way. What a talented athlete. What a daredevil. Doesn't seem afraid of death. Just like the media claims. That's good. I like dealing with people who aren't afraid to die."

Kelsey closed her eyes and pulled Mo's head into her neck, praying for help and strength. She was afraid of death, but more than anything, she was terrified of anyone hurting Mo. She'd happily die if Mo could live.

"So this is what he texted through the local I hired in Cozumel to find him and let him know we'd kidnapped the two of you." He started reading. "'Hudson Delta says to tell you he is coming. He says if you touch or hurt the woman or boy, he will send special military teams after you, and his trained family will come, and he

71

will hire mercenaries. You will never escape him if you hurt them.'"

Kelsey looked up at him, her heart beating high in her throat. He arched an eyebrow.

"Then he said to me personally once I got his phone number and texted him to get here if he wants you two alive, 'If they are harmed in any way, I promise I will tear you apart. There's no place you can run, no place on earth you can hide.' Hmm. Sounds like a lover and a father to me. Sounds like a man who will protect his own." He stared at her.

Kelsey could hardly catch a breath. Hudson's fierce and protective words made her heart leap. Luckily Mo was cuddled into her and wasn't saying anything because she didn't know how to respond to anyone right now. She loved Hudson. She always had and always would. Could he really care about her and Mo that deeply after all this time, or was he just being a Delta man? Was he still her Hudson? Her Brave? Hope she didn't know that she could afford to feel made her lighter and warmer. Would Hudson really come for them?

She buried her face in Mo's soft curls and prayed desperately.

Please let him love us like I love him.

It was silly to hope like this. It was even sillier to place her trust in a man who'd let her down so horribly when she had needed him the most.

She needed him even more right now. And at this moment, the hope that Hudson would finally come for her, as well as her deep love for Mo, for his absentee father, and for heaven was all she had.

Chapter Eight

The hours of travel were finally, finally almost over. It was two-thirteen a.m. and Hudson was racing along I-70 to meet Papa. He wasn't one bit tired, his body pumping with adrenaline. He was itching to move, to do, to knock some idiot who kidnapped Kelsey and Mo out cold, and then kiss Kelsey long and slow. The last kiss hadn't ended the way he'd hoped, but maybe if he rescued her, he could change her mind about him. Maybe she'd call him Brave again. Maybe without Jason in the picture he could finally carve a future with Kelsey and her little guy. Mo. He loved the kid's name. He could easily love Kelsey's son like his own.

He pushed all the hopes, thoughts, memories, and worries away. All that mattered right now was Kelsey and Mo's safety. Pulling off the highway at the base of the canyon that led to Summit Valley, he followed Papa's directions to a secluded spot up a dirt road, parked the rental car, and leaped out.

"There he is!"

It was his dad's voice. A small camp light turned on, revealing a circle of family members and a couple guys he didn't recognize.

Hudson rushed to his dad and got a tight hug. Relief poured through him. He was home. He'd been the guy who ditched home and those he loved because he didn't want to think about Kelsey and go insane longing for her. Now she was all he could think about. Of course his family would welcome him home with open arms and mobilize to protect Kelsey and Mo and help him, even if it meant pulling protection away from the secret and the cave. These incredible people would help him rescue Kelsey and Mo. He was surrounded by his dad's arms, support from the best family on earth, and God's love—and hopefully His inspiration, too.

He hugged his Papa, brothers, his sister Esther, and his cousin Jessie. The hugs helped settle his angst a little, but nothing but Kelsey and Mo safe would relieve him of the worry and stress. Aiden and Thor teased him about being an insane show-off, which made him smile for a second, and then he was introduced to the two men.

"Hudson, this is Petty Officer Zander Povey, a Master EOD and elite special ops support, and Captain Zeke Hendrickson, elite Navy SEAL with more advanced training than anyone I know with an emphasis on hand-to-hand combat," Aiden introduced them.

Hudson shook their hands. "Nice to meet you, and thanks for being here."

"Of course. It's all part of the fun, right?" Zeke said, grinning at him. He was a tough-looking dark-haired guy with a glint in his eye that said he looked forward to any fight. He would definitely fit in well with the family.

"For sure." None of this was fun for Hudson, but this guy wasn't emotionally vested.

"I'm a huge fan," Povey said.

"That means a lot," Hudson said. "Thank you." Hudson had over fifty million followers on each of his social media sites, but it was still humbling to think a special ops demolition expert would be his fan. He'd assume a tough military guy would think Hudson's stunts were a crazy waste of talent. He'd heard that line a few times.

"Okay, down to business," Papa said. He handed Hudson some pants and started showing him different hidden compartments. "Knife, tracking device, all-utility tool, backup knife, backup tracking device."

"Close your eyes, Jessie and Esther," Hudson told them.

They both laughed as they averted their eyes. He hurried to slip out of his Sanuks and change into the pants. They fit well and were most likely a combination of spandex, cotton, and canvas, similar to some of his rock-climbing pants that could take a beating but also stretched well.

"Hopefully they don't find any of your devices," Papa continued. "If they do, it's fine. We can track you with or without them. It would just give us all peace of mind and if we're close at all times, we can intercept if things get dangerous for Kelsey or Mo. I'm sure they won't try anything if you lead them to the cave. I know my boy is an expert at directions and navigation."

Hudson smiled. Luckily, he was. He traveled far and wide and always seemed to know which direction to go. He hadn't been to the cave since he was a teenager, but he could find it.

"We'll have Thor and Aiden follow you at a safe distance. The rest of us will wait along the path and near the cave. When you hit the fog, make sure you're close to Kelsey and Mo. In the confusion, we'll rescue you all and dismantle them." He smiled grimly. "It's starting to get routine taking these mercenaries out."

"Speak for yourself, Papa," Thor interjected. "It's still fun for me. I didn't get a military stint, remember?"

Everybody laughed.

"But you're the hero of the universe, protector of the free world," sweet Esther reminded him. "So of course it's fun for you to fight."

Aiden groaned.

"Ah, that's why I love you, sis." Thor pulled her into a bear hug.

Hudson smiled. He appreciated that his family could always tease, but he was ready to get to Kelsey and Mo. "All right. I'm going to text the kidnappers and get their location."

"Do it," his dad said.

Hudson pulled his phone out of the pants he'd dropped on the ground and hated that his fingers trembled slightly. He could launch himself off any cliff in nothing but a wingsuit, mountain bike on a ledge that most people wouldn't crawl across, or surf a sixty-foot wave, but knowing Kelsey and her son were in a demented mercenary's hands had him shaky.

I'm here, he texted. *Where do I meet you?*

The response was quick. *Mile marker sixty-eight on highway 50.*

That was in the canyon, only a few miles from where they were.

On my way.

If we think anyone is following you, you bring any kind of weapon or your phone, or you're wearing a tracking device, we'll kill the boy first. You only need one of them around as a motivator.

Hudson read the text and his stomach felt like a boulder had settled in it. He read it aloud and then stated, "No one follows me. It's not worth risking." He quickly slid out of the pants, handed them to Papa, and put his own pants back on, then slid into his shoes.

Nobody said anything. He didn't care if they agreed, but they probably all understood. He texted back, *On my way.*

He couldn't think what else to say when he wanted to just rip this scum apart.

"All right." Papa clapped him on his shoulder. "We'll head to defensive positions near the cave. Keep them safe until then. We'll be praying."

"Thanks. Love you." Hudson hugged Papa, his sister, Jessie, and his dad, waved to everybody else, and hurried to the rental car. He hated driving off, feeling more alone than he'd ever been in his life. He clung to the steering wheel to stop his hands from shaking.

We'll kill the boy first. You only need one of them around as a motivator.

What kind of a lowlife would threaten to kill a child so

callously? Had the man said something similar to Kelsey? How horrifying would that be for a mother to have someone threaten her son? His stomach churned and his muscles tightened. Mo might not be his, but he would protect him like he was.

Please keep Kelsey and Mo safe. Please help them feel thy peace and comfort. Surround them with angels from heaven. Please help me be able to hear thy voice and act without pride to do what's best for Kelsey and Mo.

Hudson had always struggled with pride, and being a sought-after sensation didn't help. He was lauded throughout the world for his talents and daredevil stunts and pursued by gorgeous women everywhere he went. It was easy to get caught up in the celebrity life, but all his spiritual and self-control training back as a twenty-year-old after he'd slept with Kelsey had helped a lot. He also prayed daily for humility and tried to be grateful and give credit to the Lord for his talents and the blessings of financial success and the many people throughout the world he'd been able to help with that.

Right now he felt completely stripped of pride and was begging for heaven's help. None of his supposed talents or charm would help him rescue Kelsey and Mo. He had to rely on the good Lord and trust that his family would be there. The most terrifying thought was ... what if something set the kidnappers off and they hurt Kelsey or Mo before Hudson could get them to the cave and to help?

The thought of being humble instead of thrashing the idiots who dared kidnap the love of his life and her son was almost too much. He prayed again that he wouldn't react and pummel these men. Nothing had ever sounded better than that ... except Kelsey and Mo safe, and Kelsey in his arms. He'd have to focus on that end goal and dream, and he'd have to pray hard that some of his self-control training would stabilize him so he wouldn't take a swing.

Chapter Nine

Kelsey was chilled clear through in the little tent they'd shoved her in with no blanket or sleeping bag. Stefan seemed intent on keeping them miserable and afraid.

When the camp had settled and the lights in the van disappeared, she'd whispered for Mo to be sneaky quiet and then she'd tried to quietly open the tent zipper. Poking her head out, she'd been confronted with a big gun and the simple barked command, "*Nein*!"

She'd retreated quickly, zipped the tent back up, and hadn't dared try to escape again. Curled around Mo to keep him warm from the cold, late-September night in the mountains, the only reassuring thing was her little boy's slow, even breaths. She'd prayed with him and sung him his favorite songs about Jesus and he'd calmed down and fallen asleep. Thank heavens.

Now she shivered and prayed and tried to thank heaven that they were unharmed, but this was the most horrific spot she'd ever been in during her twenty-four years. She'd thought Hudson never responding to her text about being pregnant and ditching her had been devastating. It had, but in a very different way. Nothing could be worse than her son being threatened like this.

She prayed harder and suddenly a warm feeling surrounded her, like the angels of heaven were hugging her. Peace and love poured into her, and she knew that many people who loved her were praying desperately for her. She thought of her mom and prayed she was being comforted as well. She closed her eyes and savored the sensation and holding her precious boy. Mo was all that mattered. The good Lord knew that and would protect him.

The van door opened and shut and then footsteps pounded toward her tent. The good feelings and reassurance dissipated at what might come, but she still felt some of the warmth and peace. Her stomach took a tumble as the footsteps stopped in front of the tent. She sat up, cradling Mo against her chest.

The zipper went up and Stefan's voice came, "Let's go. Your man is coming to meet us."

Kelsey struggled to her feet, saying nothing, and followed him to the van.

Her heart leaped at the thought of Hudson coming for them. She shouldn't let the charming playboy with a death wish affect her and get her heart broken again, but it meant everything to her that he would leave his celebrity life to save them. He'd made it clear he didn't want her and Mo in his life. Was he coming now for duty or just being a typical Delta gentleman? At least he cared enough to step up and protect them when they desperately needed him.

Stefan shoved her more than helped her into the van and

settled her on the leather seat. Even his hand on her elbow was like the sensation of a spider crawling over her flesh.

Luckily, Mo didn't stir. The van's engine turned over and they pulled slowly out of the camping spot, leaving the tents and tables and chairs behind. Obviously they didn't care about any of that.

Her thoughts immediately swung back to Hudson. If he could really rescue them, she would give him a long kiss of gratitude before he ditched her again. She knew he would ditch her again, but what if being around Mo changed his mind about being a father? Everybody fell in love with Mo. Well, everybody but the evil Stefan and his men. What if Hudson changed his mind about being a father and wanted to split custody? Would a court award that to him after he had deserted them?

Oh, my. She was worrying about things that wouldn't matter at all if Stefan shot one of them. She'd take a bullet for Mo over and over again.

Her eyes widened as something clicked in her mind. Maybe that was heaven's plan and the explanation for the reassurance she'd felt in the tent. Hudson could fall in love with Mo, Kelsey would give her life for her son, and then Hudson could raise their boy. Could she beg him to move home, or would he take Mo all over the world on his adventures? Mo would probably love it, but he needed a stable life and home, his Grammy Lori and the Delta family's support, especially after losing his mother tragically.

Once again, Kelsey's thoughts were racing and wouldn't do her any good. But she was a mother. Of course her son was all that mattered. She wondered how her own mother was faring right now. Ah, that made her chest hurt thinking of how scared and inconsolable she would be.

The van turned onto the main road and sped up. A few minutes later, they stopped.

"There's your man," Stefan said.

She could see the dark silhouette of a parked car outside the van windows. The door sprung open and Hudson straightened out of the vehicle. Her heart and stomach both lurched. The vehicle's interior light illuminated his handsome face and well-built body. He'd come! He'd really come for them. Her head started spinning all kinds of fantasies, stuff that only happened in the movies. Hudson fighting and dismantling Stefan and his men, Mo running to his father, Hudson tossing him into the air and catching him as Mo giggled. Then father and son would focus in on Kelsey. Hudson's blue eyes and handsome face would fill with love and determination. He'd stride to her, wrap his free arm around her, and kiss her until Mo pulled them apart, begging, "Throw me again, again!"

Sheesh. Her imagination had never been so overactive. None of that was going to happen. Even if Hudson did heroically rescue them, he'd be gone before the sun rose. She was obviously exhausted, distraught, stressed, and out of her mind.

Stefan opened the van door and winked at her. "Come on in, Death Wish Delta," he called.

Hudson strode across the gravel and stepped up into the van. His gaze immediately focused on her. "Kelsey." Her name came out in a husky breath that made her tingle all over. "You're all right?"

She tried to nod bravely and not cry. He looked so good and so tough in a dark blue T-shirt and gray pants. His blue eyes were full of her. His gaze dropped to Mo, luckily still sleeping in her arms. "They haven't hurt either of you?"

"No," she managed.

He nodded and gave her a reassuring look. Then he turned to Stefan and every line of his face and body tightened. He should really give up extreme sports and be an action hero in movies, because he was more appealing than any actor she'd ever seen. With his talents and abilities, he could do his own stunts. He could swing through the trees with her in his arms, land on a branch, and kiss her deeply.

Oh, my, please stop with the random imaginary scenes, Kelsey commanded herself.

"Nice to finally meet the famous Death Wish Delta," Stefan said, all smiles. "I'm Stefan. Now shut the door behind you and lie down on the van floor so I can check you for trackers and hidden weapons. Wouldn't want to shoot your son for you disobeying orders."

All the good feelings Hudson had stirred in her fled. What if he had a tracker on him? Papa, who had been in the military, probably would have something like that and would've put it on him. What if Stefan found a tracker and shot Mo? The tears she'd been trying to fight stung her eyes.

Hudson gave her an encouraging nod, shut the door, and lay face-down on the van floor. Did that mean he didn't have a tracker? It hurt to see this strong, brave, no-fear man prostrate like that, but it also touched her. He seemed to be humbling himself. For her? Or to keep her safe?

The van drove off onto the highway. Kelsey thought they were heading southeast, out of the canyon. What did that mean?

Hudson hadn't been carrying a suitcase of money or anything, but she imagined in this day and age it would be all about banks transferring funds electronically.

Stefan kneeled and pulled a wand out of a nearby van drawer. He passed it carefully over Hudson, starting at his head and going methodically down his body. Kelsey was tense and clung to Mo. If that sensor beeped ... Stefan couldn't possibly shoot a little boy. Could he? If he pointed a gun in their direction, Kelsey would cover Mo with her body and pray the bullet didn't pass through.

The curves of the canyon stopped and within minutes, they turned onto the main highway. She thought they were going south, but she wasn't great with directions. Mo was still asleep. That was a blessing.

"Roll over," Stefan commanded.

Hudson complied and Stefan started at his head again with the sensor. It was dim in the van's interior, but Kelsey could still see the blue of Hudson's eyes as they focused on her and he gave her a warm look. That look promised so many things, but most of all, she thought he was promising she and Mo would be okay.

Hudson was truly here, looking at her as if she meant the world to him, and had come for her and Mo. Many times over the past four years, she'd tried to deny how deeply she loved Hudson Delta. She knew now that was all a lie. She loved him. No matter how he'd gouged her and deserted her and their son, she still loved him. He'd leave again. She knew that, but he was here now, and she could never thank him enough.

She forced a smile, and he returned it. He pumped his eyebrows at her. It was his signature smoldering look that every woman probably died over. She'd never forget Hudson claiming his eyebrow lift and smoldering look was always intended for her and her alone.

Her smile become genuine at the memory and the fact that he was really here. It was all going to be okay.

Then the wand in Stefan's hand beeped.

Kelsey gasped, horror tracing through her as she sheltered Mo in her arms. Hudson frowned and Stefan cursed.

"Did you think you could hide a tracker from me?" Stefan demanded.

"I promise you I have no tracker on me," Hudson said in an even voice.

Kelsey knew Hudson was honest to a fault, but Stefan wouldn't know that. If there was no tracker, what had beeped?

"You think I'm going to believe you?" Stefan snarled.

"You should. I don't lie. It's probably something in my pocket." Hudson spoke slowly and calmly.

Kelsey had no idea how he was so calm and reasonable. She was trembling from head to toe, every muscle tense, her stomach rolling, her heart racing, and her palms clammy. She was afraid she'd wake Mo she was clinging to him so tightly. Maybe Hudson faced death so often it didn't bother him. Maybe it was that he didn't know and adore Mo like she did. Mo wasn't his entire life, so he could be calm when this man had threatened to kill their son.

Stefan glared at Hudson, but he shoved his hand in his pocket and yanked it inside out. A penny fell into his hand.

"No tracker," Hudson said, still level and calm. "A little guy gave me his lucky penny in Puerto Rico a few weeks ago. I completely forgot it was in the pants and I didn't feel it as I emptied my pockets. Check it and you'll see it's nothing more than a coin. The metal must have set it off."

Stefan only stared at him. Kelsey begged heaven to have Stefan believe Hudson was telling the truth, but would a hardened criminal be affected by heaven's influence? She was terrified that he wouldn't.

He held up the worn penny and looked it over carefully. Kelsey couldn't catch her breath and she covered Mo with her body. If Stefan tried to shoot their son, she would make sure the bullet hit her. Then he'd have to let Mo live to keep manipulating Hudson. Right?

Please let me protect Mo.

Her heart thudded so fast she hoped she wouldn't pass out and not be able to shelter Mo. Her head pounded and her fingertips tingled. Signs of hyperventilation. She pursed her lips and forced a breath out over a count of three.

"It's okay, Sunshine," Hudson said softly. "It's just a penny. Stefan can see that."

Stefan still said nothing. He stood abruptly and Kelsey couldn't catch a breath. The man eased the van window open, tossed the penny out, and then shut the window. He kneeled next to Hudson again and passed the wand over Hudson's hip. No beep.

Kelsey breathed again, but her heart still raced. Was he going to hurt Mo, or did he believe Hudson? Stefan said nothing, and the silence was tense as he finished going over the front of Hudson's legs and shoes with the sensor.

Finally he stood, put the wand back in the drawer, and sat across from Kelsey and Mo. Kelsey's pulse calmed considerably, and she straightened and didn't cling to Mo quite as tightly. They'd survived. For the moment.

Stefan gestured to Hudson. "Please ... sit with your family."

Hudson quickly stood and sat next to Kelsey. He wrapped his arm around her and cradled her against his side. He smelled like that irresistible cologne—spicy, sensual, and perfect. His firm torso, chest, arm, and leg pressed against her was as reassuring as his warm lips brushing her forehead. "It's okay, Sunshine. I'm here now. It's all going to be okay."

She looked up at him, and she insanely had the urge to kiss him. His hand tightened around her arm, and he smiled and whispered, "Soon you can give me that kiss of gratitude."

Kelsey almost laughed. This was the Hudson she remembered, far too cocky and loving to tease her. "We'll see if you earn it, Brave," she teased back at him, saying his nickname aloud for the first time in years.

"Oh, I will." He winked, and all the previous horrors seemed to disappear. Her Brave Warrior was here for her and their boy. He wouldn't stay, but at least he'd come. Everything would be okay. Prayers were answered and miracles still happened.

"Isn't this sweet?" Stefan interrupted.

The uneasiness and fear returned, but it was much less all-encompassing with Hudson's strong body and brave personality right here to counteract Stefan's evil.

Hudson pinned Stefan with a determined and cold look. "I will take you to the secret. But I warned you what would happen to you if you dare harm them."

"No cameras rolling right now, tough guy. But she is gorgeous enough. I can see why you want to stay on her good side." Stefan gave them a searching look. "And here she claims you aren't the father of her little guy."

Hudson's body stiffened against her. His gaze remained on Stefan and the muscles of his jaw tightened in a way the Kelsey couldn't interpret. "I'm not," he said flatly.

Kelsey was confused. The honest Hudson she knew wouldn't lie, but was there some reason he wasn't claiming Mo? She didn't like it. She wanted Hudson to claim, love, and be there for their boy. More importantly, at the moment she was afraid if Hudson didn't say he was Mo's father, Stefan would think keeping her alive was the better motivator and it would put Mo in danger. Stefan only cared about getting his money or ... what secret was Hudson going to lead him to? That seemed like an odd way to describe millions of dollars.

"But that doesn't mean I won't protect Kelsey's son from a loser like you," Hudson continued.

"Brave words, seeing as nobody can follow us, you're unarmed, and have two liabilities to protect. I have the superior fighting and combat experience, and I'm obviously in control here."

"I guess we'll see how it plays out." Hudson smiled confidently. "But I wouldn't be so sure you have superior fighting or combat experience."

Kelsey didn't know how he did it, but her Brave Hudson made her feel so safe and confident in his ability to protect them.

"This is how it's going to *play out*," Stefan said in a chilling voice. "Admiral Davidson Delta, your beloved Papa, is going to retrieve the weapon and bring it to me."

"Excuse me?" Hudson's body stiffened against her and she could hear the surprise in his voice.

Oh, no. What was happening? Weapon? Secret?

"No," Hudson said, his voice full of confidence again. "Papa doesn't have the weapon in his possession. I'm going to lead you to it. That's the only way you'll get it."

What were they talking about? What weapon? And what did this mean for Mo and Hudson's safety? Please say Hudson's confidence wasn't all because he had a plan that Stefan was now throwing all out of whack.

Stefan's easy, ugly laugh came. "You'd like that, wouldn't you? Do you have any idea how many well-prepared men have tried to get to that cave and the fabled weapon and they all failed, captured by your family?"

Cave? Fabled weapon? Kelsey had so many questions, but now wasn't the time to voice them.

Hudson didn't answer, but the wary look in his eyes and the furrow in his brow worried her. They worried her a lot.

"I am much smarter than the rest of the soldiers who've been enticed by the fifteen-million-dollar reward to secure the weapon for our revered King Frederick."

King Frederick? The tyrant destroying Banida, Germany, and Poland? Kelsey shivered, and Hudson rubbed his hand along her arm as if to reassure her. She loved that he was here, but clearly this kidnapping was about something much, much bigger than a ransom attempt.

"I'm sure you are smarter," Hudson said blandly, as if he didn't think the man had a clue what he was talking about. "So what's your foolproof plan?"

Stefan grinned and said, "We're going to hunker down in a safe spot while we wait for Admiral Delta to pick up that weapon and meet me with it. When he does, I set the little family free and you two can have a serious paternity discussion." His eyes narrowed and his smile fled. "If the Admiral doesn't ... I will kill one of you for every hour he makes me wait."

Terror rolled through Kelsey, despite Hudson's reassuring presence and arm around her. Did Papa even have this weapon? She knew Papa Delta was a revered military hero, but was he still involved in the military? The weapon they were referring to sounded like a huge deal. Why would the Deltas be responsible for it instead of locking it up in Fort Knox or something?

"It's almost three a.m." Stefan studied Hudson carefully. "It's a two-hour drive from your valley to Denver. How much time do you figure your old man needs to get the weapon and bring it to a rendezvous point?"

"I honestly don't know," Hudson said. "I've never seen the secret, and I don't know why you keep calling it a weapon. For all I know, it's a mythical legend."

"Excuse me?" Stefan demanded, his voice rising. He pulled the pistol from his hip holster and pointed it at them. "You'd better hope and pray it's not a legend or you three will die."

Kelsey panted for air and prayed she wouldn't vomit. What if there was no weapon and Stefan shot them right now?

Mo shifted in her arms, and she prayed he wouldn't wake up, then prayed harder he wouldn't get shot.

Stefan set the pistol next to him, opened a drawer, pulled something out, and threw it at them.

Hudson's free hand darted out, and he caught the object before it hit Kelsey in the face.

"Thanks," she managed shakily.

"I have quick reflexes," he said, teasing in his voice.

She wasn't sure how he could tease at a time like this, but she appreciated it and it reminded her of the Hudson she missed from her younger, innocent days.

"I've seen that," she said, referring to the snake rescue and other times he'd reacted quickly.

"Call your Papa," Stefan demanded. "Call him right now, on speaker, and let's see what he says about this 'mythical' weapon and how quick he thinks he can get it to me. Or maybe he doesn't care about you enough to bring it to me." He gave them an ugly leer.

Hudson wrapped both arms around her and held the object in front of her. It was a small flip phone. He flipped it open and dialed a number from memory. She was glad he knew the number. With all of her numbers programmed into her phone, she wasn't certain she'd know any of them from memory.

The phone rang, then she heard Papa Delta say cautiously, "Hello?"

"Papa, it's me," Hudson said, sounding relaxed in the face of all this danger.

"Hudson." Papa breathed out in relief. "What—"

"I've got you on speaker," Hudson cut him off. "I'm going to need you to bring the Delta weapon to Denver. You'll be given the meeting place, but I need to know how long that's going to take you."

"Um ..."

Kelsey was so full of horror she rocked slightly in Hudson's arms. She'd never heard Papa say "um."

"It's a two-hour drive to Denver," Papa continued, "and the journey to obtain it is a couple hours each way, and of course I'll have to go through the protocols of retrieving it and preparing to move it safely."

"How long, old man?" Stefan demanded.

"At least seven hours," Papa said, his voice decisive and strong again.

"All right. You'll meet me at the Denver Botanical Gardens, by the teahouse, at eleven a.m. That's twenty minutes more than you need. If you aren't on time, your great-grandbaby gets shot first, the beautiful woman is gone by noon, and your famous grandson is dead at one p.m."

Kelsey had no doubt Stefan would shoot them.

Papa started to say something, but Stefan cut him off. "You will show me how the weapon works, do a demonstration, and then I'll have my men let these three go. If you try to bring help or the police, if anybody follows you, or you try to bluff me with a fake weapon, I will have all three of them shot at the same time and then I'll kill you."

He sprang across the small space between them, snatched the phone out of Hudson's hand, and snapped it shut as Papa Delta tried to say something. He went back to his seat, opened a window, and threw the phone out. Slamming the window shut, he smiled at them. "That went well."

Hudson ignored him and looked down at Kelsey. Something in his eyes terrified her. He either didn't believe Papa would bring the "weapon" or maybe he didn't even believe it existed. She wanted to ask question after question, but she could hardly process or think straight.

"It'll be okay," Hudson said softly, keeping her in the circle of his arms.

Kelsey looked down at Mo's soft, sweet face relaxed in sleep, then back up at Mo's father. In a lot of her dreams, she'd imagined them all cuddled close like this, but not like *this* at all. Even with Hudson here and the peace she'd experienced in that tent earlier, she could feel the end of her world coming. And there was nothing even a super athlete and charismatic tough guy, her Brave, could do to stop it.

Chapter Ten

Hudson's gut was in a knot as they drove into downtown Denver and the van parked in the service entrance of the Four Seasons Hotel. He tried to keep a calm façade for Kelsey, but this guy, Stefan, was throwing him completely off.

His family kept him up on news regarding the secret and he'd been informed after the family meeting where Chandler and Colt had asked Papa if the secret was indeed a weapon and he'd confirmed that it was. But as far as he knew, every other mercenary had either tried to find the cave on their own, or tried to force a Delta family member to lead them to the secret weapon.

This wasn't good. He should've let Papa find a way to follow them from the rendezvous point.

He and his family would've had a ninety-nine percent chance of keeping Kelsey and Mo safe if they'd hiked to the cave. The fog sensor would've activated to disorient and distract the men. The entire family and the future in-laws and Reed's men from the

Sheriff's department, and the elite SEAL team would've been there to take these losers out.

Dang. It was smart of this scum to demand Papa meet them with the weapon and give him a demonstration of how it worked. There were more than a few problems for Kelsey, Mo, and Hudson with this change of plans. These guys would kill them regardless. He'd seen that in Stefan's chilly blue eyes. And even if there was a chance of the mercenaries setting them free, Papa would never remove the weapon from the cave. He couldn't. If that weapon got into King Frederick's hands, it was only a matter of Frederick's men getting the weapon safely off U.S. soil before nuclear warheads rained down on America.

Hudson despised the thought of Kelsey and Mo being in such danger. He had to come up with a solution on his own, and soon.

He hadn't been home since Thor's wedding, but as often as one of his family members could catch him in cell phone coverage, they updated him on the Frederick and Delta secret situation. Hudson knew exactly how precarious it was. They couldn't risk the Delta weapon, not even to protect the woman he loved and her little boy cuddled so sweetly in her arms. It was a beautiful picture, contrasted so sharply with the evil and danger they were surrounded by. It was up to Hudson to keep them safe. And somehow, someway, he would. He swore it to himself and to the angels above.

But please, a little help would be incredible, he asked in his mind.

The van door opened and two men appeared. The man sitting across from them warned, "Don't try anything. At least two of you are expendable." He pointed his gun at Kelsey to prove his point.

"We'll be quiet and do what you say," Hudson said, though it hurt to grit the words out. He prayed for wisdom, humility, strength, and inspiration. He'd have to get some signal from heaven for the perfect time to escape, because there was no other option for Kelsey and Mo's safety now.

He helped Kelsey up, and they followed the man out of the van and across a concrete landing dock. Stefan led the way into a back hallway that was deserted. It was probably four a.m., so that made sense. Hudson could smell bread baking and hear some people talking and dishes clanking in what must've been the kitchens not too far away.

It was so tempting to fight his way free, but even though he was confident in his fighting skills, he couldn't possibly keep Kelsey and Mo safe while he took on three armed men. At least one of the losers would be smart enough to go after Kelsey or Mo.

They walked into a large cargo-type elevator and Stefan pushed the button for the forty-fifth floor and then passed a keycard over a sensor. The elevator slowly lumbered up. It was stuffy and uncomfortable inside. Hudson kept his arm around Kelsey, grateful the little guy was still sleeping soundly. He wanted to offer to hold him as Kelsey looked tired enough to fall over, but the transfer might wake him up.

The door finally opened, and they walked into a service hallway with plain white walls and thin industrial flooring. They crossed to another door. One of the men held it open and they entered a different world. A plush, wide hallway with low, soft lighting, thick carpet, crepe-colored walls, a smell like an exclusive spa, fresh floral arrangements on tables, and expensive artwork decorating the walls.

They walked past a few doors and then stopped and passed a keycard over a set of double doors. The man pushed the doors open and led the way into a luxurious suite with a full living area and kitchen, a large deck through the glass wall with a blue sparkling hot tub and patio furniture. The city of Denver spread out below them, thousands of twinkling lights in the dark night.

"This way," the guy barked.

Hudson escorted Kelsey after Stefan. They walked into a bedroom that had a king-sized bed and a small bathroom and closet attached. Hudson could guess it was the smallest of the bedrooms as it didn't connect to the balcony or have windows that opened and the bathroom only had a shower-tub combo, a sink, and toilet, not a jetted tub or large walk-in closet.

The man nodded to them. "You can rest." He looked out the windows at the city lights below and the over five-hundred-foot, life-ending drop, and smirked. "Good luck escaping." With that, he strode past them and slammed the door shut.

Hudson turned Kelsey into his chest. The little man was still in her arms so they couldn't get too close. He wanted to comfort her, hold her, kiss her if he were being honest, but he had to find a way to escape first.

She shuddered and leaned her head against his shoulder. His protective instincts fired. He would get her and her son home safe. Somehow. If he couldn't escape, hopefully Papa had some idea to bluff the guy into thinking he had brought the weapon. But Hudson planned to be gone from here long before eleven a.m.

He forced himself to look around the room for a few seconds

and get his bearings. On the forty-fifth floor, scaling down the windows or even horizontally along the building to the closest balcony with Kelsey and her little man might be rough. That's if he could break the window. These windows were made to withstand a lot.

But ... he saw a heavy decorative vase, and a plan started forming. He cocked his head to look into the open closet and felt even more reassured. He'd have to wait until he was certain the main guy was gone, but it would probably work. He prayed for help. It had to work. These two were far too important to take any risks on.

Hudson slipped one hand under Kelsey's legs and the other at her lower back. He gently lifted her and her boy off the ground and against his chest. She blinked up at him with those large brown eyes he loved. His Sunshine. She was tired, obviously terrified, stressed, disheveled, and so irresistibly beautiful to him. He wanted to kiss her, but he had to keep his head on straight right now.

He walked over to the bed and laid her and Mo down on it. She blinked up at him. Kelsey was as appealing as any scenery he'd seen throughout the world. To look at the woman he loved holding a precious child in her arms made him feel like he'd just leaped out of a helicopter.

He didn't even care that the boy was Jason's any longer. At this moment, he was cursing himself for ever letting that upset him or be an issue. He shouldn't have ever told Jason to take care of her, which the failure of a man hadn't done anyway. Hudson shouldn't have angrily walked away that fateful night. He should've gone to her and talked it all out, found out why she slept with Jason and then promptly forgiven her. He should've begged her to give him a chance, then spent every day proving he'd be there for her, until she believed him and loved him like he loved her. She was his Sunshine and he couldn't be without her any longer.

He kneeled next to the bed and brushed the hair from her cheek. Her cheek was as soft and alluring as he remembered. He had time before he could initiate the escape plan. Right now, he could focus on Kelsey and pray they could reasonably and logically work everything out that had been bitter and hard between them for four long years now. He'd stayed busy and accomplished his dreams, but without her, those dreams meant nothing.

"Thank you for coming for us," she said.

"Kelsey ... ah, Sunshine. You know I would always come for you."

Her brow wrinkled at that, and it hit him as hard as that criminal threatening to shoot her son and then her that she didn't believe him. That hurt, but he guessed he could understand. She'd asked him to come when she was pregnant. She'd needed his help. He'd come, but in his immature twenty-year-old mind, he'd thought he was doing the honorable thing by forcing the father of her child to take responsibility for her and her son. And the loser Jason had failed.

"I'm sorry," he began.

"For?" Her eyebrows rose and her dark eyes searched his.

He tried to think of where to start. "So many things." He tenderly traced his finger along her jawline. She quivered under his touch. He wanted to kiss her, but it wouldn't be right with her holding her little guy. He tried to focus. They had some time to talk this out. He didn't think Stefan would leave for at least a few hours to go scout out his meeting place with Papa and most likely set up his escape and contingency plans.

"I'm sorry I didn't fight for you," he said. He drew in and out a breath, focusing on calm and self-control when he wanted to rant and rave about that idiot Jason ever touching her and then for some reason deserting her. "I thought I was doing the honorable thing, letting Jason marry you and the two of you raise your son together."

"Excuse me?" she hissed at him. It wasn't a yell, but it was forceful.

Hudson's eyes widened, and he rocked back on his heels.

"Mama?" a sleepy little voice questioned.

"Shh, baby. Shh, it's okay." Kelsey rolled away from Hudson, transferred a soft pillow under Mo's head, and cuddled him. She sang softly, "Jesus said love everyone ..."

Hudson rose to his feet and stared down at them. Kelsey didn't look at him, but he could see her body was trembling. A tear rolled across her nose and down the other cheek. What had he done? What had he said?

Horror and sick understanding punched him in the gut as he stood there looking at beautiful, angelic Kelsey and her adorable little guy. Had Jason ... taken advantage of her?

No! He prayed he was wrong. He'd never let his mind go there. He had always thought that despite his personal annoyances with Jason, the guy was honorable. In high school, Jason had never mistreated a woman to Hudson's knowledge. There was also the fact when Hudson had seen them hugging that night four years ago she'd been clinging to Jason and crying. She wouldn't have done that if he'd hurt her. Right?

Hudson didn't know, and he was confused and sick and angry. After he somehow busted them out of here, defeated these mercenaries, and then made sure Papa was okay, he was going to track Jason down and follow through on the threats he had made that night. His hand clenched into a fist.

He gazed down at Kelsey and Mo and felt it all the way through. This perfect mother and child duo were his to love and protect. He'd have to get the story out of Kelsey, apologize more for letting his pride and anger rule him and not being there for her, and then hold and love and reassure her.

Oh, Kelsey. What had she been through and endured at Jason's disgusting hands? His stomach pitched.

Kelsey released Mo and slid carefully off the bed. Hudson backed up a step to give her room. Mo stayed asleep. Kelsey lifted the bedspread and laid it over his little body. Hudson should probably let Kelsey get a few hours' rest before he initiated his escape plan, but first they needed to talk. Maybe he could hold her and let her rest after she shared what had happened with her and Jason.

She spun to face him. Her dark eyes flashed so angrily at him that he blinked and almost backed up in surprise.

"Are you all ri—"

"Don't," she warned. "I am going to use the bathroom while you watch over Mo and *then* you are going to explain that ludicrous comment to me."

Hudson backed out of her way, staying close to the bed and watching her storm to the bathroom and shut the door behind her. She didn't slam it, but probably only because she didn't want to wake Mo again.

He took a deep breath and studied the little guy. He was super cute. His dark hair was wavy and brushed his forehead. His cheeks were chubby and looked soft. Hudson could love and make this boy his. He knew he could.

He grimaced. Now how to calm down Kelsey enough to figure all this out? Ludicrous comment? She must hate Jason, and the guy must've hurt her. If not initially, maybe later on? Maybe Jason had turned abusive and that's why they weren't together. Hudson needed to not let his thoughts race, but he was more than ready to hunt his former friend down.

The bathroom door opened, and Hudson strode toward her. She was still glaring at him. She walked over to the windows and faced the night sky instead of looking at him. Clenching her arms tightly across her chest, she hissed out, "You brought up Jason at Thor's wedding and I had no idea why. You somehow believed Jason was Mo's father?"

"Well ... yeah. Why wouldn't I?"

"What?" She turned to face him, anger radiating off of her. At him or at Jason? "Who *ever* planted it in your head that Jason was Mo's father?"

"He told me he was."

The anger changed to disbelief in an instant. Her dark eyes searched his face, but she knew he didn't lie. At least he hoped she still knew that about him.

She leaned against the window as if her legs were about to give out. She kept staring at him, and Hudson had no idea what was going on. She was either furious with him, with Jason, or with ...

Was someone else Mo's father? Why would Jason have lied to him about it? All these years he'd been livid with Jason, but maybe there was another man out there who had hurt her. If so, Hudson had to track him down and dismantle him.

As they locked gazes, he realized she was as upset as he was. She was obviously fighting to control it. He'd never been more confused in his life.

"Why would Jason lie to you?" she demanded. "When did you see him? How could you believe him? You thought I slept with *Jason*?" She looked disgusted and disturbed.

"I don't know why he would claim he was Mo's father," he said, holding up his hands. "But he always wanted you. Maybe he was jealous of the other guy you were with. Whoever Mo's father is."

Had that other guy taken advantage of her? Hudson could hardly stand to think about that.

Her eyes got huge, and her mouth dropped open. "Whoever Mo's ..." Her body and face got tight as if she were ready to explode. She looked to be keeping a very tight lid on her anger. He wouldn't blame her if she did explode, but he worried about Stefan or his guys coming in or Mo being woken up.

Instead of ranting, raving, and hitting him, she poked a finger in his chest.

"Hudson Delta," she said between clenched teeth. "I have never, ever, been intimate with anyone besides *you*."

Her tightly controlled anger and obvious frustration registered in his mind, but the one thing that stood out to him very starkly at this moment was ...

"You've never ... do you mean ..." He looked to the bed and

then back at her beautiful face. Excitement and a joy he hadn't felt before instantly intermingled. The best kind of shock he'd ever experienced in his life. "Mo is my *son*?"

Hudson's body felt light and his head felt like it was going to explode. Was it really possible? Could he be ... Mo's dad? And the only man that Kelsey had ever been with? The only man she loved?

"Of course he's your *son*," she said in a voice full of frustration and disbelief. "Are you nuts?" Her teeth were clenched again, and Hudson realized he was in deep trouble. "Why would you ever believe I was sleeping around? Four years waiting for you. How could you think ..."

Hudson knew they needed to talk this out, but at the moment he was too ecstatic. He barely caught himself from whooping happily and doing a standing backflip. He was at least a little aware of their situation and didn't want Stefan rushing in here to interrupt this incredible, happy, perfect, unexpected moment.

He lifted her off her feet, swung her around, and then kissed her hard on the mouth. She didn't return the kiss, but that was okay. She was probably furious with him for believing Jason, and she had every right to be upset. He was upset at himself and at Jason, but right now the ecstatic realization that he was Mo's father overrode everything else.

Pulling back, he stared at her in awe. "Kelsey I ... Oh my heck, I've been an idiotic fool. Jason ... he ... you ..."

He shook his head to clear it. He needed to explain everything that had happened, apologize over and over again, hear her side of the story, and kiss her for a long, long time, but first ...

He looked at the sweet, perfect, adorable, amazing little boy on that bed and then back at Mo's mother. Hudson's Sunshine.

"Oh, Kelsey ..." He ran for the bed, sinking down next to Mo and wishing he could sweep him up and hold him close. He stared at the little guy in awe.

Kelsey's footsteps approached. He tore his gaze from his son—his son!—and stared up at her. "He's so perfect." He looked back at Mo. He carefully touched his soft cheek with just his fingertips. His baby boy. He wanted to laugh and cry and do so many things with Kelsey and Mo. He'd missed so much. He calculated quickly in his mind. Mo had to be almost three and a half.

Tears rolled down his face as he studied his son. Hudson couldn't think of the last time he'd cried. Even when he'd walked away from Kelsey, he'd been so angry he hadn't cried. But now ...

His flesh and blood. Lying on this bed. Innocent. Perfect. So unbelievably cute.

And in so much danger.

Fear made his gut tighten. He'd been willing to protect and sacrifice himself for Kelsey and her son before he knew. Now ...

He still needed to wait for the perfect moment, but those men out there didn't stand a chance. Hudson would dismantle them. Nobody would hurt his son. Nobody would hurt his Sunshine. The only woman he'd ever loved.

He looked back up at her. Her eyes were wide with surprise and most of the frustration had disappeared from her beautiful face.

"Brave." She wiped his tears with the pad of her thumb. "All this time. You really didn't know he was yours."

He shook his head. He should've been embarrassed about the

tears, a sign of weakness, but he didn't care. He was weak for her, and for his son, and he didn't care at all. He stared back at Mo for a few more seconds, then forced himself to tear his gaze away and stand. He wanted to reach out and hold her, but he had to somehow explain first.

"Kelsey, I'm so sorry. I'm confused and ecstatic and yet angry at myself for believing Jason and furious at him for lying to me and ..."

She grabbed his arm and tilted her head over to the corner of the room and two chairs. He could read in her dark eyes that she was every bit as upset as he was, possibly more. She'd raised their boy alone, thinking Hudson was a deadbeat who never came for her for four long years. He couldn't even imagine. She had to hate him. Would she forgive him?

They needed to talk this out, but somehow quietly so they didn't wake Mo or incite an early attack from the other room. All was quiet out there. Were the men sleeping? He knew at least one of them would be guarding the door. He'd instigate his plan and they'd escape unharmed. He prayed to know when the time was right.

Then he prayed in gratitude. For his son. For Kelsey. Everything was a mess, and they were in extreme danger, but he couldn't stop the happy, bubbly feelings and the gratitude. The anger and frustration at Jason and all Hudson had missed out on and what Kelsey must have gone through thinking Hudson had deserted her and raising their boy alone was all there, too. He was a mess of emotion right now.

He escorted Kelsey to the chairs and they each sat in one. Hudson didn't know if he could really sit right now, but it was probably smarter than him pacing, maybe punching the wall, maybe flipping in the air in his excitement.

"Why don't you tell me everything from your perspective," Kelsey said. Her voice seemed calm and reasonable, but her dark eyes were still on edge, wary, and angry. Did she believe him? It seemed like the entire nightmare hadn't sunk in yet.

He couldn't even imagine what she was thinking. He was such a jumble he hoped he could get the story out without crying again. His brothers would tease him, but he didn't care. All that mattered right now was Kelsey and Mo.

Looking over at the bed again, he catalogued that mop of dark hair, squishy cheeks, and the small body under the comforter.

His boy. His.

His entire life had just been uprooted. He was a father. It was surreal. He'd never been so happy.

Now to explain to Kelsey how he'd messed this all up so badly with a lot of help from that loser Jason. He could beg her to forgive him, kiss her, and finally hold her close.

And then he had to get them out of this hotel room and away from these mercenaries safely.

If only he'd let Papa have someone tail them. He was on his own, and not willing to risk one hair on either of these beloved heads. He prayed hard for help and strength to keep them safe, the right words to tell Kelsey the story, and then the miracle of him, Kelsey, and Mo being a family.

Nothing was more important than his Sunshine and their son. Nothing.

Chapter Eleven

Kelsey stared at Hudson's handsome face, incredulous at how he kept turning to stare at Mo, a look of wonder and awe in his eyes. She loved that he'd cried and that he was so happy and excited. So ... Hudson. It was getting harder to stay angry with him when he was so genuinely thrilled to find out he was a father and upset about the time he'd missed.

But her stomach and neck were tight and her body burned with the injustice of it all. She was upset, confused, and very frustrated. What could possibly have happened for Hudson to ever believe she would sleep with Jason Spackman? Then to make it worse when she told him it wasn't Jason, he'd asked about "the other guy"? Really? Really? Did he know her at all?

She was holding everything tight to her chest right now so she didn't explode and have Stefan run in here, but she was on the edge of exploding like she'd never done in her life.

Four years of pain, loneliness, and thinking the love of her life had turned his back on her because of a misunderstanding? It made no sense. Her blood boiled. How could Hudson possibly have thought she was sleeping around? Did he think after he went on his quest to find his self-control that she'd given up every scrap of hers? Ugh!

Yes, she'd lost control with Hudson that night, but that was because it was *him*. Hudson was the only man she couldn't resist. Jason Spackman? Never! She'd never even kissed the guy. Why would Hudson have trusted Jason's word and not talked to her about it?

Her mind was spinning so hard she couldn't settle on one thought or a direct way to get to the answers she needed and process the lost time and lost dreams. Added to the drama of Hudson not knowing he was Mo's father and his messed-up facts about the past was the horror that they were stuck in this hotel room with terrifying killers on the other side of the wall.

She wanted answers, and she wanted them now, but she would not let Mo get hurt because she and Hudson were distracted by the drama of the past.

"Before we ... figure this out." Could they figure it out? Could she trust Hudson again? This had better be some story. "Are you not worried that Papa won't get to the meeting place in time with some weapon? Even if he does, don't you think they'll kill us anyway?"

"Papa definitely won't bring the Delta weapon, and yes, they would kill us regardless of what he brings." Hudson looked completely unconcerned.

"Hudson!" Kelsey forced herself to keep her voice down, but it was rough. So many emotions right now, and she felt like she had control of nothing. "Hudson," she begged. "Mo ..." She looked at their son sleeping innocently, unaware of any danger.

Hudson leaned forward. Their knees pressed together, and he took both of her hands in his. "Sunshine, I'm here now. Nobody will ever, ever hurt the two of you again." He looked at Mo, then focused on her again. "Never. I promise you that."

She loved Hudson's intensity, bravery, strength, impulsiveness, and the devotion he used to have for her and in the blink of an eye seemed to have again. Not just for her alone any longer, but also for their precious son. Could she get through the turmoil of emotion and questions and trust in the words he'd just said?

She had so many, many questions she needed answered right now, but first she had to make sure he knew. "I'm trusting you to keep him safe, Brave." She used her mom voice.

He smiled slightly. "Good. You should. I'll keep our boy safe, and I'll keep his beautiful mother safe too."

A quiver went through her. Four years of wishing Hudson would come for them and not only own up to being a father but give her and Mo all the love and devotion she'd always thought her Brave would have for them. Was it truly happening? She wanted to trust and love him, but this was too much to process and she'd doubted him for too long. She needed to somehow change her mindset, but she honestly might explode from all the emotion first.

"I've got a plan and it will all be okay," Hudson reassured her. "We have to wait until Stefan leaves to meet with Papa before I implement it. Not that I wouldn't love to take out that pathetic waste, but I'm not risking either of you for anything." He grinned cockily at her. "And that includes my pride in wanting to show off how well I fight to you."

She almost smiled. He was still her Hudson. She'd tried to convince herself he'd changed, but here he was. The show-off who adored her. He had always backed up his cocky words, and she had to trust him now. Trust him to keep them safe. Could she fully trust him with her heart again? With Mo's?

"Okay." She nodded cautiously. "We've got time to ... talk this out, then?"

He nodded. "And plenty to talk about." He straightened, leaning back against the chair cushions, but held on to her hands. "I can't believe I missed out on over three years of his life." Regret laced his words, and his gaze strayed to the bed again.

She instinctively squeezed his hands. If somebody would've told her yesterday she'd be trying to comfort Hudson about missing out on Mo's life, she would've guffawed at them. But she knew Hudson didn't lie, and he had insanely believed all this time that she was with Jason. At Thor and Shelly's wedding, when he asked her where Jason was, she had been so confused. She was even more confused now. She searched for which question to ask first.

"Why did you take off running at Thor and Shelly's wedding instead of talking to me then?" She was skipping ahead. That wasn't the most pressing question.

His blue eyes pierced her. "Well, you'd just slapped me and were yelling at me and all I wanted to do was kiss you again. I'm not sure how much talking would've gotten done that night."

"Don't," she warned.

He smiled. Of course he was teasing her, but she was still too upset to tease right now.

"Papa issued a Delta Protection alert. General Carl Phillip used the wedding as a distraction to infiltrate the valley."

What in the world was he talking about?

"Aiden needed help rescuing Melene Collier from the three-legged skunk. Sorry I ran. It was literally a matter of life and death."

She could only stare at him. She was only getting more confused, and the anger was still pounding at her chest, trying to get out. "Hudson," she said as calmly as she could. "General Phillip died in friendly fire days before the wedding. It was world-wide news."

He shook his head. "Fake news. He was after Melene and after the Delta secret weapon." He trailed his thumb along the back of her hand, making it difficult to concentrate. Which made her mad at herself. Hudson had always been irresistible to her, but she needed far too many questions answered to let herself be distracted by his touch and charm.

"I thought Melene was an international charity worker?"

He nodded. "Phillip almost kidnapped her back in Banida where he'd trapped her as she tried to save a teenage boy. Aiden rescued her, but Phillip wanted her badly, so he put a million-dollar bounty on her head. He almost captured her in Jamaica, but Aiden was protecting her full time at that point. Aiden kept her safe and they fell in love. Phillip faked his own death to get her and the secret weapon. But we all came together the night of Thor and Shelly's wedding, stopped him and his men, and Aiden killed him."

This story was insane. They were being held by maniac killers who were after the secret weapon and Hudson was always honest, so she didn't think this was some made-up tale, but this was huge and unbelievable. It was a spy movie with a far too complicated plot for the quick synopsis he'd just given her.

Despite the serious subject, Hudson's gaze strayed to Mo. A look of wonder and an irresistible smile curved his lips. Her heart thumped happily at the sight. Hudson was in their lives and seemed genuinely moved and ecstatic about being a father. Could they really work this out and work through their messed-up past to a future together?

She tried to focus. It was so easy to get distracted when Hudson was around.

"What is this secret? Some weapon? Why didn't you ever tell me about it?" She'd thought before they were separated that she knew everything about Hudson.

"It's a weapon of some sort. I wasn't lying to Stefan, but maybe misleading." He shrugged. "I've never seen the secret and have no idea what it is. Only Papa and whoever he names Secret Keeper know what it truly is. But it's very serious and a huge responsibility for all of us, especially the Secret Keeper. Yes, I've known about it since I was twelve."

She leaned back against her chair and released his hands. "Wow. I thought you told me everything. You know, back before …"

"Sorry." He pushed a hand through his hair, disheveling it just the way she liked it. "None of us could share it with anyone until we were married. It's … huge. Like, end of the world, starting or ending World War III kind of huge."

"I imagine so if King Frederick is after it," she tried to say the words calmly but her voice shook. Her mind tried to grasp the implications of it. World War III? What kind of nightmare had she entered?

He nodded, more serious than he usually got.

Her stomach rolled, and she stared at Mo. "We're in a lot of danger, aren't we?"

He bobbed his head, obviously unable to lie to her, but then he captured her hand again and squeezed it. "I've never lied to you, Kelsey. You know that, right?"

"I've always known you couldn't lie." Even though this was all a lot to take in, and she hadn't trusted Hudson because he'd never come for her, she still believed he would tell her the truth.

"Then believe me when I tell you I will get us out of here and I will keep you and Mo safe. Always." His blue eyes were intense and captivated her like they always used to do.

She let his words and the depth of his feelings wash over her. She loved his passion. She loved his protectiveness of her and Mo. She loved him. But there was still a lot to talk about and a lot of trust to rebuild. He hadn't been there for her before. He'd been lied to, but it cut her down deep to think he'd stayed away for four years, no matter what Jason had told him. She could not comprehend it and the pain of that separation cut deep.

"I believe you will keep us safe," she said. She had no idea how he'd rescue them and her stomach was tied in knots with fear and worry over Mo and Hudson's safety, but she would trust Hudson. He had let her down before, but she could see now it wasn't intentional. He'd been hurt and confused too.

"Thank you." He lifted her hand and brushed his lips over her knuckles.

Kelsey quivered from the sensation. She loved him. She could never deny that. She trusted Hudson would do everything he could to keep them safe. But Stefan and his men were horrifying. They were in a treacherous situation and the terror hovered around them like a thick fog.

She also had no idea how Hudson had believed she could be intimate with someone else. They'd spent four, long, lonely years apart and it was more sickening and unbelievable now than ever. If her Brave didn't have the most incredible excuse in the world. Could she truly trust him with her heart again?

Chapter Twelve

Kelsey wished they were safe and had talked everything out and could just kiss for a good, long time. But she feared neither safety nor kissing was going to happen. Saying a quick prayer for trust, faith, and forgiveness she tried to focus on the past while they could. "Now let's go back to how in this messed-up world you could believe I would sleep with Jason Spackman." Her voice rose unintentionally and frustration tightened her chest.

Hudson lifted his free hand and brushed her lips with it. "Shh, Sunshine. We don't want them coming in here ... yet."

Yet? That scared her. His plan was to lure them in here? The scary-looking guys with big guns?

"So you sent me that text that you were pregnant and needed me to come," he started with, distracting her from their current situation.

She nodded.

"I was so excited at first." He released her hand, sprang to his feet, and paced in front of her chair. Hudson had so much energy. She let him pace.

"At first?"

He paused and turned to her, using his hands to talk, but thankfully not pacing and making her dizzy. "I was stoked to be a dad, and I dropped everything and got on a plane to get to you. I wanted to call you or text you, but that seemed hollow and the news felt so ... huge and amazing. I just had to be there to hug you, kiss you, celebrate, and reassure you that our path might be different now, but we would make it all work. Together."

That was what she'd hoped for, well before that woman answered his phone and she Googled him and realized he'd lied to her about being off the grid. That still confused her. Why had he lied about that?

"As I traveled, I studied the text and I worried about your phrasing. Wondered why you said you were pregnant but never said the baby was mine and the 'break away from my busy schedule' was kind of snippy and not like you. I also wondered how you wouldn't have known you were pregnant for over three months and that made me worry the pregnancy was more ... recent than when we'd been together. But I hated that I doubted you. We loved each other completely and I knew you'd never cheat on me. But I have to admit the doubts kept working their way in."

He paused, and she stared up at him. "I don't have regular periods, so until I started feeling the signs of pregnancy and realizing it had been a while since my last period, I didn't think to take a test. I was snippy because when I called, some girl answered your phone."

"What girl?" His brow furrowed.

"I don't know. Whoever had your phone."

"When I did my final two weeks of self-mastery high in the Peruvian mountains, I left my phone with some friends. I didn't see your missed calls or get the text until it was a week old. One of their girlfriends must've answered the phone when you called."

"No." She shook her head. "Nope. You've got more explaining to do about that one."

He cocked his head to the side. "Okay?"

"You asked me not to Google you early in your career because women would post things that didn't portray the whole picture. Remember?"

His blue eyes were grave. "I remember. That redhead who kissed me and her friends took a photo that she posted and made you upset."

"Yep." She was getting upset now. "Then after we ... created Mo." His eyes widened and filled with some heat at that one, but she rushed on. Now was not the time to dwell on that. "You went off the grid to learn self-mastery and didn't do your stunts for three months. Right?"

"Yeah."

Her neck was getting hot, and she started to stress. If Hudson had lied to her about that ... "When I called to tell you I was expecting," she tried to keep her voice level, "that girl answered your phone, and I got upset."

"I bet. I'm sorry."

She held up a hand. He could hold his apologies until the end. Her hand unfortunately was trembling, and his blue eyes got wary. "I was so upset I decided to Google you. Imagine my surprise when you weren't off the grid at all but in fact were doing stunts the entire three months and 'mingling' with the women in the crowd in some of the pictures." She stared pointedly at him.

His brow squiggled. "Kels ... I wasn't doing stunts that three months. I was doing self-mastery and all kinds of mind-body fighting classes."

A hard knot formed in her gut. "You never lied to me before. Never." She almost shrieked the last word.

"I'm not lying now." He held up a hand. "Please, hear me out. Since the start of my career, I've always had my guys record extra stunts and interactions with the crowd so when I was visiting home or got injured or something didn't go right we'd have extra footage to post. For example today they'll post some fabulous stunt I'm doing." He semi-smiled. "They'd die to have the footage of how I'm going to break us out of here."

She could only stare at him. "You pre-record ..."

It actually made sense and was pretty smart.

"Yeah." He shrugged. "Fans want constant content. To keep building and growing, we try to give it to them even when we aren't giving it to them."

"Oh." That explained a lot. Her anger cooled, but the frustration was still there. If only they could've talked this all out four years ago.

"You believe me." He searched her gaze, his blue eyes clear and guileless.

"Yes," she admitted. It was so easy to think, 'if only,' and they were just getting started. She wanted him to get the story out and prayed she could understand and get past it all. She gestured for him to keep going.

"Okay, so I finally made it to your apartment complex. It was late at night. I saw some couple hugging at your door. I didn't want to interrupt, but then I realized it was Jason, and a few seconds later I saw your face. You were crying." His voice was both sad and angry at the same time. She could tell these memories hurt him and she knew how passionately Hudson felt everything.

"I asked some girl walking past if you two were together and she said 'all the time.'"

Kelsey's eyes widened, and she tried to think of how to defend herself. Now she knew how he'd felt about her accusing him of being with that redhead.

"Jason was there for me," she said cautiously. "As a friend. He tried to talk me into marrying him. Until I started showing and my rear end grew bigger than my baby bump. He disappeared pretty quick after that."

"The stinking, idiotic waste of a human heart," Hudson muttered. He clenched and unclenched a fist. He paced back and forth a few times. She watched him, appreciating him being so upset that Jason had been a shallow jerk, but she waited to hear what Jason could've said or done to convince Hudson she was with him and Jason was the father of her baby. Some girl saying she and Jason were together wasn't enough proof, though it probably planted more doubt. She'd known Jason was interested in her, but if he had outright lied to Hudson that he was Mo's father? That was sneaky and stupid. Hudson could easily thump Jason Spackman.

"I was pretty upset seeing you hugging him and that girl confirming you were together. I ... Well, I went behind some cars and spewed, thinking about you two being together."

Her eyes widened, but she could relate. She'd felt similar feelings when that girl had answered his phone and then she'd seen social media posts of him with other women and assumed that her Hudson had lied to her.

"I was just trying to figure out what to do, what to say to you," he continued, "when Jason came through the parking lot. I asked him if he was the father of your baby and he happily told me he was." He drew in a breath.

"And you believed him?" She was stunned.

"I did." He hung his head. "I'm sorry."

Her neck got hot and righteous indignation boiled inside her. How could Hudson believe she'd cheat on him? He was the only man she'd ever loved, and he hadn't trusted in their love.

"I tackled him and started thumping him until he begged me to stop. I was so angry I couldn't see straight, but I'd been working for all those months on self-control, my relationship with my Savior, being humble, and not being a selfish bugger."

She lifted her eyebrows. His quest for control was why they'd been isolated from each other in the first place.

"I might've killed him, but I forced myself to let him go and I was convinced that I had to take the higher road and let you be with the man you'd chosen. The father of your baby."

"What?" She jumped to her feet to face him.

Hudson spread his hands and nodded. "I threatened him with dismemberment if he didn't marry you and love, protect, and spoil you and your baby. Then I stormed away so I wouldn't tear him apart then and there. Leaving you was the hardest thing I've ever done." He blew out a breath. "I went back to my work and put everything I had into it, trying to stay away from home and any memories of you and filled with more recklessness than ever. Death Wish Delta." He shook his head.

He studied her, obviously wondering if she was going to explode. She didn't want to disappoint him like he'd disappointed her by never coming for her. All the bottled-up emotion of this conversation, or more likely of the past four years, came rushing out.

She flung herself at him and started hitting his chest with her fists as hard as she could. She wanted to scream and rant and rail on him, but she couldn't wake Mo up or risk Stefan coming to investigate, so she just silently hit him as tears streamed down her face.

Delivering her baby without Hudson there by her side. Staring at the birth certificate for almost an hour before leaving the space for "father" blank. Every time she was so exhausted from work and taking care of a newborn, but woke up with Mo repeatedly in the night as a baby, or held him, pacing or rocking when he was sick and inconsolable. Hearing sweet little Mo tell people, "I ain't got no daddy," and seeing the sympathy in their eyes as they looked at him and often the disdain as they focused on her.

She hit him and let out all the pain and loneliness and lost time. He let her. He stood there and took it until she wore herself out and abruptly stopped and laid her head against his chest. She pulled in hard, fast breaths and the tears kept trailing down her cheeks.

Hudson wrapped her up and held her as if she were a priceless possession.

"How could you? How could you leave me? How could you miss out on Mo? How could you believe that idiot Jason?"

"I'm so sorry, Sunshine. So sorry." He shook his head. "I can't even stand to think about missing out on this time with you and our son. There are so many what-ifs running through my brain. I can't believe I was such a trusting dupe, trying to take the higher road and all my principles that weren't even correct. I should've pounded on your door and forced you to confirm Jason's story. I was immature and an idiot and I was honestly convinced in my idealistic brain and with my broken heart that I was doing the right thing."

She ran her hands around his back and cuddled in closer. How she'd missed him. She could hardly believe all those painful, lonely, miserable hours without Hudson were because Jason wanted to make a play for her and had blatantly lied to Hudson. And Hudson had stupidly believed him.

Groaning, she shook her head against his chest, more tears running down her face. "Four years. You stayed away for four years because of that lying, sneaky, jerk."

"It's sickening. All that time I missed with you. With Mo." He pressed his lips to her hairline. "Will you ever forgive me?"

"I don't know. I can't wrap my mind around it. Didn't your mom or somebody tell you I wasn't with Jason? That I was in the valley raising my son alone and working as a home health care nurse?" She looked up at him, gauging his response.

"No." His blue eyes begged her to forgive him and understand it was all an awful mistake. One that could've been avoided, and their life plan and dreams could've stayed on course, but she'd come to realize that life didn't go according to her plans very often. "Didn't you notice I never came home? And if I did, I stayed away from church and town. If my mom or anybody tried to bring up your name, I would change the subject, pretend I lost cell coverage, or find some other way to end the conversation. It hurt too much to hear about you and Jason."

"There was no me and Jason," she said vehemently, but she realized he'd been deeply hurt and kept on hurting for four years. What a tragic loss for both of them.

"I can't tell you how relieved I am." His face tightened. "But I can hardly stand that I believed him that night. If I would've just gone and knocked on your door, talked to you ..."

"It would've been so different." She pressed her lips together and then said, "I'm going to find him and tear him apart."

Hudson chuckled and hugged her tighter. "We'll do it together."

"Together." She looked up at him. Were they really going to be ... together? This was truly going to happen? They could both forgive and move past this?

"Yes, Sunshine." Hudson bent down low and grazed her lips with his own.

Her heart started beating out of control and the ache she'd fought for four long, lonely years threatened to burst. She needed Hudson. She'd always needed and loved him no matter how she'd tried to make him an unfaithful loser in her mind.

"I won't be stupid and let you go ever again. I'm not missing out on another minute with you and Mo." His blue eyes were full of light and love. For her. For their son. "I love you, Kelsey. I love you and I'll do anything to prove to you—"

She stood on her tiptoes and pressed her lips to his, cutting him off. She loved his words, but right now she needed his mouth on hers and his strong body circling her.

Hudson responded fervently, kissing her with all the pent-up longing and love and devotion that she'd dreamed of feeling and seeing from him. He sank down into the chair behind him and tugged her onto his lap. "You make me weak, Sunshine."

She ran her hands through his hair, mussing it up like she loved it. "I know that's a lie, Brave. You're tougher than any man I know."

He grinned. "You obviously haven't met Aiden's elite Navy SEAL buddies."

"Couldn't hold a candle to my Brave."

He chuckled, but then he kissed her again. She wrapped him up tight, and he wrapped her up tighter, and they kissed and kissed, trying to make up for lost time, pushing the pain and the loss behind them. They might never make up for the loss, but she would savor each touch, kiss, word, tease, and moment. She'd never take time with him for granted. Would she ever tire of kissing him?

The room was getting lighter in the pre-dawn when she pulled back to catch her breath. His blue eyes glinted at her and he said, "Need to rest, Sunshine?"

"Nope. I could kiss you all day and all night."

He pumped his eyebrows in that smoldering move that made her stomach heat up. "We'll do that soon, just as soon as we can get married."

Married? Married to Hudson. It was the dream she'd never thought would become a reality. She melted against him, and he captured her lips with his. The passion and love overwhelmed her.

They were captives of evil men and their son was in danger, but at this moment she focused on the slice of heaven of her Brave man holding her close. Somehow, Hudson would protect and free them from Stefan and his brutes. Then they'd get married and be a little family.

Despite the danger and uncertainty of their current situation, she'd never been so happy.

Chapter Thirteen

Hudson was drowsily content as he held Kelsey against his chest and watched her sleep. He'd slowed their kisses down, not because he was anywhere close to thinking he'd kissed her enough, but because they weren't married yet.

He cuddled her close and wanted to beg her for stories about Mo, but she'd fallen asleep. He didn't blame her. Being kidnapped with their son—*their* son—was probably the most stressful, terrifying, and exhausting event of her life.

Looking over at Mo cuddled into the pillow and blanket made him so happy. He focused back on Mo's beautiful mother and the happiness only grew. His Sunshine and their little boy. Mo needed a nickname, but Mo was a pretty great name already.

One thing he knew for sure was Kelsey and Mo both needed Delta as their last name. As soon as they got out of this mess, he would buy a wedding ring, get a wedding license, and beg her to marry him tomorrow if possible.

Closing his eyes, he let himself bask in the feeling of having her close. He hadn't heard anything more than a few muffled movements and minimal exchanged words out in the main area. The sun had risen but these rooms faced west, so it wasn't shining directly into the windows. He prayed hard to know when the right time was to implement his plan and get Kelsey and Mo to safety. He'd shown her ultimate confidence like he did with all his stunts and to reassure her, but he'd never had a stunt that was so important to him. He'd have to pray desperately and rule out every variable where either of these two might get hurt. Knowing his family were all praying helped a lot. If only one or two of his brothers would show up. He loved that idea.

He looked over at Mo. His son looked so small burrowed into the covers of that king-sized bed. Protectiveness welled in him. He kissed Kelsey's forehead and then closed his eyes again. He prayed for the help, strength, inspiration, and execution he needed to get Kelsey and Mo out of here unscathed and these men apprehended.

He didn't hear a voice from heaven, but he did hear a cute little, "Mama?"

Hudson straightened and looked over at Mo sitting up on the bed.

The little guy blinked at him. "Hey, Thor's brother. Whatcha doing to my mama?"

Hudson should've smiled at the cute words, but he was blinking back tears. He loved listening to Mo talk and wanted to beg him to keep talking. He wanted to know about every friend he had, every sport or activity he loved, and every funny thought in his head. Hudson wanted to know if he dreamed of riding a horse, a dirt bike, a mountain bike, or a four-wheeler. Hudson would buy him one of each. If Kelsey was okay with that. He wanted to know if Mo wanted a little brother or sister first. Hudson could hardly wait to get started working on that.

Kelsey blinked awake. "Mo? You okay, love?"

"Yes, Mama, but I'm hungry."

Shoot. Hudson wanted to make sure his son learned to work hard and wasn't spoiled, but he didn't want him to lack anything. Right now he couldn't even give him one of the basics of life—food. They didn't have any food in this room, and he doubted the men would give them anything.

Kelsey slid off his lap and walked over to the bed. Hudson stood but didn't know if he should follow her or not. He was treading in unfamiliar waters and needed to follow her lead. When could he hold Mo? When could he tell him he was his dad?

Mo held out his arms, and she swooped him up. She turned to Hudson and his breath caught. He rubbed at his chest, amazed at the incredible picture they made together. He'd traveled the world and seen such beautiful scenery it could move a man to tears, but nothing—nothing—compared to Kelsey and Mo together.

"Can we have rollies?" Mo asked.

Hudson wondered what rollies were.

"Sorry, love," Kelsey said. "We have to wait a little while for breakfast."

Mo wrinkled his nose. "That's dumb." But instead of complaining about it, he looked at Hudson. "You Thor's brother?"

Hudson smiled and walked a few steps closer. "I am. My

name's Hudson." He eased in close to them and extended his hand.

Mo sized him up and then put his soft little hand in Hudson's palm. "Nice to meetcha."

"It's very nice to meet you, Mo." Grinning, Hudson wrapped his hand around his son's. He never wanted to let him go.

"I gotta pee," Mo announced, pulling his hand back.

"Oh, my." Kelsey shook her head but hurried her son to the bathroom. She looked over her shoulder at Hudson before they entered and gave him a soft smile. He could swear his heart squeezed.

His family. His wife. His son.

Okay, his Sunshine wasn't his wife yet. But he'd get to work on that very, very soon.

Hudson paced the small room as he waited for them. He wanted so many things right now. He wanted Mo to know he was his father and call him Dad. He wanted to kiss Kelsey again. He wanted to talk to his mom and dad and tell them everything that had happened.

Most importantly: he wanted to get Kelsey and Mo out of here and somewhere safe and spend a whole lot more time talking to and holding both of them.

He heard water running and a few seconds later, the bathroom door burst open. Mo ran to him with his hands up. "Will you throw me like Thor does?"

Hudson couldn't hide his grin as he swooped his son off the floor and tossed him up in the air and then caught him.

Mo laughed and Hudson noticed Kelsey watching them with a smile.

Hudson threw him up again and then caught him and couldn't resist holding him close. His little body was light and fit perfectly in the crook of his arm. Mo put his hand on Hudson's shoulder and said, "You throw good."

"When we get outside, I'll throw you higher than Thor can." Hudson winked at Kelsey.

"Not too high. He's a daredevil just like his daddy," Kelsey responded.

Hudson loved that his boy was a daredevil, but then it hit him. Had she told Mo who was his ...?

She shook her head quickly.

"I ain't got no daddy," Mo said.

That twisted his heart. He looked into the little man's blue eyes and wished desperately he could change the past. But he couldn't, so they had to move forward.

Kelsey walked over to them. He put his arm around her waist and held them both close. This moment was the stuff dreams were made of.

If only they weren't stuck in a hotel room being guarded by murderous losers.

"Mama, can we go outside so Thor's brother can throw me?"

"Hudson," she supplied. "We'll go outside ... soon."

Soon. He had to get them out of here. The clock on the night-stand said eight-thirty. How soon would Stefan leave? Hudson would have Kelsey hide with Mo in the bathtub while he pounded on the window with the vase or metal rod from the closet. Either the men would burst in and he'd perform some of his parkour moves using the ceiling fan and the bed and take them out, or the window would break and when they came in he'd throw them out of it. He seriously doubted the window would break, but he liked the idea of it. Making his stunts more dramatic was half the fun.

Kelsey looked up at him with such trust and love that his heart raced out of control. Being with her and Mo was more exciting and fulfilling than any crazy stunt he'd performed. He wondered if she wanted to settle down in Summit Valley or travel for a while with him. He could do more responsible stunts close to home. He didn't care where they lived or where he worked. Only that they were together. He wanted to change his nickname from Death Wish Delta to Father of Mo and Husband of Kelsey.

"Rollies?" Mo asked, breaking their concentration on each other.

Kelsey's smooth forehead crinkled. It hurt to think of their son being hungry. He instinctively needed to protect, shelter, love, and provide for his son, and at the moment he couldn't feed him.

"What are rollies?" Hudson asked to distract their boy.

"You don't know rollies?" Mo exclaimed. He put his little palms on Hudson's cheeks and said in a funny voice, "Did your mama not like you?"

Hudson laughed at that. "My mama is the best, and of course she likes me."

"No way," Mo countered. "Cause my mama's the best."

"I can't argue with you on that one." Hudson's gaze traveled over Mo's beautiful mama's face. He was more in love than anybody had a right to be. How quickly life could change for the best.

The door sprung open behind them and a slightly accented voice said, "Oh, isn't this a pretty picture?"

And how quickly it could change for the worst.

Hudson slid Mo into Kelsey's arms, gave her what he hoped was a reassuring look, hating the terror in her dark eyes. He pivoted and planted himself in front of them and stared Stefan down.

Stefan grinned, pointing a pistol at Hudson and seemingly unaffected by Hudson's glare. Hudson was usually happy, smiling, and easygoing. When he was upset and he glared, most men quavered in their shoes.

"I'm heading out early to set up everything to meet with your Papa."

Hudson didn't let it show on his face, but he felt relief. Once Stefan was out of here, he could confidently take on the other two.

"Just to make sure you don't get any ideas while I'm gone." He gestured with his hand and the two brutes walked in. The one held an A.R. The other held zip ties.

Hudson's gut tightened. That might put a wrench in his plan.

"Sit in the chair," Stefan commanded, gesturing with his pistol to the spot by the window where Hudson and Kelsey had talked and kissed. The innocence of that moment was tarnished by these losers in the room.

Hudson wanted to fight, but he had no weapon and the two most important people in the world were in harm's way. He restrained himself and was grateful as always for the self-control training he'd pushed himself through. Well, until he realized that was part of the reason he'd missed out on so much time with Kelsey and Mo.

He held up his hands and half-pivoted to Kelsey, giving her what he hoped was a reassuring smile. Mo was quiet. That worried him. The little man had fear in his blue eyes. Hudson prayed for strength to not lash out at Stefan and escalate the situation. Fear in Kelsey's dark eyes and Mo's blue ones made him furious.

He gestured with his head toward the opposite corner of the room. Kelsey nodded and strode toward the bathroom door. He hoped if things went south she'd lock herself and Mo in there, though it wouldn't provide too much protection as they could easily blow through that door with their A.R.s. Would Stefan's men really shoot and draw the attention of other hotel guests and the possibility of somebody calling the police? Hudson wasn't willing to find out. Especially with Kelsey and Mo's safety.

Hudson stalked to the chair. Stefan said something in German to the man and he came behind Hudson, yanked his arms back, and secured his hands with the zip ties. Then he shoved him down into the chair, which was luckily cushioned enough he didn't break an arm with them in an awkward tight position behind him while being forced to sit down. The guy secured each of his ankles to the wooden leg at the bottom of the chair with the zip ties, then stood. Unfortunately, the wooden bottoms of the chair had decorative claw feet, or he could've simply lifted the chair and slid his legs free.

"All right." Stefan clapped his hands together. "If the zip ties aren't enough deterrent, Jaron will be waiting outside your bedroom door. Any attempts to escape and he'll shoot through the door until he kills one or all of you." He shrugged as if it didn't matter.

Hudson's stomach churned. The zip ties were definitely a deterrent and them shooting through the door would change his plan. If he was being honest, it might even ruin his plan. He glanced over at Kelsey. She had Mo cradled against her shoulder, rocking him slightly. Mo stared at the men and their guns with wide eyes.

"I'm off to get King Frederick's new weapon." Stefan grinned. "And don't stress too much about the fact that you can't escape us. Most of America will be dead in a few days anyway." He saluted them, spun, and strode from the room. His men followed, slamming the door behind them.

Kelsey rushed toward him, her dark eyes frightened, but also flashing anger. "Those idiots. Are you okay? Did that hurt either of your arms?"

Hudson leaned forward, taking the pressure off his arms digging into the chair. It tightened the zip ties against his ankles, but he'd been through much worse pain. "Of course I'm okay, Sunshine. Everything is going to be awesome."

He prayed he wasn't lying to her. He'd never lied to her, but he didn't want her to worry. The look on her face said she thought he was sugarcoating. The zip tie situation did put a damper on his plan, but he had plenty of time and he'd spread his wrists just right to give him the space he needed.

Papa wouldn't be at the meeting spot until eleven. Right?

What if Papa was early and that was why the guy had left already?

Ah, crap. Why hadn't he insisted that his family figure out a way to follow them from the canyon? They'd all been so certain that Stefan would instruct Hudson to lead them to the cave. This was not working out according to plan. He said a prayer and brainstormed solutions to the current problem, getting him out of these restraints and all of them safely out of this hotel.

Most of his days didn't go according to plan. The unexpected surprises made for great footage and got him more views. This was just another challenge. The most dangerous challenge he'd ever faced because Kelsey and Mo were at risk. He'd get through it. He had to get through it with them safe. The option for failure was zero in his mind.

He looked at Kelsey and Mo in her arms. He grinned at them. "Hey, big guy, you gotta smile for me."

Mo cocked his head and then asked, "Why?"

"Because your smiles are rays of sunshine," Hudson said. "Did you know I call your mama Sunshine?"

"Sunshine?" Mo giggled. "Sunshine Mama?"

Hudson laughed, glad to distract his boy, though Kelsey still looked far too scared.

"You are my sunshine, my only sunshine," he sang in a silly but low-toned voice so it wouldn't carry. "You make me happy, when skies are gray."

Kelsey finally smiled and Mo laughed. Hudson winked at her, giving her an overconfident pump of his eyebrows while his mind scrambled to know how to get out of this one. The most important performance of his life. And at the moment ... the most destined for failure.

Chapter Fourteen

Kelsey studied Hudson, this incredible man she loved. She knew he didn't lie, but she felt like some false bravado was happening—or more likely, he was trying to insulate her and Mo from worrying. How in the world was he going to get out of being zip tied to a chair and rescue them with a brute on the other side of the door with a machine gun in his hand, willing and ready to end all of their lives? She held Mo closer. Her boy was still smiling at Hudson's silly singing.

"What are you thinking?" Kelsey asked quietly.

"Thinking?" Hudson pushed out his chest and gave her an incredulous look. "Thinking, Sunshine? I'm planning, plotting, and executing."

She wasn't sure what to say to him. "Overconfident much, Brave?"

"Never." He suddenly pushed to a standing position, the muscles in his legs straining against his pants and the muscles in his arms even more evident with his hands positioned behind his back.

Her eyes widened, and he grinned.

"Whoa," Mo said. "You's got lots of muscles."

Hudson chuckled, then he twisted his arms and shimmied them back and forth a little bit. Kelsey and Mo watched him. His left arm came forward and then her jaw about came unhinged when his left hand was free and then his right. The zip tie fell to the chair behind him. He put up both hands like he'd just completed an impressive trick.

"Whoa!" Mo started to scream.

Kelsey put her hand over his mouth. "Shh, sweetie."

"Sorry," he whispered against her fingers. She pulled her fingers back. "I be quiet."

Hudson looked unconcerned. He winked at her and slipped off his shoes. "Kelsey, can you help me lift this chair?"

"Sure." She set Mo down and hurried to him.

"Lift up one side," he instructed.

She tilted it to the side, and he pushed at the zip tie around his ankle, trying to maneuver it over the clawed wooden foot of the armchair. It didn't budge and was held fast to his ankle.

"Okay, new idea." He straightened. She caught a hint of frustration on his face, but it was there and gone quick. He winked at her. "The challenge just makes it fun, right?"

A challenge? Fun? She loved him, but he was insane if he thought this was a fun challenge. As she looked into his blue eyes, she could see ... he was trying to keep it light for her and Mo. He was very, very concerned.

"We'll have to bust apart the chair in a minute," he told her.

"Unfortunately, that might make too much noise and bring the losers running, so we need to be prepared. Right now I need a little help from my beautiful people." He looked down at Mo.

"Mama's beautiful. I'm cute," Mo told him.

Hudson laughed as if they didn't have a care in the world. "Okay, cute, tough guy."

Mo nodded as if that were acceptable.

"Sunshine, I need you to see if the metal hanging rod in the closet will come out."

"Okay." She walked to the small closet with Mo following her. She grasped the metal bar for hanging clothes and lifted it out. Taking Mo's hand, she hurried back across the room to Hudson.

"Perfect. Set it down behind the bed." She did. "Okay, now can you also set that decorative vase by the rod?"

Her brow wrinkled, but she didn't question him. She picked up the vase from the dresser, surprised at how heavy it was, and carried it to the bed, setting it down next to the rod.

"Thanks, Sunshine." He looked at Mo. "Hey cute, tough Mo."

"That's me." Mo stuck out his little chest just like his dad would do and tried to flex his arm muscles. Kelsey couldn't help but smile.

"Do you like to play hide and seek?"

"Yep. I'm good at it."

"Sweet. When we get out of here, we'll play it for real. Right now I need you to go into the bathroom and hide in the tub. Your mama is going to come hide with you in just a minute. You keep her hidden in that tub, keep your heads down, and you hug her tight until I come for you. Got it?" He extended his fist for a pound.

Mo hurried over and gave him a pound. Then he impulsively hugged him around the leg. Hudson's face softened and his eyes brightened. He wrapped his arm around their little boy and held him close for a second. Mo tugged free and looked up. "I'll hug Mama tight," he said bravely.

"That's my boy," Hudson said softly.

Mo obviously didn't understand that reference, but it made Kelsey's stomach fill with happy butterflies. If they ever got out of this situation, they could truly be a family. She knew how fun and exciting life could be with Hudson. It was a dream for her adult life she never thought could happen. If only they could escape.

"You'll get the bad guys?" Mo asked.

"Yes, I will."

That seemed to be enough for Mo.

"Now go hide in the tub. Your mama will be there soon."

Mo nodded and skipped to the bathroom.

Kelsey didn't know how she could leave Hudson alone, with his legs zip tied to a chair, and think he was going to lure in and somehow beat those awful men with guns. What was his plan, and how could she help? Her mama heart was tugging her toward the tub and covering Mo with her body and praying fervently until Hudson somehow miraculously rescued them. Her Hudson-adoring heart was begging her to help him somehow, not let him sacrifice himself for them. What if that was his plan? Create enough noise and distraction that somebody called the police and the bad guys got captured before they could get to her and Mo, sacrificing himself in the process?

Hudson gestured her close. "Okay, Sunshine. Things are going to move fast in a minute. First, I want you to use all your lovely muscles and carry the other armchair into the bathroom. You're going to put it in front of the closed door to insulate you and Hudson more. Can you do that?"

Could she carry the chair, or could she leave him here alone to fight those gun-toting cronies while she and Mo cowered in the tub?

Studying her carefully, Hudson said, "I love you so much, Sunshine. Please do this for me. Keep our boy safe. Please."

She met his gaze, and she couldn't say no to him or to keeping Mo safe. She bobbed her head.

"Thank you," he breathed out. "Can you lift the chair?"

She flexed, trying to act as brave as he was. *Please let him have a foolproof plan and not get himself killed to protect us.*

"Nice." He gave her an appreciative look.

Walking over close to him, she picked up the other chair, relieved that she could. It was heavy, but not impossible.

"That's my girl."

She slowly carried the decorative armchair toward the bathroom. Her fingers started cramping and she could feel it slipping. If she dropped it, those men would hear. What if they started shooting, or came bursting in and saw that Hudson was executing … some kind of plan?

She bent her knees and set the chair on the ground, flexing and un-flexing her fingers.

"You okay?" Hudson asked quietly.

She looked back at him and gave a saucy wink that she wasn't feeling. "I'm better than okay."

"At kissing," he said back.

Her stomach filled with warmth. She pumped her eyebrows at him and hefted the chair again. She hurried forward and made it into the bathroom. There wasn't a ton of space, but she set the chair in the middle of the room next to the open door.

"Mama?" Mo looked up at her from the bathtub. He was on his back in the porcelain tub. If he'd done that at home fully clothed, she'd have taken a picture of him and they would've laughed. Right now, she was just grateful he was safe.

"Hey, love. I'll be right back, okay?"

"Okay."

She was impressed how well he was dealing with all of this. Hopefully his lack of exposure to awful situations would keep him innocent and relatively unafraid. She blew him a kiss, then hurried back to Hudson.

He gave her a smoldering look as she reentered the bedroom. How she wished they were safe. She could picture it now: Mo tucked in bed after scriptures, stories, prayers, and some teasing and wrestling with his daddy. Hudson walking out of Mo's bedroom with that smoldering look in his eyes. Him teasing her, lifting her into his arms, and kissing her thoroughly.

"Good job," Hudson said. "Now after you help me with a couple more things, I want you to lock that bathroom door, shove the chair in front of it, turn on the fan and the faucet, hide in that tub, keep you and Mo's heads down, and don't move until you hear me, or the police, coming for you."

"Okay," she squeaked out, but she didn't like it. "How are you going to ..." She gestured to his legs zip tied to the chair and then the metal rod and decorative vase by the bed. She realized they

143

were hidden from view of the door. Was he somehow going to lure them in here, hide from their bullets, and take them out with a rod and a vase? It wasn't a great plan, but it was a million times better than any idea she had.

"Don't worry, the most beautiful woman in the world and the love of my life. It's a foolproof plan."

His confidence was ultra-appealing and terrifying at the same time. How had he guessed that she wasn't understanding or seeing his vision of a plan?

"Please don't take any unnecessary risks," she begged.

Hudson chuckled. "Sunshine. Every day of my life is an unnecessary risk. Don't you watch my YouTube channel?"

Sadly, she didn't. It had hurt too much while they were apart. Now she'd go back and watch everything she could. Unless she could be close to him and watch the real thing.

She shrugged. "I may have missed the one where you defeat two evil brutes with your legs zip tied to a chair and no weapon besides a vase and a closet rod."

"That explains it. It's a fabulous and inspiring episode. Too bad Noah and Giles aren't here to film and take still shots."

"Honestly, Brave." She begged him with her eyes. "Please. I just want you safe. For once in your life, will you not be the crazy risk-taker?"

His blue gaze went warm and serious at the same time. "C'mere, Sunshine."

Kelsey went willingly. She crowded into his space, and he wrapped his hands around her waist and dipped his head down toward hers.

"You've heard my nickname? Death Wi—"

She put a finger across his lips. "I hate it when they call you that."

"Then it's in the past, love. You've made me a father, and someday soon, a husband. We'll stick with Brave for a nickname."

She quivered with the anticipation of him never leaving them again, them being married, the three of them being a happy family.

He softly kissed her and said, "I'm going to take these guys out and get you and Mo out of here safely. I promise I will do all I can to stay alive. Utilize every bit of real-world experience and training from my parents and Papa and all my vast array of talents and resourcefulness." His blue gaze searched hers. There was nothing cocky in his gaze. He was simply assuring her that he was ultra-talented and exceptionally trained. His eyes filled with love for her. "I've never had so much reason to live, to grow old and gray and crotchety ... with you by my side and Mo and ten little brothers for Mo to be a good example to. All those boys will make you insane dirtying up the house and wrestling each other and they will make me laugh with all their crazy antics and stunts."

"Ten?" She drew in a shaky breath. She loved everything he was saying, except four or five children would be plenty. She didn't care if they were boys or girls, but she would love to see a little girl with pigtails who had her daddy wrapped around her little finger.

He smiled, but then he captured her lips with his. The kiss stole every rational thought from her mind and the oxygen from her lungs. He pulled back much quicker than she wanted him to.

"Okay, Sunshine. I hate to break up this incredible activity, but it's stunt time. We'll return to the main event later." He winked, a hundred percent confidence and swagger. She loved him so much. "You remember your instructions from earlier?"

"Door locked, chair pushed against it, fan and faucet on, me and Mo hiding in the tub until you come for us."

"Me or the police," he reminded her.

"You," she said fiercely, wrapping her arms around his neck, clinging to him, and begging him to agree. She couldn't lose him again.

"So demanding, I like it. Okay. You only come out for me."

She kissed him hard on the mouth. He returned it, but she forced herself to pull back. "Okay, what now?"

"We need to quietly get my chair closer to where you set my weapons." He winked. "So when I break it and they hear the noise, I can be ready to fight back."

"Okay." Her stomach took a tumble. He was going to fight two men with machine guns with a metal rod and a decorative vase. What if the chair didn't break and they simply gunned him down?

"We've got this," he reassured her, probably sensing her fears. "God's on our side."

She nodded, prayed for protection and strength and miracles as she went around behind the chair. At his instruction, she pushed as he pulled with his legs. It was slow-going, but they moved it the five feet he wanted, then he said, "All right. Now this is the tricky part."

This was the tricky part? She didn't even understand his plan, but it all seemed tricky and like it wouldn't work. She prayed for faith in heaven above and in the man she loved.

"So I'm going to lean into a handstand."

"A handstand? With a chair attached to your legs?"

"That's the tricky part, but I've done much trickier stunts. It's more of a headstand anyway, so easy peasy." He didn't even look concerned. "I'm going to need you to help lift the chair off the ground and balance the front of the chair on the back of my legs, then you'll help me flip the chair back. It will break, but the cushions will protect me from getting hurt. You run for that bathroom and follow your instructions. All right?"

"Hudson. What if the chair doesn't break?" She couldn't desert him and lock herself in that bathroom. Maybe she could lock Mo in the bathroom and help him fight.

"It's all going to work out," he reassured her. "The quick movement, weight of the chair, and our strength propelling it will break either the chair itself or at least the zip ties will pop with how tight they're secured on my legs. But the noise is going to bring the men running. I need you to promise you'll hide with Mo as soon as you help me slam that chair back."

"Hudson ..." This was insane. "What if the zip ties or the chair don't break?"

"They will," he reassured her, no doubt in his face or his voice.

She had a lot of doubt and a lot of fear.

"Now give me a kiss for good luck, and don't forget to pray for me."

"Hudson, please ..." Tears stung at her eyes and traced down her cheeks. This wasn't a plan. It was insanity. Those men were probably going to blast him with their machine guns after the chair crashed to the ground and he'd be a sitting duck still attached to the chair with the zip ties.

"It's Brave to you, my beautiful Sunshine." He wrapped his

hands around her hips and tugged her closer. "Kiss first, then it's time for stunts and tricks."

Kelsey willingly kissed him, but she had no idea how this stunt would be the time he didn't defy death. Death Wish Delta.

Please don't let his awful nickname come true.

She couldn't stand by and let him get himself killed.

Chapter Fifteen

Hudson had no clue how he was going to survive the next five minutes, or possibly less time than that. He wanted to keep his word like he always did and be the one to get Kelsey and Mo from that bathroom, hug them, and lead them out of this prison.

He had to have faith that it could happen, but it was a really stupid plan. Unfortunately, he couldn't think of anything better. Most of his plan was to create enough noise and distract the two men outside for long enough that somebody in the hotel called the police. If he could stay alive long enough for the police to arrive, that would be brilliant, but if not ...

He prayed like he prayed before each of his stunts. Then he looked into his gorgeous Sunshine's dark eyes and thought of their adorable son in the bathtub, and he easily straightened his back with resolve despite the discomfort of his legs being attached to this stupid chair, the zip ties digging in so hard he was losing feeling in his feet. He had the best motivation in the world. He would fight to protect what he loved, and God would make up whatever he lacked.

"Promise me, Sunshine. As soon as I tell you, you run for that bathroom, bar that door with the chair, and don't come out until I come for you." He stared deeply into her eyes. She wasn't going to do it. She couldn't leave him. He loved her for it, but she had to protect Mo and herself.

"Promise me," he begged. "For Mo. For our son."

She swallowed, and he watched her smooth neck bob. He saw the moment she knew she had to leave him to fight alone. For their boy.

"I promise," she said softly.

"That's my girl." He tried to hide the emotion in his voice, but his throat was thick. *Please, Lord. I've just found them again. Don't let this be the last time I hold her close. If it be Your will, let us raise our boy together.*

He gave Kelsey one more kiss on the lips but pulled back before he could get lost in her and forget the ultimate goal— Kelsey and Mo staying safe. He winked. "Let's do this."

Her dark gaze was full of concern, but luckily she didn't argue with him or try to talk him out of his plan. There sadly wasn't another option. His family didn't know where they were and as soon as Stefan discovered Papa didn't have the fabled weapon, he would order their executions and probably try to kill Papa too. Hudson planned to get free, find a safe spot for Kelsey and Mo, and intercept the exchange with Stefan and Papa shortly.

He leaned all the way forward, planting his hands solidly on the carpeted floor, fingers spread wide for ideal balance. Hudson was not only incredibly strong and talented at extreme sports, but his balance and flexibility were unparalleled. He was counting on all his strengths, but more importantly his humility and trust that the Lord would make up what he lacked.

"Okay, Sunshine, let's lift this chair."

"'Kay," she said, her voice shaky.

Kelsey hefted the chair up and he strained with his back and legs to help keep it aloft. He bent his elbows and rested his head on the floor, using every bit of stability he could. Kelsey maneuvered the chair until the front of it rested on the back of his thighs and butt.

"On the count of three, you shove it hard backwards with all your strength and I'll spring off with my hands. The zip ties will pop when it slams into the floor and then you'll be hiding in that tub." He hurried on before she could protest. "One, two, three."

He thrust upward quick with his hands and arm strength as he flung himself back against the chair as hard as he could. At the same time, he yanked his legs forward to hopefully pop the ties on his legs. Kelsey must've pushed with a lot of strength and the angels in heaven as well. The chair crashed back with a tremendous bang. His head slammed into the cushion, which was good. The chair's spine broke and his right leg burst free of the restraint. His left leg was still attached to the chair.

Kelsey scrambled toward the bathroom as he heard shouts in a foreign language from the other room. Would they start shooting like Stefan had claimed, or burst through the door to see what they were shooting at?

Kelsey paused by the bathroom door and looked back at him.

"Go!" he yelled. He grabbed the metal rod and slammed it

against the leg of the chair attached to his leg. Two quick slams and he broke the wooden leg and slid his foot free.

Kelsey met his gaze and disappeared into the bathroom, shoving the door closed behind her. She'd kept her promise and left him. Thank heavens.

He heard the fan and faucet start and the chair scraping across the tile.

The bedroom door burst open and one of the men appeared with his A.R. in hand. Hudson sprang to his feet and hurled the metal rod as hard as he could. It drove into the man's chest, almost like a spear. Unfortunately, it didn't embed but popped back off. The impact and surprise worked, though. The guy stumbled back against his buddy, not firing a shot. Yet.

Hudson grabbed the vase, ran at them, and chucked it with all his strength. It smacked into the first guy's head and snapped it back. The vase crashed to the floor. The guy's arms flailed, and he dropped his gun.

Hudson's eyes widened in surprise. That had worked much better than he thought it would. He sprinted at the open bedroom door and hurled himself at the guy in front with his head and shoulder down. He drove straight into the chest of the man he'd just hit with the rod and the vase.

The man screamed out as Hudson's weight and momentum slammed him and his buddy back onto the wood floor. The bottom dude's head made a sickening thud on the unforgiving marble flooring. Hudson prayed the guy on the bottom was unconscious, but he wasn't going to count on it.

He ripped the weapon from the hands of the guy on the bottom. Hudson was on top of their odd triple stack. He slammed the metal of the gun into the top guy's head and then slid the A.R. onto the floor and away from the three of them.

Slamming his fists into the top guy's face, he was surprised that he was still awake and fighting back. The man shoved him off and lumbered to his feet. Hudson sprang up, leaped into the air, and kicked the guy in the chest. The guy was flung away from him and crashed against a table, staggering.

Hudson scrambled to his knees, sliding into the other man on the floor and grabbing the gun that the first guy had dropped. The guy looked like he was down for the count, but he sidestepped away just in case and brought the gun away to point it at the other man.

The man straightened away from the table and muttered something.

"Hands up," Hudson commanded.

The guy looked at him like he had no clue what he was saying, and he edged toward the other gun on the floor.

"Don't do it," Hudson warned him. "Get your hands up."

The guy looked down at his buddy on the floor, and then he smiled. Hudson felt a hand close around his ankle as the other man dove for the gun.

Hudson prayed desperately, *Protect Kelsey and Mo,* then he dropped his weight onto the arm of the man holding his ankle as the world exploded.

Chapter Sixteen

Kelsey followed Hudson's instructions and within moments she was curled around Mo in the tub trying to hold and shush him to comfort him, but also so she could hear what was happening to Hudson. She realized now he'd told her to turn on the fan and faucet as well so she and Mo couldn't hear. Dang it.

He'd gotten his other leg free, right? She'd been trying to make sure he was okay, get in the bathroom, and somehow tell him she loved him with her eyes at the same time.

Please protect him, please protect him, she repeated over and over again in her head.

She heard different sounds: maybe a door bursting open, some thumping sounds that sounded like fighting, voices saying or commanding different things ... It was hard to know exactly what was happening, especially with cute Mo peering up at her and saying, "Mama? Hudson?" over and over again.

"It's okay, love." She kissed his forehead and cuddled him

close. "Just a few more minutes. Let's play the quiet game and see if you can beat me."

He gave her a look that said he knew exactly what she was doing. That was the problem with an only child surrounded by adults all day. They understood far more than they should. He cuddled into her shoulder and didn't say anything. Kelsey was cursing herself for leaving Hudson without at least making sure he was free of the chair and had a fighting chance. Why had she promised him she'd go? She held their son closer and knew exactly why she had. Mo had always been her priority, and Hudson expected her to protect their son while he protected both of them. Especially if everything went south. She prayed everything wouldn't go south.

Then the ugly sound of gunfire filled the other room.

Kelsey screamed in horror. She could hear shooting, bodies slamming into objects, bullets ripping through walls or furniture.

"No!" Hudson! Brave! No!

Mo clung to her and didn't say anything. She froze and listened as the gunshots stopped and all was quiet. Too quiet.

Please let Hudson be okay, she begged. *Please!*

Footsteps came toward the bathroom door. Her heart raced. What should she do if it wasn't Hudson? It had to be Hudson. He had to be okay.

But if it wasn't … She couldn't cower in the tub and pray they didn't push the door open, but she had no idea what to fight with, how to stop them.

A rap on the door then, "Kelsey? Mo? It's me. Let me in."

"Brave!" she screamed, relief making her feel lightheaded.

"Hudson?" Mo's little face brightened and all the fear

vanished from his eyes. As soon as they got out of this mess, she and Hudson would tell Mo Hudson was his father and then they'd plan a very, very quick wedding.

Kelsey lifted Mo onto the tile floor, then scrambled out of the tub. She yanked the chair back, hurried around it, and flung open the door.

Hudson stood there looking like a superhero warrior. He had a scary-looking gun in one hand, his clothes were ripped, blood dripped down his ankle from a painful-looking abrasion, his hair was disheveled, his muscles were all on glorious display, and all she wanted to do was kiss him.

She flung herself at him. He caught her with his one arm and kissed her hard and fast, then he pulled back and asked, "Mo? You okay, buddy?"

Mo ran at them. Hudson released her and scooped up their boy. Mo flung his arms around Hudson's neck, buried his head in the crook of his neck, and just clung to him. It worried Kelsey that he wasn't saying anything, but it was an incredible picture seeing Hudson holding their boy.

She wanted to savor the picture, but her gaze scanned Hudson for more injuries. She could see scrapes and future abrasions but no blood besides the ankle and she was pretty sure that was from the zip tie.

"We've got to go," Hudson said. "Stick close to me, Sunshine." He gave her a reassuring smile and turned. She hurried forward, keeping her hand on his lower back as they walked back through the bedroom. "Keep your eyes on me, please," Hudson said. She wasn't sure if it was to Mo or her or both of them as they entered the main area.

She kept her gaze and hand fastened on Hudson's back, but swore she could smell gunpowder, blood, metal, and death.

They were almost to the suite's main door when a sharp rap came on it.

Hudson froze. He gestured her to the nearby wall and handed Mo to her. "Go hide behind the couch," he said softly.

She obeyed, scurrying around the couch, then dropping to the ground behind it and cradling Mo close. How many bad guys were there? Would they ever be safe?

"Housekeeping?" a highly pitched male voice called.

Kelsey made the mistake of looking across the living area and saw one of the kidnappers sprawled on his back with blood covering his chest. He wasn't moving. She gasped.

"Housekeeping?" the man repeated.

Kelsey thought Hudson should answer or they'd probably just come in, see the dead bodies, and report them to the police. At least it wasn't more criminals.

"We coulda used some housekeeping about ten minutes ago," Hudson called, lowering the gun and shaking his head.

Kelsey's brow squiggled.

"I think you still do," the voice called back, now deep and with a cowboy drawl. "I think you need a whole heap of help from a superhero like myself."

"Thor!" Mo tried to yank himself from her arms.

Kelsey stood with him but didn't let him go yet. Hudson opened the door and Thor lunged at his brother, hugging him tightly. She hurried toward them.

"How'd you find us? What took you so long? Decided not to

wear your French maid costume?" Hudson threw questions and teases at his brother.

Thor released him and turned to Kelsey and Mo. He was in a white button-down shirt, black pants, a pistol holstered to his hip, and holding a feather duster. He grinned at them.

Mo strained to get out of her arms. Kelsey handed him off to one of his favorite men in the world. Thor hugged him. "There's my little man." He looked at Kelsey. "You're okay?"

Hudson's free arm came around her and she leaned into his strength. "I am now," she said, her voice choked with emotion. They were safe. Hudson had saved them and Thor was here.

"Let's go." Thor looked into the room and his eyes widened slightly. "Poor housekeeper that finds that mess."

He led the way through the hall and used a key to get into the service hallway. They walked to the large cargo elevator they'd come up in. Kelsey's gaze darted around, expecting Stefan to pop out and kill them, but it was quiet.

Thor pushed the button for the cargo elevator, then pulled out his phone with his free hand. He pushed something on it. "Papa, I've got them." He paused. "Yes, it is. Thank heaven for sure. Aiden and I will be at your position soon."

"Tell Papa that Stefan will be well prepared and try to kill him," Hudson interjected.

"Careful of Stefan, the guy after the weapon," Thor said. "He's with-it and will be out for blood. I agree we need to capture him." He paused. "Okay, see you soon." He hung up, then pushed another button. "Aiden, I've got them. Main level service exit in two."

Pocketing the phone, he grinned at them.

"Is Granny Vance okay?" Kelsey had to know.

"Yeah." He nodded. "She's at Joseph and Holly's now and safe."

"Thank you."

The elevator dinged on their level. Hudson stepped in front of them, leveling the A.R. at the doors as they opened. Thankfully, it was empty.

They hurried inside and pushed the main level button. Thor passed a keycard over it. He looked them over. "We might want to hide that obnoxiously big gun," he teased Hudson. "Man, you look good with it though."

Hudson smiled. "I always look good."

"That you do. Almost as good as me. We have to make up for all the ugly Aiden brings to the table."

Kelsey smiled at their teasing, but her legs felt weak. They'd just escaped. Hudson had done it. Her Brave had rescued them. Could they just go home and live their happily ever after? Couldn't the police go after Stefan? At least Hudson could stay with her and Mo.

"How'd you find us?" Hudson asked as the elevator slowly descended the forty-five floors.

"Papa left Aiden and I at the mouth of the canyon just in case the kidnappers took a different route. When we saw that van go by, I just knew. I don't know, bro. I could feel you in it. Does that make any sense?"

Hudson nodded.

"So we followed you at a distance and luckily were able to keep the large van in our sight, even in the city, because it was the middle of the night. We had to wait to come into the hotel and then we had to steal housekeeping carts, male uniforms, and keys and start checking rooms. I actually had to clean a toilet or two when I went into a suite that was occupied and they wanted me to clean and not come back later." He gave a shudder. "Saw a few things I want to get out of my head when they didn't answer the door and I went in."

Kelsey could only imagine.

"We searched floor after floor. It's been a long morning. And look, you didn't even need me." He winked.

The elevator stopped at the main level. Hudson pressed the A.R. between them to semi-hide it as Thor checked the hallway. He nodded, and they all eased out of the elevator. Everyone in the area was too focused on their own business to notice the group. They walked down the hallway and to the exit. Aiden was waiting.

He had a broad smile for all of them and a quick hug for Hudson. "You're all okay?" he asked as he led them out the door, his pistol in hand.

"Yes," Kelsey said. "Brave rescued us."

Hudson squeezed her waist.

They walked across a docking platform and down some steps.

"Brave? No more Death Wish Delta?"

"No," Kelsey said firmly.

"Okay." Aiden grinned. "Brave is almost as cool as Aquaman."

"Not as cool as Thor," Thor interjected as they hurried through a parking lot.

"Thor's tough," Mo crowed.

"Brave's a lot better looking, though," Aiden argued.

"Don't get down on your ugly self," Thor countered.

"I'm talking about your scary face," Aiden said. He winked at Mo.

Mo grinned. "You're the goofy face," he said.

"That's right," Thor laughed. "My buddy knows who the handsome one is."

"You," Mo crowed, pointing at Thor.

They all laughed at that.

Aiden stopped at a silver Lincoln Navigator, clicked the door locks, and then pulled the door open. Thor handed Mo to her, and Hudson helped her slide into the backseat. She edged over and he slid in next to them, setting the large gun on the floor.

Aiden and Thor climbed in up front. Aiden started the motor and they drove away, still teasing about who was the ugliest.

Kelsey leaned into Hudson, and he wrapped her up tight while she held Mo. They had no car seats or seat belts on, but they were driving slowly through downtown traffic. Were they really safe? With Hudson, Thor, and Aiden around, she actually felt safe. Though she kept waiting for a tank to T-bone them and then a rocket launcher aimed their direction.

No. She had to have faith in heaven, and faith in her Brave.

Tilting her head up, she looked into Hudson's handsome face. He pumped his eyebrows at her. "Told you I would rescue you, Sunshine."

She gave a shuddering laugh and arched up to kiss him.

Their lips met in a kiss of relief and promise. The world exploded with happiness until Mo tugged at her arm and said, "Mama, stop!"

She could hear Aiden and Thor chuckling up front. "Sorry,

love," she said to Mo, "but you're going to have to get used to me kissing Brave."

Hudson grinned at her. Mo shrugged his little shoulders. "I guess."

"So that's how it is?" Thor asked, glancing back at them.

"Oh, yeah." Hudson tugged her close. "That's exactly how it is."

Chapter Seventeen

Hudson only gave Kelsey a brief kiss before releasing her. Mo would have to get used to them kissing, but not while he was right on her lap. He was flying high from defeating those men, rescuing Kelsey and Mo, and having his awesome brothers appear. Now Kelsey and Mo were in his arms and safe. It was a better rush than any stunt he'd performed.

As they pulled into the parking lot for the Denver Botanical Gardens, his euphoria took a hit. Papa. Stefan. Who knew what kind of plans that guy had made? Hudson did not want to underestimate Stefan. He was a sadistic loser but he was smart.

He glanced at the Suburban's clock. Ten a.m.

"We've got plenty of time," he said.

"For sure." Aiden drove away from the entrance and to the far edge of the parking lot shaded with trees. He turned off the vehicle and turned to look at them. "Kelsey, how many men have you seen with this Stefan?"

"Well, the two in the hotel that Hudson took care of, then whoever drove the van to the camp spot and traded us for the Suburban."

"Okay. So we know there's at least one other unfriendly, but I'm assuming this Stefan isn't stupid and wouldn't try this with only one other guy."

Hudson nodded. "He knew about the other mercenaries' failed attempts to get to the cave. That's why he demanded Papa bring the weapon. But he might be cocky enough to think he can get out of here after the exchange if he has a great sniper covering him and a helicopter waiting. Maybe he doesn't want to share the reward money."

"Maybe." Aiden mused. "Papa is being covered by dad, Uncle Joseph, Greer, and Reed. He has the weapon and is already at the rendezvous point in the gardens, so Stefan can approach him at any time. I'll have everybody look for a helicopter and a shooter."

"Papa has the ... what?" Hudson demanded. His chest tightened and his head started to pound. "He didn't bring the actual ... No! Why would he do that?"

Thor and Aiden both looked at him as if he were the most important human on the planet. Thor gestured to the three of them cuddled in the backseat. "He had no time to come up with a way to fake a 'demonstration' with an A.R. or machine gun. What was he supposed to do? You three are more important than any weapon."

Hudson leaned back against the seat, feeling like he'd just landed on the ground from a two-hundred-foot drop with no parachute. He couldn't catch a breath.

"You okay?" Kelsey whispered.

"What's up?" Mo asked.

Hudson tried to smile at the two of them reassuringly, but that weapon should not be out of the cave. What on earth? Why would Papa risk it? He could've brought a case with an impressive .50 caliber machine gun and claimed it had a special … something. Okay, he couldn't fake a demonstration. He was at a loss, but … the weapon.

"No matter how far you've traveled from us, Huddy," Thor said softly. "We all adore you and would give anything for you."

Hudson looked at his brother's faces. He wanted to explain why he'd stayed away, but there wasn't time right now. "I love you both too," he managed. "But the Delta weapon? Out of the cave?"

"You okay, Brave?" Mo asked.

Hudson really wanted him to call him Dad, Daddy, Pops, whatever he wanted, but hearing him use Kelsey's nickname was cute.

"I'll be okay," he lied. He might not be. The entire world might not be. Papa had truly moved the weapon from the safety and protections of the cave.

He looked back at his brothers. "I know Papa would do anything for me and the family all cares for Kelsey and Mo, but he didn't know Mo was his great-grandson. Did he?"

Thor and Aiden's blue eyes both widened. They looked from Kelsey to Mo to Hudson and back. "He's yours?" Aiden whispered.

"He doesn't know," Hudson cautioned, referring to his son.

They both nodded but kept on staring. "How did we not see it?" Thor asked.

"I didn't want you to," Kelsey said.

"It's a very long story," Hudson said. "We'll share it after this is all resolved." He ran his hand along Kelsey's arm and she nodded up at him. He wanted to kiss her and just hold her and Mo, but he had to focus. This stunt was far from over. "Okay," he said to his brothers. "What's the plan? How are we going to keep Papa and that weapon safe and get the weapon back in the cave so I can breathe again?" And not blame himself if the entire world exploded in nuclear warfare. He'd probably be dead, though, so that was a moot point.

Thor and Aiden stopped gaping at Mo, and Aiden explained, "The entire family is here." He shrugged. "First time in how many years somebody hasn't been protecting the cave?"

Hudson blew out a breath. The implications of this were huge. What if other mercenaries were watching the family and had followed them to where they were exposed? What if some of his family members died protecting the weapon out in the open like this? He looked around at the thick foliage of the gardens. Who was hiding out there? Chills pricked at his spine. Hudson usually ignored all fears and worries, but today they were being brought out for him, big time. He needed to get Kelsey and Mo far away from here, but he knew he could be a big asset. If he walked up to Papa and Stefan at the moment of the exchange, it would shock Stefan and give them the distraction they needed.

"Papa should just get the weapon out of here and we'll all capture Stefan and whoever else he brought," Hudson insisted.

"Papa's already waiting there. If he walks now, Stefan will disappear and come back to try again. We'll get him and get the weapon back to the cave."

Hudson drew in a breath. He had to trust his family. Papa

would obviously do anything for him. It was overwhelming and made him feel valued and loved.

"Okay," he said. "Let's ... I need a safe place for Kelsey and Mo."

Kelsey's dark eyes studied him as if she knew he was leaving them. He couldn't leave them again, but the weapon, and Papa. His mind scrambled for some solutions or ideas. There was no way he could leave Kelsey and Mo until he was certain they were safe. But the clock was ticking.

"Just one second," Thor said. He checked his phone and then grinned. "The most beautiful cowgirl in the world is almost here. My wife."

"And the most beautiful philanthropist in the history of the world. My fiancée," Aiden put in.

Why would Shelly and Melene be here? They didn't have the fighting experience the rest of the Deltas did. Why would Aiden or Thor put their wife or fiancée in harm's way?

A white Lexus sport utility pulled up next to them.

"Dang, I wish I could get a kiss," Thor said, waving at Shelly who was in the driver's seat.

She winked and waved back.

"Kelsey." Aiden was more serious than his brother, as usual. "Our mom, Klein, and Alivia are in the car as well. We hoped we could rescue you but didn't know it would work this well. You and Mo will go with them, and they'll get you back safely to the valley. Two elite Navy SEALs who've recently joined our cause will follow you in a car you won't notice. Four of Reed's deputies are waiting at Papa's house with your mom and Granny Klein. My mom will arm all the security in the house and she and Alivia are as proficient with a weapon as Thor is."

Hudson caught a full breath again.

"What about you?" Thor asked. "Alivia and Mom are as good as you too."

"Come on." Aiden rolled his eyes. "I'm a Navy SEAL."

"Guys," Hudson redirected. Kelsey and Mo would be safe. That was all that mattered.

"The other SEALs and Reed's deputies will patrol outside the house until we all get back. You'll be safe there." Aiden smiled. "And we won't be long. So kiss your man and then we'll open both vehicle's doors and you'll slide into the other vehicle."

Hudson hated to let her go, but he was grateful this plan was a lot better thought out than his crazy escape back in the hotel room. Kelsey and Mo would be safe. He praised heaven above.

Kelsey glanced up at him, her dark eyes bright. "I'm afraid if we're separated, it'll be a lot longer than four years before we see each other again."

He felt her worries all the way through. "Trust me. I'll stay safe and I'll come after you. I promise."

"You promise?" she asked fiercely.

"I promise."

She looked close to desperation, but she finally said, "Be careful. No death wishes today."

"Ah, Sunshine. You know I'm done with that nickname." He kissed her before she could say anything. He kissed her desperately then he pulled back and kissed Mo's forehead. "Take care of your mama," he told their boy.

"'Course," Mo said, all happy and adorable.

The other car door opened and Hudson forced himself to open his door and escort Kelsey out and into the other car.

"There's my baby boy," his mom said from the far side of the middle row. A car seat was in the middle and Alivia and Klein were squished in the smaller backseat.

"Love you, Mom." He blew her a kiss, kissed Kelsey quickly again, and then shut the door and slid back into the other car before he clung to her and Mo and refused to let them go. It was much too soon after being reunited to have to let either of them go again. They were safe. That was all that mattered.

The Lexus drove away, Shelly waving jauntily.

Hudson watched it go, feeling like a lovesick sap and wondering which of his brothers would take a jab at him. He glanced at the front seat and noticed his brothers watching the car and looking as sappy as he felt. He wanted to smile and tease, but everything was pretty heavy.

Thor handed him an earpiece. "Put this in so you know where everyone is and what's happening."

Aiden and Thor's earpiece must've come alive because they both said, "Yeah?" Aiden shoved open his door as Hudson got the earpiece in. "Stefan's approaching Papa. Let's move."

Stunt time. He grabbed the A.R. and scurried out of the car.

At least Kelsey and Mo weren't in danger this time.

Papa was.

Hudson knew his family and two more elite Navy SEALs were scattered throughout these gardens. They'd keep Papa safe.

He prayed hard that he wasn't wrong.

An uneasy tingling was spreading throughout his body. Should he not have sent Kelsey and Mo away? Was more danger waiting in the valley, or would someone follow their car and attack them? Would Papa or one of his other family members get killed here today? Would Stefan and his people somehow get the weapon, take it to King Frederick, and kill millions of Americans?

He didn't know the answers or why he was so uneasy, but he followed Aiden and Thor at an all-out run. Right now, he had to trust his mom and everyone else would keep Kelsey and Mo safe. He had to trust that heaven above was watching over all of them. And he had to keep Papa and that weapon safe and get that dang weapon back in the cave.

There were no other options.

Chapter Eighteen

There was no time to worry or overthink anything as Hudson raced with his brothers toward the meeting spot by the Japanese teahouse. They approached, and he could see Papa through the foliage. Papa was standing on a grassy spot nestled against some thick trees, holding a large rectangular gun case.

Hudson stopped and shoved his A.R. at Aiden. "Get hidden so he doesn't have a reason to shoot Papa," he told his brothers. "It has to be me that distracts Stefan."

They both nodded and faded into the flowers and trees lining the path.

Hudson had a prayer in his heart and his head held high as he strode down the path toward Papa. His grandfather's gaze moved to him and he gave him a relieved smile. "Hudson."

He increased his pace, anxious to be by Papa's side before Stefan arrived. Too late. Stefan came out of a sidewalk from the north, angling straight for Papa. He held a pistol in his right hand, but Hudson couldn't see any other guns on him. He wondered where his other man was, and if there were multiple.

"Stefan!" Hudson shouted, breaking into a run to intercept him.

The man whirled to face Hudson, pointing his pistol right at his chest.

Hudson slowed his steps, holding up his hands to show he wasn't armed.

"Hudson," Papa cautioned.

The mercenary's eyes widened in surprise, but then he smiled that ugly smile of his. "So you escaped. I'll kill Kyle and Jaron for failing."

"Too late." Hudson kept walking toward them.

"Oh? Nice work. You can stop moving now."

Hudson obeyed, but he swore it was the last time he would obey this loser.

"Where's the beauty and your little boy?" Stefan asked.

"Safe. You'll never get close to them again."

"We'll see." He gave an ugly laugh. "The weapon, old man. Bring it to me or your famous grandboy dies."

Papa walked slowly toward him, holding the weapon in the gun case. Hudson could hardly believe he'd brought the actual Delta weapon. It made him feel overwhelmed with his grandfather's love but also terrified him to think of that weapon, whatever it was, being outside the cave it had been sheltered in for the past twenty years.

A female gardener walked around the corner of a clump of trees, holding several potted plants and a hand shovel.

"Get over here," Stefan demanded, gesturing to her.

The gardener squeaked in fear and slowly walked to Stefan. He grabbed her and dragged her in front of him, using her body as a shield.

"Come on," Stefan hissed at Papa. "Before you get innocent people killed."

The gardener let out a terrified sob.

"You'll be okay," Hudson reassured the girl, easing toward Stefan and Papa.

"You won't be," Stefan snarled at him. "Stop moving." He glared at Papa. "You move faster."

Papa walked up to him and extended the gun case. He said nothing. Hudson kind of felt it was his duty to.

"You'll never get out of here with that," he taunted Stefan.

"Watch me."

"You and what army?" Hudson asked, easing closer still. The Deltas would easily stop him.

"He's got a helicopter in the next clearing," Uncle Joseph said into the earpiece. "Colt and I will go secure it."

"I don't need an army," Stefan said. "Just a distraction." He pivoted and shot Papa just below his neck, right above the bullet-proof vest he should have on.

High shots came from different spots. Papa was hit multiple times.

"No!" Hudson screamed, hearing his cry of horror echoed throughout the nearby trees and gardens as Papa slammed back onto the ground with blood spurting from his wounds.

Multiple shots rang out and a thud and then another. Hudson knew the shooters had been tagged out of whatever tree they'd been hiding in.

Stefan was shuttling away with the weapon, dragging the girl like a human body shield. Did nobody have the shot? Hudson ached to go for Papa, but Jessie was already there, pushing her hands against the wounds to stop the blood. His youngest cousin must've been hiding right next to them in the trees.

Hudson took off at a sprint after Stefan. The man lugged the heavy case and the girl. He suddenly shoved the girl at Hudson, firing a shot at the same time.

Leaping into the air, Hudson grasped a tree branch, dodging the girl and the bullet. He flung his body forward and nailed Stefan in the abdomen with both feet. The man folded forward and then hit the ground in a crumpled heap. Hudson leaped onto him, ripping his gun from his hand, tossing it, shoving him onto his back, and then hitting him with jab after jab to the abdomen where he'd kicked him.

Stefan fought for air and tried to hit back, but he was no match for Hudson.

Aiden and Greer were right there. Greer stripped the Delta weapon from the man's hand and headed back toward Papa.

"Helicopter's secure," Joseph said in the headset.

"Get back here," Maddie begged her dad, her voice catching on a sob.

"Maddie?"

"Papa," she got out.

Papa! Hudson echoed the cry. He shoved Stefan into the ground.

"I've got him, Hudson," Aiden said, touching him on the shoulder. "Papa's asking for you."

"He's alive?" Hudson leaped up.

Stefan reached for his leg, trying to trip him. Hudson kicked his hand hard enough he heard bones crack. The man yelped in pain.

Aiden flipped Stefan face down and growled, "Don't move. Don't even breathe. I'd love an excuse to kill you."

Hudson ran to the group kneeling or standing around Papa. Any in-laws stood respectfully nearby. The two Navy SEALs he'd met the other night had guns up and were guarding the family from any other threats.

His dad and uncle were on each side of Papa's head. Jessie had a couple of bloody shirts, pressed into wounds right below his collar bone and on his hip. Blood ran down his thigh as well but the rest of the bullets must've hit his bulletproof vest. Thor, Aunt Holly, Esther, Colt, Maddie, and Chandler were all kneeling as close as they could get.

Hudson dropped to his knees next to his dad. "No," he groaned. "Papa. I'm so sorry." He'd baited that idiot. If only he'd let him walk away with the weapon. They would've caught him.

Papa's eyes were open but glazed, he focused in on him. "Huddy, this was ..." His breath gurgled and with sickening realization, Hudson knew blood was filling his lungs.

"This was for you," Papa finished.

"Oh, Papa." His throat was thick with emotion and tears stung his eyes. "I'm so sorry. I shouldn't have—"

"Stop," Papa said quietly. "I love you." He pulled in a breath. "Take care of Kelsey and Mo."

"He's your great grandson, Papa. I just found out."

Several of the family cried out in surprise. Hudson's dad squeezed his arm in a show of support.

Papa smiled. "I wondered." He gurgled for air. "He's perfect."

"He is."

Papa grew serious. "I love ... all of you so much." He paused for breath and Hudson hated the awful gurgling sound of every breath. "Keep the weapon safe. Keep this family safe."

He was leaving them. He really was. Hudson's chest was tight, and he couldn't swallow past the emotion. He wanted to scream out his agony and somehow save his Papa. Police sirens were approaching. They were close, but not close enough to save Papa.

"It's okay," Papa said, looking around the group of somber faces. "I'll be with Rachel."

Hudson knew that was true. He knew how Papa had missed Granny. Death was an awful thing, but in ways it was beautiful.

His gaze sharpened. "Hudson. Jessie. Aiden. Joseph. Keith."

Aiden came running over. Hudson wondered if he'd bound Stefan, killed him, or if somebody had taken the man off his hands.

"Get the weapon out of here," he paused to breathe, "back to the cave. Go now, before the police. Too many questions." He rushed all the words out, then gasped through several rattling breaths. Then he demanded, "Go ... now!"

Hudson saw no other option but to stand up and go. Colt slid his hands onto the T-shirts and Jessie lifted her hands away. She bent and kissed Papa's cheek, and he smiled softly.

"I love you," he told her.

"I love you," Jessie sobbed out.

"I love you all," Papa said, then he smiled and said, "Rachel?"

His eyes closed. The rattling breaths stopped. He was gone.

Hudson knew he was gone. Knew it as strongly as anything

he'd ever known. Pain ripped through his chest and he wanted to scream out his anguish.

"No!" Jessie screamed and laid her head on Papa's chest. "No," she whimpered, her body shaking with sobs.

Quiet crying and sniffling was overridden by police sirens growing far too close.

Greer handed Aiden the Delta weapon.

Uncle Joseph gently lifted Jessie off of Papa and to her feet. "We have to go love."

She leaned heavily into him but she didn't say anything.

His dad squeezed Hudson's arm and tilted his head to the side. "This way."

The five of them hustled through a thick stand of trees. They had to get the weapon back safely in the cave.

Papa was gone.

It hurt like Hudson hadn't hurt since he'd lost Kelsey. Sharp, throbbing pain in his chest. Jessie's quiet sobs added to the hurt. Aiden, his dad, and Uncle Joseph didn't cry out loud, but he could see tears streaming down their faces and he could feel them on his own.

Pain. Regret. Loss. Agony. He felt it all. Yet somehow inside there was light, warmth, and hope too. Papa was with Granny now. Papa was with Jesus and their Heavenly Father now. He wasn't in pain. He wasn't the Admiral directing and fighting this long, hard battle. He wasn't worried and losing sleep at night.

Papa would watch over them from heaven. He knew that as strongly as he knew his family would keep this weapon safe. He was still overwhelmed at the gesture of Papa bringing the actual weapon to bargain for Hudson, Kelsey, and Mo's safety. Putting his family first. Always. He loved his Papa so much, and he knew Papa loved him in return.

They hustled through a gate and around the edges of the garden toward a back parking lot. They'd get the weapon out of here. And they'd honor Papa's legacy and life's work. There was no other option.

There were a lot questions pinging through his brain:

Were Kelsey and Mo safe?

How soon could he get to them?

Were the rest of the family okay?

How would they calm Jessie down?

How would they protect the Delta weapon without Papa's connections, influence, experience, and convincing power?

Who was the next Secret Keeper?

And the worrisome, nagging question ... What if Papa hadn't assigned one yet?

Chapter Nineteen

Kelsey was trying to share with Hudson's mom and family members about everything they'd gone through, Mo chirping in details, as they sped away from Denver and toward the mountains to the west. Their mountains. She couldn't wait to go home. But she wanted Hudson. Would Hudson really come for her? She hated them being apart. It wasn't that she couldn't stand on her own. She'd done it and proven to herself she could. But it was past time to figure out a future with her Brave. Both of them loving Mo and loving each other.

In the back of her mind, those worries that he'd be gone before the sun came up tingled. She refused to let him surface, but they were so embedded in her thinking she couldn't completely eradicate them. She wanted to fully trust he'd be racing after them as soon as he could. His loyalty and promises to her and Mo were beautiful. She probably just needed time to heal the wounds of the past four years and have Hudson show her that he would come for her.

She thought about Hudson, Papa, and the Delta family facing Stefan, and whoever was with the monster. The fear overrode any worries about Hudson following them home. *Please let him and everyone be okay,* she prayed. Stefan had been very confident in his plan and his abilities to kill and fight. She shuddered. He was a monster. Were her awful worries about Hudson not following them because he was going to get hurt or killed? She hugged Mo and prayed harder.

Myrna's cell phone rang. The Lexus was her car, so the phone was connected. The car's audio system chirped, "Thor, supreme leader of the universe and the best son of all time."

"Oh, that boy." Myrna laughed. "He's always programming something into my phone."

Shelly laughed with her. "I know. I won't tell you what some of mine say." She winked and pressed a button on the steering wheel as they all raised their eyebrows or smiled at that.

"Hey, handsome husband. You're on Bluetooth, so—"

"Shell ..." Thor's voice was so full of sorrow that the entire vehicle quieted.

"What's wrong?" Myrna demanded, leaning forward so her voice could be heard.

"Oh, Mama ..." Thor choked up.

Kelsey's heart was hammering out of control. Hudson! Not Hudson!

"Papa's ... gone," Thor got out.

"No!" Alivia let out a heart-wrenching cry of pain. Klein wrapped his arm around her and held her.

Myrna had tears streaming down her face. Her mouth flopped open, but she didn't say anything. She buried her head in her hands and just sobbed. Kelsey felt awful and wished she knew how to help. She loved Papa like everyone in Summit Valley did, but she wasn't his family.

She looked down at Mo, who was staring at her, wide-eyed.

"Mama?" he whispered.

She cradled him as close as she could with him in the car seat. Mo was Papa Delta's great-grandson. Admiral Davidson had never known that truth. Kelsey had kept the secret because she'd refused to force Hudson into stepping up and taking care of her and Mo. But she could admit now that she'd been deeply hurt by Hudson not coming for her, immature enough to hide her secrets, and scared of more rejection from Hudson.

Now that she knew the truth of why Hudson had never come for her, guilt jabbed through her like a scalpel. If she would've just been honest about who Mo's father was, Papa Delta would've spent time with Mo as a great-grandpa. Myrna and Keith would've loved him from birth on up as his paternal grandparents. All the Delta family would've made Kelsey and Mo their own. Despite the fear of rejection she'd felt in the past, she knew the goodness of these people and knew they would've loved her and welcomed her. And she also knew they would've hunted Hudson down and forced him to fulfill his responsibilities. And he would've happily done it. She groaned inside. All those wasted years of Hudson and his family not knowing he was Mo's father. Regret and pain overwhelmed her.

"Sorry, Papa," she whispered to the heavens.

"What, Mama?" Mo asked in a small voice.

"Papa Delta went to heaven," she said softly, not wanting to interrupt the details Thor was brokenly sharing with Shelly and the entire car, and Myrna and Alivia's soft sobs.

"The murderer was running with the weapon and dragging an innocent gardener as a body shield. We were trying to move to get a clear shot when he took a shot at Hudson," Thor said through the speaker.

Kelsey cried out, cold chills covering her body.

"He shot my Hudson?" Mo yelled.

"No, Mo," Thor rushed to say. "No, buddy. Hudson's okay. He did one of his crazy leaps, grabbed a tree limb, slammed his feet into the guy's stomach and took him out."

"Yay!" Mo cheered.

Kelsey relaxed a fraction. Hudson's mom squeezed her arm and then released it.

"My little bro is quite the superstar," Thor bragged, and despite the sadness in the car, it was nice to have something to celebrate. Hudson was all right. "Almost as cool and tough as Thor, ruler of the universe."

"Yay, Thor!" Mo called out.

Melene smiled back at the little boy.

"I gotta go talk to the police," Thor said. "And deal with the ... details."

"Thanks, love," Myrna said.

"Of course, Mama. Be safe. We'll be home as soon as we can."

The mood in the car was somber and reflective as everyone said their goodbyes and the phone call ended.

Kelsey couldn't help but feel a little awkward. She wasn't

really a family member. Myrna didn't even know Mo was her grandson. though she knew the woman had always wondered.

While the family quietly talked, comforted, and shared stories about Papa Delta, she held on to Mo's hand and wondered how soon she'd see Hudson. How should they tell his family that he was Mo's father? With all the sadness surrounding Papa Delta's death, a funeral to plan, and whatever the family would need to do for the Delta Protection Detail ... Wasn't that what Hudson had called it?

She thought Mo would fall asleep, but he listened to stories, sometimes interjected funny comments or asked questions. It was comforting to see how much he was loved by the Deltas.

It was a relief when they drove into Summit Valley.

They passed through the valley. She wouldn't have minded going home, but she wasn't about to ask for anything right now. They drove up to the Deltas' valley. Several of the Summit Valley sheriff's deputies and she assumed the Navy SEALs she'd heard about were stationed outside. They must've gotten the news too, because they looked very somber.

They unloaded from the Lexus and went into Papa's house. That was a rough moment, everybody realizing that Papa wouldn't return here.

Her mom was waiting in the kitchen, stirring soup with all kinds of sandwich fixings ready on the counter. Granny Vance was napping in a large recliner.

Her mom squealed when she saw Kelsey and Mo and ran at them. She hugged them over and over again, crying and wanting to know everything that had happened. But then she interrupted her questions to hug the Deltas and express her sadness about

Papa. Granny woke up, but Klein and Shelly were right there for her.

Everyone was kind but serious, and Mo was a great distraction. At least for Kelsey.

The group assembled sandwiches and tried to eat while Kelsey and her mom talked quietly about everything that had happened and Mo tried to entertain the crowd with silly made-up jokes and his best stunts, his headstand and his cartwheels and somersaults, which were pretty impressive for a three-year-old. He'd probably be as talented as his daddy someday. Maybe more so as Hudson would want to work with him and train him. She missed him. When would he come? He would come. He'd told her he'd marry her, that they'd have ten boys—that made her smile—and he was changing his nickname from Death Wish Delta to her Brave. Of course he'd come.

After lunch, Mo seemed to be slowing down and Kelsey felt the Deltas could use some time alone. She'd love to get Mo down for a nap, shower, and pack some things to bring back for their stay here. Who knew how long it would be? She didn't care as long as Hudson was here.

She approached Klein and Alivia. "Since Stefan is arrested and Mo and I aren't in danger any longer, my mom could run us home and I could get Mo down for a nap, take a quick shower, and pack some things."

Klein and Alivia exchanged a look. Alivia shrugged and Klein said, "I think it'd be okay if you went, but I'd like to have the SEALs or a couple of Reed's guys go with you. The men who kidnapped you might be arrested or dead, but new threats seem to arise every day, and with Papa gone, we don't have the layer of protection that his reputation and vast network of contacts in the military and government gave us."

"Oh." Kelsey hadn't thought of that. She had a lot of questions about the Delta weapon, but Hudson had said even he didn't know what it did. It made sense that King Frederick would still be sending people after it and maybe even accelerate his attacks with Papa Delta gone. That wasn't great. What would that mean for her and Hudson? She missed him.

He'd show up soon. He'd hold her close, and she'd know all her crazy worries were ridiculous. They'd have to wait on getting married and it made her stomach tumble to think of more Stefans coming to this peaceful valley, attacking, trying to get that weapon.

Hudson would keep them safe. When he came. But she wasn't ready for more danger.

"Let's go talk to Officer Leandro." Klein squeezed Alivia's hand, then stood.

Alivia was sitting with Granny Vance. She gave them a smile and a wave as Kelsey, her mom, and Mo walked out of the living area. Kelsey was grateful Alivia hadn't held a weird grudge for Kelsey trying to date Klein last summer.

They walked outside with Klein, and he walked them over to a Spanish-descent man who was powerfully built and holding a scary-looking gun.

"Hey, tough guy," Mo said in his silly voice.

"Hey little man." The guy waved and smiled.

"Would you and Officer Christensen mind escorting them home and watching over them while they shower, pack a few things, and then bring them back?"

The guy pursed his lips. He didn't seem to like leaving his post.

"I think everything's pretty settled here," Klein said. "The group is already headed up to the cave, and Thor texted that the rest of them are on their way."

Where was Hudson?

Leandro looked her over and then said, "I don't like spreading the protection detail out. Can you go pick up what you need from your house, and then we'll escort you back here and you can shower here?"

"That's fine." It looked like Mo wouldn't be getting a nap at home, but she didn't want to put anyone out. She didn't feel awkward with the Deltas per se, but they were focused on their grief right now and she didn't want to be a burden to any of them. If only Hudson would get back. Then she'd know her place. She looked at her mom.

"What about my bakery?" she asked. "I've already had it closed the entire morning."

"Ma'am. You might have to keep it closed until we figure out a few things. I want to keep you ladies safe."

Her mom didn't seem to like it, but one look at Mo and she nodded. "You're right. Kelsey and Mo being safe is all that matters."

Kelsey's heart warmed. She knew her mom adored them both. She wanted to be alone with her and share the details she'd kept back about her and Hudson's time in that hotel room. Well, maybe not all the details, but she'd at least tell her they'd figured out about how everything got so messed up four years ago and the fact that they'd kissed. She smiled to herself. They'd kissed a lot.

Of course Hudson would come. It wasn't just the intense kisses they'd shared. It was the way he'd looked at Mo. He'd never leave the two of them again.

"All right. Christensen," Leandro called. "We're going on a drive."

"Thanks, Klein," she said.

"Sure thing."

"Bye, Klein," Mo called.

"I'll see you real soon, Mo," Klein told him.

They loaded into her mom's car, Christensen driving and Leandro sitting up front. Her mom said, "How did you boys get involved in this Delta weapon thing?"

Leandro smiled. "It's a crazy story, ma'am, one I don't know that I'm at liberty to share. You do understand that you can't tell anyone about the Delta weapon?"

"Oh, yeah." Her mom leaned back against the seat and gave an exaggerated nod. "I got that loud and clear."

Mo started peppering the SEALs with questions about their guns and if they were G.I. Joes and did they like to shoot bad guys? The drive passed quickly. The SEALs searched their house, then let them go in and pack bags. In no time at all, they were headed back to the Deltas.

Kelsey wondered where Hudson was and why she hadn't heard from him. She didn't want to take him away from any important Delta family duties, especially with the huge hit of Papa's death, but she needed to hear from him. Her mom had picked up her phone at Granny's and she assumed he'd gotten his phone back, but who knew? He could be off doing something important with the weapon or ... what if he had to go back to his crew and film some stunt or video that his producers were waiting on? He wouldn't do that right now. But if he had to, he'd tell her. Right?

Two days ago, she wouldn't have trusted Hudson as far as she could throw him. Today she'd trusted him with hers and their son's lives and her heart. He'd come through big time. Where was he now? She prayed for strength and patience and selflessness. The issues right now were all about Papa Delta's death and the weapon they needed to protect from the horrible King Frederick. Her worrying where her long-lost love could be was selfish and silly and showed a lack of faith in Hudson she didn't want to have anymore.

The SEALs escorted them back into Papa Delta's house, carrying the bags they'd packed as if Kelsey, her mom, and Mo were going to be permanent house guests. Would this nightmare with the weapon ever be finished? Kelsey thanked them for taking them, and they faded back outside.

The house was full to bursting. She searched for Hudson, but she couldn't see him, his dad, Aiden, Jessie, or his uncle. It looked like every other Delta family member or future family member was here. Along with some more military-looking guys.

Thor immediately came to take Mo from her. The little guy said sleepily, "Thor, can you throw me?"

"Of course." Thor grinned and started tossing the boy into the air.

Kelsey's heart clutched at the sight. She could picture Hudson doing the same thing, promising to throw their boy higher when they were outside. Where was he?

Her mom went into the kitchen to help Myrna, Holly, Greer, Emery, and Klein.

Kelsey felt lost, alone, and wanted to beg anyone or everyone for news of where Hudson was. She was uneasy about the future of this entire family with Papa gone. If Alivia was right, they'd have more evil men coming without Papa's protection. It all sounded terrifying, but she'd gone through something more terrifying and been fine. Because of her Brave.

Where was he?

Esther came to her and gave her a brief side hug. "Are you doing okay, sweetie?"

"Yes, thank you."

"Mama said we'll have you, Mo, and your mom stay at their house. Is that all right with you?"

"That's great. Thank you. I hate to put anyone out."

"They have plenty of room. There are always people on guard duty in the valley, and we have sensors and cameras outside and through the main areas. You and Mo will be safe."

"That's good to know." Safe was good. Hudson close was even better.

"I'm staying there too. Until Reed and I get married." She grinned happily, holding up her gorgeous engagement ring for Kelsey to inspect.

"That is beautiful," Kelsey said.

"Thanks. Let's grab the bags and I'll walk you over and show you the rooms. It's a little loud here for me."

"Perfect." She wanted an excuse to get out of here and not look for Hudson to appear every other second.

They picked up hers and Mo's bags and her mom's. She

looked to Thor. "Are you okay with Mo if I walk our bags over to your mom's house and take a quick shower?"

"For sure," he said. "Me and Mo are buddies. Take your time."

Mo gave her a thumbs up, then begged Thor, "Play horse."

"Oh yeah. Gotta get you ready to be a real cowboy," Thor said.

Kelsey smiled as she watched them. Thor dropped to all fours and Mo perched on his back, riding him around like a horse.

She turned to Esther, and they carried the bags out the front door, across the driveway, through the gravel, and up the driveway of Hudson's parent's house.

The sheriff's men and the SEALs were out front, almost as if they were making their presence known should anybody try anything with this family that had just lost their patriarch.

Esther waved to the men. They all gave her manly chin lifts back.

Neither she nor Esther said anything as they walked. Esther was a lawyer and a very calm person. Kelsey thought the charming Sheriff Reed fit her perfectly.

They walked up the sidewalk, across the wide porch, and into the house. It was an airy two-story country house with lots of windows and open space. She followed Esther up the stairs.

"Okay, this one is for your mom." Esther set the bag down and then walked into the next room. "This one is for you and Mo. This used to be Hudson and Chandler's room. My mom had to completely redo it with all the holes they put in the walls and mud and burn marks they made in the carpet."

Kelsey laughed and looked around. It was painted a light gray with white trim. A large king-sized bed had a cool leather headboard behind it. There were two large windows with views of the lake and the mountain.

She wasn't ready to go face the crowd again. "Do you care if I shower and rest for a few minutes before I head back for dinner? My mom will take care of Mo if Thor gets bored of him."

"I'm sure you're exhausted after all that stress. You rest. We'll all watch over Mo." She smiled sweetly. Kelsey wondered if Thor or Aiden had told Esther that Mo was her nephew. Kelsey didn't want to get into it right now. Not without Hudson here to share the happy news with his family.

"I'll just let Captain Hendrickson know you're in here and to keep an eye out for you."

"Thanks."

Esther turned to go.

It just burst out of Kelsey. "Where's Hudson?"

His sister turned back and searched her gaze. "He had to go ..." She paused as if she shouldn't say it out loud.

Kelsey's heart seemed to stop pumping blood to her head. She got dizzy and lightheaded and sat down on the bed. She was exhausted and things weren't clear right now. Had Esther paused because it was another secret thing for the Deltas, or because she didn't want to break Kelsey's heart in two?

Esther bent in front of her and asked, "You sure you're okay, sweetie?"

She tried to nod, but her head wasn't complying. "Where did he go?" she managed to ask. She thought she kept the angst out of her voice, but it was sure building inside.

"You don't know?"

Kelsey stared into Esther's blue eyes, so like Hudson's, and she hated herself for thinking it, but she feared that she absolutely did know.

"I know," she finally said. He'd gone. Back to his stunts. Back to his life. Really? Could he really leave when Papa had just died? Could he ditch her after they'd just reconnected? Could he leave Mo after how ecstatic he'd been to find out he was Mo's dad and all the sadness of what he'd missed out on?

Brave! She wanted to cry out to him and have him run back to her.

Could he really leave them? Without saying goodbye? Without making future plans?

With grim realization, Kelsey admitted to herself that was his pattern. Despite all his promises and their incredible reconnection. She could still see the intensity of his blue eyes, feel him close as he said, *Sunshine. I'm here now. Nobody will ever, ever hurt the two of you again. Never. I promise you that.*

He'd been there to protect them, but now that they were safe, he'd had to go. Hudson was intense and impetuous, and she loved that about him. Maybe he'd just had to go do a stunt quick or help with something for Papa or the weapon that he'd been so concerned about. Maybe she was blowing this all out of proportion because of how exhausted and overwrought she was.

He'd come back. Right? He had to come back. It hurt so much that he could leave like this, and she was terrified of what it meant for them. What if the dream life she'd created in her head would always be just that—a dream?

Esther nodded encouragingly. "Yes, so you know ... why he can't be here. Why he had to go?"

Kelsey bit at her cheek to keep from crying. "I know," she said again. She wanted to be alone and try to think clearly.

Esther straightened as if that settled it. Hudson had to go. His sister didn't blame him or second guess it. He couldn't be here. He had to go. He must be doing something very important. Could it be for Papa and the Delta weapon thing, or was there a stunt that was so huge and planned out that he couldn't stay away?

She wanted to ask if he would come back? No. He'd come back. He had to. It was just *when* he'd come back. Right? She hated her lack of faith in her Brave. She didn't dare ask Esther for a time of his return, because if the answer wasn't tonight or at the worst tomorrow she would dissolve into a heap. If he was gone for a while, on an assignment for Papa while he was dying, or maybe back to his important, successful life ... what would she do? She was suddenly glad she hadn't told Mo Hudson was his father yet. When he came back, they'd tell Mo together. Why wasn't he here? Why hadn't he cared enough to let her know why and where and how long he'd be gone?

"I'll let you rest." Esther walked out of the room, shutting the door softly behind her.

Kelsey lay on the bed and let the tears come. He'd really left her and Mo? How could he be so incredible and attentive and sweet with them, risk his life to rescue them, and then just leave? Could she have misunderstood Esther? She thought back over the conversation. She didn't think so, but what did she know? Hudson was doing what he always did, and Esther didn't seem to question it. That was a depressing thought. Hudson back to Death Wish Delta with women chasing after him. No! He wouldn't do that.

She was probably so overwrought and exhausted she wasn't seeing or thinking clearly. Closing her eyes, she prayed for strength and prayed for Hudson to be safe and happy wherever he was and prayed for her and Mo to somehow keep going if he didn't come back for them.

That was silly. He'd come back. She prayed for more faith in heaven and trust in Hudson. He was the only man she had ever and could ever love. She had to trust him.

Sadly, she had four years of experience not trusting him, and all those embedded memories, heartache, and longing were at the forefront right now.

She tried to refocus her prayer outside of herself. She prayed for the Delta family's safety and emotional and spiritual well-being with Papa gone and to protect the Delta weapon.

The tears kept coming, but the prayer at least distracted her from her fear of another desertion. Her heart was breaking in two.

Where on earth could Hudson be?

Chapter Twenty

Hudson, Jessie, Aiden, his dad, and Uncle Joseph finally made it back to Papa's house after a far too slow trip to the secret cave. The scene in the cave had been both enlightening and horrifying for all of them. He passed a hand over his face. The entire family would know soon. Until then, he tried to keep a lid on his own emotions and trust that Papa knew what he was doing.

He couldn't believe Papa was gone. Especially when he walked into Papa's house with each of his family members there and lots of food, drinks, and treats laid out on the counter. Papa would've loved this. The entire family together. Except him. His eyes burned. He blinked, refusing to cry again. It felt like he'd been crying since Papa had said, "Huddy this was ... this was for you." His grandfather had loved him completely. As did all of his family.

He was anxious to talk to his siblings and make a plan to go forward, but even more anxious to hold Kelsey and Mo close and make plans with her. He looked around the crowded living, kitchen, and dining area. Her mom Lori held Mo and was coaxing him to eat some broccoli. Mo clamped his mouth closed. Hudson grinned at his son, momentarily forgetting about the insanity of this day and those bullets hitting Papa.

"Hudson!" Mo spotted him, jumped off his grandma's lap, and ran at him.

Hudson caught him and easily tossed him in the air. "Hey, Mo. How's my boy?"

"Good! 'Cept I hate 'roccli," he said in a stage whisper.

"I do too," he confided.

"Yes!" Mo held out his fist to bump. "My man!"

Hudson chuckled. It felt so right, holding his son and commiserating with him.

He glanced around for Kelsey, but she didn't appear. He'd assumed she was in the restroom or something. He couldn't wait to see her, see her dark eyes light up and her lips curve in a smile for him. He'd run to her, hold her close, kiss her. Kelsey would make everything right.

"Where's your mama?" he asked.

"I no know." Mo shrugged. Dang, he was the cutest kid ever. But where was Kelsey?

His dad clapped his hands together. "I need a quick meeting in the conference room with all the Delta family members."

Could Hudson find Kelsey first?

Shelly looked at her father-in-law. "In-laws and future in-laws?"

He shook his head. "Not this time. We need to make some decisions about Papa's funeral and ... some other things."

"And that's going to be quick?" Maddie asked, staring at her uncle as if he'd lost it.

"Yes," his dad insisted. "The SEALs are outside if someone could please take them food. Reed and his men are watching over the cave. We'll trade them out after we make the decisions and let you all know." He looked at the in-laws. "Sorry to be exclusive, but this is something that Papa started with his grandchildren twelve years ago and they need to be unified on it." He looked around at his children and nieces and nephew.

Hudson already knew what was happening and could only imagine the reaction they were going to get. He didn't even want to think about it. He looked at his Aunt Holly, and his stomach took a nose dive. Ah, man, this was going to be awful.

"It's okay, Keith," Melene said. "I trust you all."

Hudson didn't know Melene well, but she seemed like the sweetest woman. Perfect for the tough Aiden. Where was Hudson's perfect woman?

Nobody said much as his family members headed for the stairs.

"Does anybody know where Kelsey is?" he called out.

"She went to shower and lay down in her room for a bit at Mom and Dad's," Esther told him. "I let Captain Hendrickson know to watch over her."

"Oh." Hudson didn't want some elite SEAL watching over her. He wanted to watch over her. He wanted her in his arms ... right now. The meeting could wait five minutes for him to go reassure Kelsey he was back safe and get a quick kiss. He just needed to see her. It would take the family more than five minutes to settle down and start the meeting.

"Hey, buddy, I've got to go somewhere real quick. Okay?"

"'Kay." Mo squeezed his neck and then squirmed out of his arms and ran for his Grandma Lori.

Hudson met Kelsey's mom's gaze. She smiled at him and waved. Mo would be fine. Kelsey was resting. Why did his stomach feel so unsettled? He had traveled across the globe, been through an insane kidnapping with the woman he loved, found out he was a father, and hadn't slept. He'd lost his beloved Papa and found out a secret that had him terrified and sick. It was little wonder he was upset.

He hurried for the front entry and said to Aiden's back, "I'm going to check on Kelsey quick. I'll be right back."

Aiden spun around on the second stair down, staring incredulously at him. "Dude. Get your butt down here. You know how important this is."

He did, he really did, but Kelsey needed him too. The protection of the weapon and the Keeper was huge for their family, but Papa always put his family first and that's exactly what Hudson was doing. Kelsey was his first priority.

"Five minutes," Hudson said, backing up.

Aiden sprang up the stairs, getting in his face. "We need you right now. Everybody's going to need you down there." He pointed down the stairs. "When ..." He shook his head in frustration. "Kelsey is either showering or asleep. She's been through a lot."

Exactly. She'd been to heck and back and she needed Hudson.

Maddie, Alivia, and Chandler skirted around them, giving them questioning looks but not saying anything.

"Kelsey won't even know you're gone," Aiden said in a low voice as Jessie, Holly, and Colt went down the stairs.

Well, that hurt.

"Come on, man. You can spare fifteen minutes for your family."

Hudson hated his tone of voice, like he was the slacker little brother nobody trusted. That sucked. Hudson had been gone, but only because of the agony of not knowing Mo was his and thinking Kelsey didn't love him.

Aiden grabbed his arm, and it wasn't a friendly brotherly grab. It was a *you'd better move your butt, little brother* grab.

Hudson slammed his fist into his brother's forearm. Aiden released him but came back with an uppercut to his gut. Hudson almost doubled over, Aiden really packed a punch, but so did Hudson. He dug deep and hit his brother hard in the chest. Aiden teetered on the edge of the steps and almost tripped.

"Boys!" His mom wrapped her arms around him from behind. "What is wrong with you two?" She came around in front of him to glare up at him. "Your dad needs you right now." Her voice broke and tears made her eyes bright.

Hudson wrapped his arms around her. He should apologize, but he was too ticked at Aiden.

"I'm sorry," Aiden said, "but we all need you. Kelsey will be okay."

"Is that what this is about?" His mom stared up at him. "Kelsey's napping, sweetie. Can you wait until after the meeting to go see her?"

His dad appeared at the bottom of the stairs. Hudson looked

past Aiden and met his dad's gaze. The heartbreak in those blue eyes wrenched at his gut.

"Everybody's ready," was all he said, but Hudson could feel it. His dad needed him. He'd just lost his father, and now he and Uncle Joseph were in charge. Uncle Joseph was an absolute mess at the moment, finding out who the Secret Keeper was. Aunt Holly would react worse than he had. Uncle Joseph had tried to stay in control in the cave but as they'd exited he'd pushed off into the trees for a minute and they could all hear him throwing up and then begging the heavens to know ... *Why?*

Kelsey was showering or sleeping. She was okay. His gut churning was because of all they'd been through, Kelsey and Mo being in danger like they'd been, losing Papa, and all that was coming for his family. It was all compiling.

He nodded to his dad and escorted his mom toward the stairs. Aiden turned and pumped down them and his dad disappeared back toward the conference room.

He'd get through this meeting, offer his devoted support to his family, find Kelsey, and kiss her for a good, long time. Then until his patrol time up at the cave, in the Delta valley, or at the monitors came, he'd hold Kelsey and sleep soundly. When could he tell Mo he was his father? When could he fulfill the dream he'd given up on four years ago of officially proposing to Kelsey? How quick would she marry him?

He descended the stairs, walked his mom over to his dad and pulled a chair out, and then sank into an empty chair by Aiden.

"We good?" Aiden asked, extending his fist.

It was interesting that Aiden even worried about it. The

brothers wrestled and fought all the time. But usually it was in fun and with lots of teasing banter.

"Yeah." Hudson forced a smile, bumping his fist into Aiden's.

His stomach was raw from hunger, and that probably added to the weird emotional emptiness in his gut. He should've grabbed a plate of food and a drink. This would be a good time to eat before he went for Kelsey. Yet as he looked across the table at his cousin Jessie, he didn't know if he'd be able to eat.

He glanced around the room. He'd never been in this room without Papa. By the lost and forlorn looks in some of the Delta family's eyes, none of them had.

His dad shut the door, then he and Joseph stood where Papa usually stood. His dad looked at his brother and something unsettling passed between them.

"You want me to?" his dad asked quietly.

Joseph nodded and sank into a chair. Aunt Holly reached for his hand. He clasped her hand tightly, looking at her. Her gaze widened, questioning, searching. He looked away, as if afraid of what she would see. Hudson thought his uncle looked like he'd aged twenty years today.

Hudson was not ready for the reaction Aunt Holly or any of them were going to give. He could only imagine how Uncle Joseph and his dad were feeling right now. Hudson needed to be here for his family and would've felt awful making them wait. Kelsey would be okay. Why did he feel like she needed him? She wasn't in danger. The sensors and cameras would reveal anyone or anything out of place. The Navy SEALs were patrolling.

Please keep her safe, he prayed.

Maybe it was just that she and Mo had been in such extreme

danger and he was tired and this meeting was going to be rough and ...

It would all work out, but sitting here was torture right now.

His dad cleared his throat. "We don't have time to waste tonight, or until Frederick is defeated, so I'm going to be as brief as I can be."

Brief sounded great to Hudson. He cringed at his selfish thought. Kelsey was okay. Mo was okay. He needed to focus on the rest of his family right now.

"Please forgive me if I seem abrupt. I'm as devastated as any of you to lose Papa." He paused, pressed his lips together, and then cleared his throat. "The only thing getting me through is thinking of him and Mom up there, finally together again."

There was a moment of silence as they all seemed to picture that. It was comforting. Papa would be happy with Granny. He was in a better place. Hudson knew that was all true. Still, it hurt. It would hurt less if he could hold Kelsey close.

"Joseph and I have decided to have a small graveside service here for Papa as soon as the mortician can prepare the body and the casket. Probably Sunday." Granny was actually buried around the east side of the lake, so that made his idea easier. "When everything settles down, we'll have a large and more formal memorial service at the church down in the valley."

Nobody said anything. It stunk. They should've had a large funeral with all the military honors and praises that Papa deserved, but the situation was precarious at best. Papa would be the first to tell them to keep the family and the weapon safe, not expose both with a huge service that any mercenary could sneak into or sneak around like General Phillip had during Thor and Shelly's wedding.

"We'll have to think of a good excuse to tell the people in town and the Navy," Aunt Holly said.

Uncle Joseph nodded to her. "We could just say in his will he asked for a private family graveside service by his wife's grave, but we're planning a memorial service for later."

"That's fine," Dad said. "Blame Papa. He can't defend himself."

There were some uneasy chuckles at that. It grew quiet quickly.

"We'll also have the pastor and Reed's guys spread the word that the family is hunkering down and wants no visitors until further notice."

"You're going to keep the church ladies from bringing us homemade bread, cookies, and casseroles?" Thor asked. "That sucks."

Everybody smiled.

"I think you'll survive." Their dad's smile was there and gone quick. "Before I move on, I want you all to know how proud Papa was of each one of you. You've all excelled as Delta Protection members, in your chosen career paths, and your relationships with each other," he'd already forgotten Hudson and Aiden's fight of moments before, "your spouses or future spouses, and your Savior." He paused and cleared his throat again. "He loved each of you very much."

There was a warm current in the room and Hudson almost felt as if Papa were there, smiling at them, teaching them, loving them. He'd been the most incredible example and champion of each of them. To think he'd actually retrieved the Delta weapon from the cave early this morning to ensure Hudson, Kelsey, and Mo's freedom... That would always hit Hudson hard and make his throat feel thick.

"Now on to something even harder."

Almost everyone looked around in question. They were all probably wondering what could possibly be harder than burying Papa.

Aiden nudged Hudson. He met his brother's gaze. Hudson nodded to him. The scene in the cave earlier had been surreal. Hudson wished he could change it, but he couldn't. Papa had made the decision, he was certain with lots of prayer and inspiration. Now they all had to somehow live with it.

They both looked at Jessie. She sat between Colt and Maddie. She looked small and young and innocent and ... Hudson squeezed his eyes shut and said another prayer.

"Some of you may have wondered why Jessie was assigned to go with Joseph, Aiden, Hudson, and I to replace the weapon."

The room seemed to freeze as more glances were exchanged. The question of Secret Keeper had been at the back of everybody's minds.

Suddenly, Aunt Holly screamed out an anguished, "No!"

Uncle Joseph pulled her close as she started sobbing. His eyes squeezed shut and his body trembling slightly as if to absorb his wife's pain.

That "no" and his beloved aunt crying hit Hudson harder than tumbling off his surfboard at the crest of a sixty-foot wave onto the concrete-like ocean below. This was awful. He still couldn't wrap his mind around it.

Alivia and Maddie had the truth sink in at the same time. They exchanged horrified glances and grabbed each other's hands. Hudson could see that Esther, Greer, Chandler, and his mom all realized what was happening. His mom started crying just like Aunt Holly, though not as loud.

Before anyone else could say anything, Colt's blue eyes grew determined. Colt was the oldest cousin, and everybody loved and respected him. He turned to his little sister and wrapped a protective arm around her. "No," he said firmly. "No! You all know how much I love and respect everything Papa did, all he taught us, what he gave his life for, but I will *not* allow Jessie to be Secret Keeper."

"Jessie?" Thor burst out with. "No way is Jessie the Secret Keeper."

Their dad gave Thor a disgusted look as Jessie shriveled into Colt.

His brother lifted his hands up. "What? I'm not saying she couldn't do it. I know she's more than capable, smart, well-trained, and talented. I've fought and trained with her all my life. She's impressive, instinctive, brave, and tough. What I'm saying, is no way on this earth would Papa do that to Jessie. She's too sweet and perfect and we all adore her, especially Papa. I don't think anyone here minds me saying she was Papa's favorite. No way would he put that kind of target on her back."

Hudson knew exactly what Thor was saying because he and Aiden had a similar discussion as they rode back from the cave with their dad while Joseph and Jessie took the two-person Razor down.

"Jessie *is* the Secret Keeper," their dad said firmly. "I watched her open the cave myself and put the weapon away. She is the one entrusted to protect the secret until ...”

Hudson had watched as well. Jessie was the Secret Keeper, ordained by heaven and their Papa. Now they all had to figure out how to comprehend that, and how to keep her safe.

The until ... was a sickening thought.

Until King Frederick succeeded and they all died.

No, he couldn't think like that. Until Jessie used the weapon, finished this nightmare, and possibly sacrificed her life in the process? Who knew what would be required of her? Papa had never fired the weapon to any of their knowledge. There had to be a reason for that as there'd been other tyrannical rulers before Frederick. What if firing it was the ultimate sacrifice? Hudson felt bile rising in his throat as he looked at sweet Jessie.

He had no idea what the weapon truly was, but they all suspected it had something to do with DNA since Chandler's girl-friend Kylee had risked so much to retrieve hair and follicles from King Frederick. Why hadn't Papa just used the weapon and ended the tyrannical reign of that monster? Hudson had no answer to that, but that was because he didn't know what the weapon did or what its capabilities or limits were.

Aiden was hopeful he could talk their dad and Uncle Joseph into letting his SEAL team and the elite SEAL team of Captain Hendrickson that was now living in the valley and protecting the secret go take Frederick and his top men out on an unsanctioned mission. Hudson didn't know if that plan would happen, but he would love for it all to be behind them. He wanted to focus on loving Kelsey and raising Mo.

What if it was never done? In twenty years, would Mo and his cousins be sitting around this table or still fighting mercenaries who were after the weapon? His gut lurched again. He wanted it done and finished and some peace for their family. He'd train Mo to fight and be tough, but he didn't want his son in a never-ending battle.

"Jessie is the Secret Keeper and none of us can change that fact," his dad reiterated, looking sadly at Colt. "I am standing behind her with my unending support and ultimate confidence, just as I did Papa." He looked around the room.

Before he could even ask who would join him, Esther, Aiden, Thor, Chandler, and their mom shot to their feet.

Hudson proudly stood and joined his immediate family, nodding to Jessie. She was the cousin closest to his age, and he adored her just like everyone else did. As he stood, he felt it surge through him. She was young and her heart was tender, but she was tough and prepared, and Papa would not have given her this ulti-mate responsibility if he hadn't felt she was ordained by heaven above and known she was the right person to fulfill it. Jessie was the Secret Keeper and she would do exactly what needed to be done.

Maddie and Alivia slowly stood, holding hands with tears streaming down their faces. Uncle Joseph stood. Aunt Holly glared up at him, then looked at her youngest child. The sobs racked her body and Hudson found himself filled with as much conflicting emotion as he had been when Papa died. This was horrible and beautiful at the same time. But most of all, it was right. Papa had longed to go to heaven and be with his wife. He'd given everything he had to this family and to protecting this secret. Now it was their time to carry on his legacy, with the youngest, most humble, and angelic among them leading the way. Jessie would be at their head.

Uncle Joseph offered his hand. Aunt Holly took a shuddering breath and then she placed her hand in his. He helped her stand. Aunt Holly's body shook, and even tough Alivia cried harder seeing their mom visibly trembling as she stood in support of her daughter to carry this huge mission forward. A mission that might never end and might require each of them to sacrifice in ways they couldn't imagine.

Everyone looked at Jessie and Colt. Jessie had silent tears running down her face, but she also beamed at their support.

Colt still had his arm around her. He looked around the room, then he looked back at Jessie and he quoted from Matthew, "'So the last shall be the first, and the first be the last. For many be called, but few chosen.'"

Hudson loved that. How appropriate. Their family had been called and chosen to do this. The youngest was rising to take the place they all assumed the oldest should take. Jessie's humility, her deep spirituality, her close relationship with Papa, and her ability to watch and learn from all of them would be only a few of her strengths. The fact that she wasn't the obvious leader would help protect her. And they would all give anything and everything to protect and support her.

Colt stood slowly, looking down at his beloved sister. "I pledge my support and loyalty to Jessica Delta as Secret Keeper."

As one, they all repeated the phrase. "I pledge my support and loyalty to Jessica Delta as Secret Keeper."

Hudson looked around the room. He was proud of his family and felt the rightness of being here. Most of them didn't know why he'd stayed away. He loved his career, but it had all been about Kelsey for him. Now he was here for his family, for the Delta Protection Detail, and most importantly for Kelsey and Mo. He was a father now, and keeping Kelsey and their son and his family safe was his utmost priority.

A tug toward Kelsey came again. He hated to be antsy at this moment, but he needed to make sure she was all right.

Jessie stood. "Thank you," she said in a quiet voice that carried throughout the room. "When Papa told me a few weeks ago that his time was short—"

Some surprised gasps followed that statement. Jessie had known ... that?

She nodded. "He didn't want me to say anything and distract or worry any of you, but he felt it coming. He also explained that he'd known for years that I was the future Secret Keeper, and he'd resisted it. He wanted to protect me, just like all of you do." She gave a sweet smile. "I know I'm the youngest and probably the weakest, but I will use my humility, my faith in God and in Papa, and my love of my family and my country to protect the secret and ..." Terror filled her blue eyes, but it quickly turned to resolve. "... use the weapon when I am inspired to do so."

Hudson was humbled and impressed by Jessie's words. Heaven's inspiration was of the utmost importance, and it was also something that distinguished them from King Frederick and his followers. The Deltas knew their Father above was watching over and would help and inspire them.

"Amen," Esther said softly.

"Amen," they all repeated.

The benediction was pronounced without a formal prayer.

That was all right. They'd have more family prayers and individual prayers. What mattered right now was going forward with faith, upholding Papa's legacy, and protecting America and people throughout the world.

The family started hugging and breaking up into small groups. Hudson hugged and waited impatiently for his turn to hold Jessie. He needed to be with Kelsey. It was of utmost importance that he find Kelsey and hold her tight, tell Mo and the family he was Mo's father, and if she agreed, plan a wedding.

Everything else would have to work itself out. The Deltas were okay. Why was he so uneasy? Was another attack coming, or was it just that he was a father now and needed to be with and protect Kelsey and Mo?

Chapter Twenty-One

Kelsey didn't know how long she laid on the bed, feeling out of sorts and sorry for herself, which she hated and had done too often in her longings for Hudson.

She forced herself to get up and take a quick shower but didn't wash her hair. She put on minimal makeup and scented lotion, looking at her bloodshot eyes in the mirror. Anybody who didn't know her would think she was hung over. Dressing in a long-sleeved shirt and jeans, she texted her mom to make sure Mo was okay and told her she'd be back soon. Her mom said to take her time; Mo was being spoiled and loved. Kelsey was sure he was.

She forced herself to leave the room and walk downstairs, then outside. It was chilly, but the cool air on her face helped wake her up. If only it could help her think clearly.

A tough-looking man with a clean-shaven head waited next to the porch, a large gun in one hand and a smile on his face. It was one of those smart-alecky smiles, like something Hudson would give. She missed Hudson. Ached for him. Could he truly be *gone* gone, or had she misunderstood what Esther was trying to say? She hated herself for doubting him. She didn't doubt he still loved her and Mo, but she had no idea how he could leave for ... whatever he had to leave for, without saying goodbye or making plans.

"Hi," she managed, feeling a little uneasy with a stranger in light of what had happened the past two days.

"Ma'am," he said, nodding to her. "I'm Lieutenant Van Udy. I was assigned to watch over you and escort you back to Admiral Delta's house when you're ready."

She breathed a little easier. She'd seen him with the other SEALs and heard a little about the elite team sent to get the secret weapon from the Deltas but instead turning their allegiance to Papa and protecting the weapon.

"Thank you," she said. Was she ready to go back? Not really. Not without Hudson there. Being around all his family would hurt. "Do you mind if I just walk down to the lake for a bit?"

"Not at all. I'd love a walk to the lake." He grinned at her and gestured for her to walk in front of him.

Kelsey would rather have privacy, but she knew it was important to stay safe and protected. She shuddered at the thought of ever being captured by someone like Stefan again. Who would come after the Delta family and their weapon next? Terrifying.

She walked down the grassy slope and along the lake's edge until she came to the dock. She walked out on the long dock and stared at the water and the green, lush mountains surrounding the lake. Hugging herself, she prayed for strength, especially if Hudson was really gone.

Tears stung at her eyes at the thought. She'd put all her trust and faith in him again. Could he really have left her, Mo, and his family when they all needed him so much? She wanted to vehemently deny it, but the Hudson of the past four years definitely would've disappeared as quick as he could.

But that Hudson had been hurting and heartbroken just like she had, and he hadn't known he was a father or how much his family needed him. Her Hudson, her Brave, wouldn't leave. Right?

Then where was he? On a mission Papa Delta had given him as he died? That would explain the secrecy and Esther cautiously asking because she didn't know what Kelsey knew. An assignment for Papa would explain why he'd had to go without saying goodbye or making future plans.

The dock creaked and she spun, praying for Hudson. It was the Lieutenant. Vance? No Van. Interesting name. He seemed like a nice guy and he was obviously handsome and tough and impressive, but he wasn't her nice, handsome, tough, and impressive guy.

Tears ran even more freely. Where was Hudson? *Please*, she begged heaven above. *Please say he just went on a mission for Papa Delta and he'll be back soon. I love and respect his career and dreams, but we all need him here.*

"Are you all right?" the Lieutenant asked, a lot more softly than she could've imagined he would talk.

"Not really," she admitted.

"It's a huge loss for your family and our nation," he said, obviously referring to Papa Delta.

"It is." She tried to stop being so selfish and scrubbed at her damp face. Of course he would think she was crying about Papa.

He came ever closer, and she focused on his unique hazelgreen eyes. He was hurting too. Deep pain. She got the impression he didn't reveal his pain often, but he was commiserating with her so it had released.

"Are *you* all right?" she asked.

His eyebrows shot up and he looked away. "I ... of course. I'm on a mission and we shelve any personal stuff on missions." He met her gaze and gave her an obviously practiced smile.

She studied him and found herself touching his arm to reassure him. "Maybe in the military you do, but you're with the Deltas now." She wanted to claim she was a Delta, but she didn't know when that was going to happen. Not until her wayward love came back to her. "The Deltas are tough, loyal, and focused, but they're also there for their own. It's okay to let down your guard, express emotion, and have feelings."

He just stared at her. Then he ran a hand over his bald head and muttered, "I'm not sure how to do that. I can't let down my guard." He searched around the quiet grassy slope and the houses above them as if they would be attacked any moment.

"I appreciate your diligence in protecting me, but I think we're safe." She looked him over and was grateful to focus outside of herself and her own pain and worries. One of the many reasons she loved being a nurse was nurturing and helping others. "I think a hug would help both of us right now," she offered. She missed Hudson fiercely and knew some human contact would help her, but she thought it would help this tough, untouchable lieutenant even more.

He blinked at her and murmured, "A hug?"

Kelsey smiled. "Have you ever had one?"

He finally gave her that smart-alecky smile from before, but it was a little shaky. "Once or twice."

"Oh, good. I don't have to teach you how then." She liked teasing with him, like one of Hudson's brothers. She wished it was Hudson she was planning to hug. Soon. She hoped.

She stepped close, feeling like this man needed an emotional connection a million more times than she did. She slid her arms around his back and he startled, his muscles tense and his gaze wary.

"It's okay," she said. "I won't hurt you."

He let out a sound that was maybe a chuckle, but sounded like it was too full of pain to be considered laughter. "That's a matter of opinion, ma'am."

She laughed, but it cut off as he abruptly wrapped his arms around her back and squeezed her tightly against him.

He was broad and tough, and his pain actually seeped into her as he clung to her. What had this man been through? She could only imagine what an elite Navy SEAL would have to see or do. Was it all related to his assignments and missions or was it deeply personal as well? Pain felt from childhood on up? Had he lost someone very important to him? Someone who loved him had broken him? She wasn't sure, but she knew his pain was raw and it was deep.

He shuddered and buried his face in her hair. Kelsey didn't have a brother, but she imagined this was how it would feel to hug one. It felt nothing like being close to Hudson, more like holding Mo. She could sense how deeply this man had needed this. Maybe through her pain and questions of the last couple of hours, at least some good could come.

If only Hudson would appear as well.

Chapter Twenty-Two

Hudson pounded upstairs first from the family meeting. In-laws and future in-laws and Lori were all watching him, waiting for answers. Some of the adults were in odd positions, bent over and semi-hiding behind furniture, clinging to the back of the pantry door, and Klein's large frame was cramped under the kitchen table.

Mo was behind Papa's leather recliner, which Granny Klein was currently relaxing in. Hudson could hear his son counting loudly, "Seventeen ... thirty-two ... fourteen ..."

He couldn't help but smile at his cute little boy and be grateful for all these people that cared for his son and were playing hide and seek with him. Hudson had promised Mo they'd play back in that hotel room. He would ... soon.

"Kelsey?" he asked urgently.

"At your mom and dad's," her mom said.

"Okay." He needed to go to her. Now. He looked at all the

expectant faces. He usually loved talking with a crowd, but he kind of assumed his dad, mom, aunt, or uncle would be the one to explain. It was urgent he get to Kelsey. She was safe, but he needed her.

"Hey," he said. "Um ... I think my dad or mom..."

His mom came up behind him and wrapped her arm around his waist, leaning into him. "I'm so glad you're home," she said.

He kissed her forehead. "Me too, beautiful Mama." He leaned down closer and whispered, "I need to find Kelsey."

"Go." She shoved him away from her and then clapped her hands. "I know you all have a lot of questions and we will answer them. Keith and the rest are coming up now." She shooed Hudson with her hand as she walked farther into the room.

Lori caught Hudson's eye. "Mo?" he mouthed to her. He'd never been responsible for anyone but himself, but he wanted to make sure Mo was watched over.

She nodded and shooed him with her hand as well. Hudson eased back toward the door, running into his Aunt Holly.

He turned and pulled her into a hug. She was still crying. He didn't ask if she was okay. She wasn't. It was a lot to ask of any mother to put their child in extreme danger. Jessie nor Holly had signed up for this, but it had been thrust on them and he knew these incredible women would rise to the occasion.

"Love you, sweet boy," Holly said into his neck.

"I love you too."

She looked up at him and took a deep breath as if steadying herself. "Where's your girl?"

"I don't know. Esther said she's at my mom and dad's house."

"Well, go find her. I'm sure you have a lot of ... talking to do."
She winked and let him go.

Hudson grinned and hurried past her and through the foyer
before anybody else intercepted him. Talking? Sure. Kissing?
Definitely.

Things were still unstable for all the Deltas, but they were at
least safe for the moment. He could focus completely on Kelsey
and Mo.

He pushed out the front door, jogged off the porch and
angled toward his parent's house. Running into the house, he
called for Kelsey. He searched each room, but there was no movement in the house at all. Had he missed her? Was she really okay?

He ran back to the main room, his heart thudding too fast in
his chest, and looked out the huge picture windows. Down by the
lake there was a couple embracing on the dock. But all the couples
were at Papa's house ...

He squinted and his gut turned over. Kelsey? Hugging the
bald SEAL? What?

Was this Jason all over again?

His gut told him he should calm down before he confronted
them. No way! He was fighting for her. He wasn't walking away
ever again. He would fight if an army stood between them.

Slamming through the laundry room and out the back entry,
he sprinted across the grass and down to the dock. Heat and anger
filled him as he ran. How could she be hugging some other dude
when all he wanted was to be with her and hold her? He couldn't
believe it.

But unlike that awful night four years ago when he'd seen her
hugging Jason, he would not talk himself into being unselfish and

the bigger man. He was going to hit the guy she was hugging—no, he was going to pummel him, and then he was going to get answers.

They must've heard him coming, because they released each other and both spun to face him. Kelsey's face lit up with delight. "Hudson! You're here!"

Hudson wasn't sure what that meant. She didn't know he was here? Where did she think he'd gone? She was hugging some other guy because she thought Hudson had left?

He'd get those answers soon. But first...

The bald guy's face went from contentment at hugging Hudson's girl to wary. Quick. Hudson knew this guy was an elite warrior and had training and experiences that even the Deltas would be hard-pressed to compete with, but Hudson was an unparalleled athlete in his own right. He was sprinting so fast the momentum would be to his benefit. He leaped into the air with his fist cocked, ready for a fight-ending punch worthy of any action movie.

The guy deflected the punch and turned to take the impact. Hudson's speed was an asset, and he used all his skills to change the trajectory of his momentum. He brought his knees into the guy's chest, shoved off the guy, and flipped up and backward. He landed easily on the dock with both feet as the SEAL wind-milled his arms for balance. His efforts were in vain, and he slapped against the water in an inglorious back flop.

"What are you doing?" Kelsey cried out, her hand over her mouth.

"What am I doing? What are *you* doing?" Hudson demanded.

The SEAL grabbed the dock, sprang out of the cold water,

and tackled Hudson to the wooden dock. Hudson landed a few kidney shots, then did a reversal and flipped him over, driving the man into the dock, dampening his own clothes and just getting started with this epic fight. It was the perfect release for all the anguish and stress of last night and today.

"Stop!" Kelsey begged, grabbing Hudson's shoulders and trying to haul him back.

"Kelsey." Hudson held her away from him. "You'll get hurt."

The SEAL bucked Hudson off of him and Hudson barely avoided taking Kelsey down. Hudson sprang in front of her and put his hands up. "Wait until she's out of the way."

The guy popped to his feet and nodded. At least he was honorable and wanted Kelsey safe. Hudson's gut churned. This guy wanted Kelsey. Fire surged through him.

Kelsey darted in front of Hudson. He lifted her off her feet and swung her behind him. He heard shouts and footsteps pounding toward them. Somebody in the house must've noticed them fighting. Or one of the SEALs stationed outside.

Grabbing his shoulders, Kelsey stared at him with those gorgeous dark eyes of hers. "Hudson ... stop! Please. I offered to hug him because he's in pain and I was crying for you and needed a hug as well."

"What?" he demanded. Why would she be crying for him?

"I'm fine," the guy grunted from behind them.

"You are not fine," Kelsey shot at the guy. "Van, you need some love and attention big time, and you really need to realize that human emotion is normal and it's healthy to release and share it."

Van needed love and attention? Not from Hudson's Sunshine he didn't. Hudson's fists clenched again.

Aiden, Thor, Greer, and a couple of the SEALs pounded up to the dock.

"What's going on?" Aiden demanded.

Hudson gestured back at Van. "This guy was hugging my girl. So I sent him into the lake to cool him off."

Van chuckled and wiped the water off his bald head. He extended his hand to Hudson. "Sorry. I wasn't trying to make a move on anyone. Kelsey was ... helping me deal with some junk. Lieutenant Van Udy."

Kelsey gave Van and then Hudson an impertinent glare.

Hudson looked at her and at his brothers and then forced himself to shake the guy's hand. "Sorry. I get riled a little too easily sometimes." His self-control training hadn't helped him a few moments ago, but Kelsey was everything to him and he still felt his overreaction was justified.

"A little?" Kelsey asked.

"Hudson Delta," Hudson finished the introduction and released the SEAL's hand.

"I know who you are, Death Wish," Lieutenant Udy said. "That flip off of tackling me and not going into the water with me was impressive. Can you teach me that?"

Hudson actually smiled at the guy. "Sure, but that nickname is in the past. I have everything to live for now."

He looked down at Kelsey, but she didn't look ready to melt into his arms.

Aiden slapped Hudson on the shoulder. "You'll have to forgive my brother. He's recently reconnected with the love of his life and he's a bit over the top and dramatic on normal days of the week."

Hudson elbowed Aiden in the gut. Aiden flinched, but barely.

"Enough of the fighting," Thor said. "I can't believe I just said that," he muttered. He gestured with his head to Kelsey. "Time to be a lover, not a fighter, bro."

"He wishes," Kelsey snapped, her arms folded over her chest and her dark eyes filled with frustration.

"I do wish," Hudson admitted.

The other men smiled knowingly and walked off.

"Thanks, Kelsey," Lieutenant Udy said as he walked past, dripping wet.

"You need a lot more help than that one hug," Kelsey told him.

His smile was sarcastic. "We'll see."

He stalked off.

Kelsey harrumphed at his back, then turned to face Hudson. She arched her eyebrows. "What was that nonsense?"

"Why were you hugging him?" Hudson had to know.

"Because he was hurting and needed a hug. It was like hugging a brother, if I had a brother."

Hudson wasn't sure what to believe. That hug had looked pretty ... tight. A hug like that at the wrong time four years ago had cost them four years of being together. At least they were talking. He'd determined before he'd gone after the lieutenant hugging her, and he felt it more strongly now. He wasn't walking away from her. Unless she pushed him into the icy lake. Nope. Not even then. He'd launch back out and beg her to love him.

"I've been a mess the past couple hours," she said. "Esther told me you 'had to go' and acted like it was some secret I would understand. I thought you'd ... left. Again."

Hudson could only stare at her. No wonder he'd felt so unsettled and stressed about her. "I went to take the weapon back with Jessie, Aiden, my dad, and Uncle Joseph. Then we had a family meeting. Esther said you were lying down at my parent's house resting and Aiden forced me to go to the meeting when I wanted to come for you first. I would've fought Aiden and come to you but ... my dad really needed me there and everyone kept saying you were resting and fifteen minutes wouldn't matter. I should've listened to my gut and run for you."

"Oh, Hudson." Her breath rushed out, and she stepped up close and put her hand on his arm. "Us and our stupid misunderstandings. I was afraid and exhausted and unreasonable. I thought you'd gone on some special mission for Papa or maybe you had a really important stunt scheduled you couldn't get out of. I was devastated because you hadn't come to tell me, kiss me goodbye, and make future plans."

His jaw dropped. "You thought I would leave you, Mo, my family?" He gestured back toward the houses up the grassy slope. "After finding out I'm Mo's dad, that you still love me, and after Papa died? What kind of an inconsiderate jerk do you think I am?" He had a history of running away, so he guessed he could see why her insecurities would flair. He wasn't running now. Never again.

Kelsey wrapped her arms around him and there was no world where Hudson could resist her. He gathered her close and relished that she was in his arms, though he was reeling. She still didn't trust him not to disappear. He'd have to fight harder to earn her trust. He could do that. He could, and he would, fight for her.

"I'm sorry. I was doubting my doubts, but they were still there. I didn't know where you were, and I needed you so badly. I realize the Delta weapon is more important than my silly insecurities. And losing Papa. I'm sorry. I know now it's not your fault, but I've spent the past four years convincing myself the Hudson I loved was gone and the new Hudson would always selfishly disappear when I needed him most. It's hard to forget that pain, and I reverted to it. Of course I know you wouldn't leave me, Mo, or your family, but I was scared and I let myself doubt."

Hudson tilted her chin up. "I'm the one who's sorry. Sorry I abandoned you when I should've run to you and fought for you. Sorry I've let these years go by with you alone and in pain. Sorry you ever hurt. Sorry that I didn't prove earlier that you could trust me. I shouldn't have doubted you and freaked out about the hug, but it was like Jason all over again. I'm not sorry that I tackled Lieutenant Udy, though. That was fun."

"Boys." She shook her head. "Are you telling me that Mo is going to be a brawler like his daddy?"

Hope surged inside him, light and happy, especially compared to all the pain and worry of what they'd been through. "Him and his ten brothers. They'll be making holes in your walls, breaking your furniture, sending each other to Uncle Colt for stitches."

"Oh, wow. What a brilliant future we have in store for us." She blinked up at him, so beautiful, so perfect. "Thank you for coming for me, for fighting for me even if you didn't need to."

"Oh, I'll always need to fight for you, Sunshine."

She smiled, but it slid away. "Do you think we can get past all the pain and misunderstandings and trust each other completely?"

Hudson studied her, hoping she could trust him. He'd spend

whatever time and energy she needed proving he would never leave her or Mo again.

"I am swearing to you right now, Sunshine. I will never leave you or Mo or our ten boys." She smiled at that, but her eyes were bright. "I am swearing to you that I will trust you and I will do anything and everything I can to earn your trust and be the man you can love, respect, and turn to while I love, honor, and protect you and our family."

He bent and kissed her softly to seal his words.

"I swear to you, Brave," she said, her words brushing across his lips, "that I will trust you to be there for us as I will be there for you. You are the man I love and respect and I can't wait to turn to you, be there for you, support you, and love you through good times and bad. With Mo and our four little girls." She winked, then arched up and kissed him. She kissed him passionately and about knocked him back off the dock.

Hudson happily returned her kiss, and he could only imagine how beautiful their little girls would be. They finally pulled back for oxygen and grinned at each other. The pain was in the past. Hudson felt like he was going to burst with joy. This was happening. Him and Kelsey and Mo.

He released her, dropped to one knee, and clasped both of her hands in his. Kelsey's eyes widened as she looked down at him. "Brave?"

"Sunshine, marry me. As soon as we possibly can, marry me. I don't have a ring yet, but I adore you and can't stand to be without you for one more second."

Tears crested her lashes and rolled down her cheeks. "Yes," she cried out. "Of course, yes!"

She tugged him up, and they kissed to seal the deal. She smiled sweetly at him. "After Papa's service and all the craziness with the weapon dies down, we'll plan a wedding and you can get me that ring."

"Why not tomorrow?"

"Tomorrow on the ring?" Her brow squiggled.

"Tomorrow on all of it."

"You're crazy."

"You already knew that." He winked and felt the rightness of it wash over him. "Let's get married here, on this dock, or on the grass, or wherever you want, tomorrow. Just our families. Papa would love that, and all the family could use the happiness of a wedding." He pulled her closer. "Then I don't have to wait to start working on all those baby boys."

"Hudson Delta." She slapped at his chest and looked properly shocked about his last comment. He hoped she wasn't shocked by the rest of it.

"Unless you want to plan a big, fancy wedding. I'm fine with that too. Or a wedding on a beach somewhere after Frederick is defeated. Honestly, whatever you want."

"What do you want?" she asked him.

"Only you." More tears made their way out of her eyes. "And Mo and those ten boys. They're gonna be so cute."

She laughed at that, wiped her eyes, and said, "Let's do it. If your family is okay with it in light of Papa's death and keeping the weapon safe."

He sobered at that. "Okay. We'll do what is best for the family and make it all work. All that matters is that we're married. As soon as possible."

"I can agree with that."

He lifted her off her feet and swung her around, lowering her to kiss her.

He heard footsteps and released her, spinning in front of her to protect her. It was most likely his family, but if anyone was coming to hurt her, or Lieutenant Udy was coming for more hugs ... he was more than happy to fight anyone.

Lori carried Mo down the grass.

"Hey!" Mo called to them. He struggled from his grandma's arms and ran to them. Hudson scooped him up and hugged them both close.

"Sorry to interrupt." Lori's dark eyes sparkled. "He saw you down here and wouldn't stop asking for you."

"It's great timing," Hudson reassured her.

She turned to go.

"Wait." He looked down at Kelsey and she nodded.

Lori turned back.

"Can I ask your permission to marry your daughter?" Was that right? He'd never done this before.

Lori put a hand to her mouth and nodded, her dark eyes looking as bright as her daughter's. "Yes," she said, pulling her hand back and rushing to them. They all hugged in a circle.

"What's up?" Mo asked.

"Your mama and daddy are going to get married," his grandma told him.

"Grams, I ain't got no daddy," Mo said.

Hudson looked to Kelsey. He never wanted Mo to say that line again. Kelsey nodded her permission.

Lori and Kelsey both stepped slightly back. Hudson held his

son and looked into his blue eyes. He was adorable; he was perfect; he was his.

"Mo. I'm your daddy." Hudson had no clue if that was right either, but he heard no objections from the women.

"You wants to be my daddy, or you are my daddy?" Mo looked confused.

"Both, buddy." Hudson tried to think how to explain to the little guy. "I want to be your daddy more than anything, and I *am* your daddy and I am going to marry your mama."

"So we'll do lots of fun stuff and you'll make me brush my teeth and say prayers and stuff like that?"

All the adults laughed.

"Yes," Hudson said. "All of that and a whole lot more."

"Hide and seek?" Mo asked.

Hudson nodded.

"Can you throw me higher than Thor?"

"Oh, yeah." He tossed him into the air and caught him.

Mo laughed and laughed.

"That was a little too high," Lori reprimanded.

"Sorry." Hudson and Mo exchanged a look, and he knew his boy thought it was just about perfect.

"Are you going to kiss Mama a lot?"

"A whole lot, but I'll try to not do it in front of you too much." He smiled at Kelsey and his body seemed to catch fire from the warm look she gave him in return.

"I guess that's okay," Mo said.

"You guess?" Hudson flipped him upside down and hung him over the edge of the dock.

Mo squealed and laughed. Kelsey smiled, but Lori didn't seem quite as thrilled.

"Are you going to roughhouse my grandson nonstop?"

"Yes, Mama James. It's a boy thing," Hudson tried to explain.

She threw her hands in the air, but there was a softness in her eyes that said she wouldn't get too upset with him.

Hudson looked down at his son. "Okay on the kissing?"

"No!" Mo yelled.

He lowered him and dipped his hair in the cold water.

"Okay, okay," Mo screamed. "You can kiss my mama."

Hudson easily flipped him upright and into his arms. "Good answer, son." Man, he loved calling his boy son. "Now the important question. Do you want ten brothers or four sisters?"

"Ten?" Lori asked as Kelsey moaned.

"Brothers!" Mo cheered.

Hudson turned to Kelsey. "He's on my side."

"I'm in trouble," she said.

"Yes, you are," her mom agreed.

They all laughed.

"How soon are we putting together this wedding?" Lori asked.

"Tomorrow," Hudson informed her.

"Tomorrow?" Her eyes went wide.

"Tomorrow," Kelsey agreed.

"Tomorrow!" Mo echoed happily.

"I need to go talk to your mom," Lori said, rushing away from them and back toward the house.

Hudson smiled, turned his fiancée toward him, and kissed her soft and slow.

Mo pushed between them. "No more kissing."

"In the water he goes," Hudson said.

Kelsey laughed and Mo squealed as Hudson dipped his hair again. He couldn't stop smiling. There was still the pain of Papa's death and the worries of protecting the Delta weapon and how sweet Jessie would fulfill all that she needed to do.

But right now, Hudson was so happy that no worry in the world could touch him. Kelsey and Mo were finally in the right spot. In his arms.

"Hudson Delta!" His mom's voice was piercing.

"Oops." Hudson grinned at Kelsey.

There were also a few details he needed to share with his mom.

Chapter Twenty-Three

Kelsey nervously smoothed the white dress. Her mom, Hudson's mom, Mo, her, and Hudson had made a quick trip to Denver this morning while everyone else either protected the weapon, prepared for their impromptu wedding, or dealt with details for Papa's graveside service and all the phone calls of condolences. Admirals Gusbane and Seamons had both called and spoken with Uncle Joseph at length.

The entire family was stressed as they analyzed where the next attack would come from. They admirals had both intoned the attacks would increase from their own military or government without Papa's influence to protect them, let alone whatever Frederick was sending their way. It was unnerving.

Kelsey focused on her wedding. The rest would have to wait. She and the women had found this beautiful fitted white lace dress at a boutique while Mo and Hudson watched Hudson's stunts on his phone, Mo screaming his approval. She, Mo, and Hudson had found the ring of her dreams at a jeweler while their moms picked up the cake and a bunch of food for the lunch after the wedding.

Hudson had the ring right now as the ceremony was about to begin, but she could picture the wide white-gold band and the sparkling two-karat princess-cut diamond.

"You ready, love?" her mom asked, looking into the mirror over her shoulder.

Kelsey smiled at her, then looked at herself in the mirror. She looked pretty. Hudson would say she was more than pretty. She was so in love and could hardly wait to marry him.

Hudson's mom had cussed him out for a few minutes yesterday evening before bursting into tears and hugging them both fiercely in turn. Then she picked up Mo and cried and hugged him for a very long time.

Surprisingly Mo let her and adorably he tried to comfort her, patting her back and saying, "It's okay, Myrna. It's okay."

When Myrna asked if she could be his granny, he lit up. "Granny Myrna?" he'd asked. "Sure!"

Myrna had burst into tears again.

The rest of the Delta family had taken the news of their fast-approaching wedding and Hudson being Mo's father with lots of cheering, laughter, questions, and hugs.

She was afraid they would think she and Hudson didn't care about Papa, having their wedding the day after his death, but everybody reassured her it was perfect, exactly what they all needed, and exactly what Papa would want.

The sheriff's men were all up at the cave, monitoring the

secret, and the SEALs were all here protecting the valley and the family. The family was off duty for the moment. By tomorrow, Hudson would be back in the rotation and working long hours to help his family. Kelsey would do what she could monitoring video surveillance, taking care of Mo and Granny Vance, cooking for a literal army, and hopefully not having to help Colt and the SEAL medic treat any injuries.

She and Hudson had both agreed to wait until after the Delta secret was safe before they plotted revenge on Jason Spackman. They wouldn't hurt him, but he needed to see them together and feel lots and lots of guilt for his lies.

"I'm ready," she told her mom. She was more than ready. For four years, she'd been ready for this day.

Her mom took her arm, and they walked through the quiet house and out the back door. The family was all waiting on chairs facing the dock. Hudson stood on the dock in the gray suit he'd worn at Thor's wedding. The slight breeze ruffled his hair and mussed it like she liked, and he had a huge, mischievous grin on his handsome face. Mo and the preacher, Pastor Sam, stood on each side of him. The wedding would be simple. She was so happy.

"Mama!" Mo called to her, jumping up and down.

The wedding party stood almost in unison and turned. They all beamed at her. She returned the smiles, but she couldn't keep her eyes off of Hudson. His grin and bright blue eyes beckoned her to him like a tractor beam.

"Slow down, love," her mom whispered. "He's not going anywhere."

She laughed. "I know. Believe me, I know."

Hudson wasn't going anywhere. At least not without her. They'd talked a little about her and Mo traveling with him and watching him film stunts around the world after the Delta weapon was safe again. Kelsey would love the adventure and planned to start online nursing school as soon as possible. Hudson had been quick to reassure her he had buried Death Wish Delta and he would focus on the safest stunts possible. He also promised they would come back to Summit Valley whenever she wanted and build a house by her mom, or up here in the Delta valley.

All that mattered to her was that she was with Hudson and Mo.

They finally, finally reached him.

"Pretty Mama," Mo blurted out.

"Thank you, love."

Her mom handed her off to Hudson. He pulled her close, softly kissed her, and whispered, "Gorgeous Sunshine."

"I love you, Brave." She looked up into his blue gaze.

"I love you, Sunshine."

They were lost in each other until Pastor Sam said, "Is it all right if I start the ceremony now or do you two need a moment?"

Everybody laughed.

"We need a lot more than a moment," Hudson told him with a confident wink directed at her. "But you'd better make it official first."

"Oh, my," Hudson's mom burst out. "Hudson ..."

"Sorry, Mama." Hudson hugged Kelsey tight, making her veil go off-kilter and her stomach fill with warmth. "But I've been waiting a long time to make this beautiful woman mine."

He kissed her again, and her lips sang happily from the sweet and fulfilling pressure. They both ignored the laughs from the family, a lot of teasing cracks from Thor and Aiden, and Mo groaning about "more kissing."

Hudson finally pulled back from the kiss, but kept her close. Ever since Hudson had proposed yesterday, it felt like she had stepped out of an alternate universe and back onto the true path of her life. The detour had been hard on her, Mo, and Hudson, but the future was as bright as it had ever been, not just for her but for her little family. The hard times apart had made them stronger and the separation and heartache would make them appreciate being together even more.

Still holding her gaze, Hudson said, "All right, Pastor Sam, do your thing. Husband and wife sounds pretty perfect about now."

"Give me a minute to get to that part," Pastor Sam said. "I've got to instruct you how to love, honor, and cherish this sweet angel."

"I'm all over that," Hudson told him. "But oh, can you do me a favor? Can you commit her to ten more boys during the ceremony?"

The family gave laughs and jeers at that.

Mo put out his fist to his daddy. "Brothers," he called out.

Kelsey shook her head.

Pastor Sam winked. "I'll add it to the vows," he said.

"Oh, boy," Kelsey groaned, but she couldn't help but laugh. Life with Hudson would never be boring, and she knew through whatever came their way, Hudson would do everything possible to love, honor, and cherish her and she'd trust, love, and support him.

Her Brave winked at her, squeezed her around the waist, and gestured for the ceremony to begin. "Make it a good one, Pastor Sam. Then we'll start working on Mo's little brothers."

His mom and hers both groaned, but everybody else laughed. Kelsey was more than willing to create beautiful babies with this incredible man. But she'd trust in heaven above that eleven boys weren't in her future. Right now, she was ecstatically happy with one adorable boy and his irresistible father.

Thank you for reading the Delta family stories! I love each of them and can hardly stand to say goodbye. I think you're going to love the epic finale, Jessie Delta and Zander Povey's story. Jessie is such an angel and Zander is exactly the kind of tough, teasing, and tempting hero she needs by her side.

Read on for the first three chapters.

Hugs and thanks,

Cami

Delta Family Romances

Deceived

Abandoned

Committed

Betrayed

Devoted

Compromised

Endangered

RETURNED

Accepted
Returned
Devastated

Devastated - First Three Chapters

Chapter One

Jessica Delta had to escape. She had no idea how she would accomplish such a feat but she wanted to run out of the back door of her beloved grandfather's house and keep running until she somehow outran the pain, the emptiness, the responsibility, and most of all her acute awareness that she could never complete her assignment and was in fact doomed to fail.

It was ... maybe Thursday evening. The entire family, minus the newlyweds Hudson and Kelsey who were taking a couple of days to themselves, and Greer, Alivia, Klein, and Colt who were on duty monitoring the cave, and Emery and Bailey who were on duty watching the cameras and sensors downstairs, were gathered in Papa's spacious living room. Everyone was talking, teasing, and eating leftovers from the wedding earlier today.

She'd lost track of time and days since Papa had been shot and killed and her life had upended. Yesterday morning. It shouldn't be hard to keep track of one day, but it felt like a heart-wrenching lifetime of pain had been driven through her head and her heart between then and now.

"You okay?" her next oldest sister Maddie sat next to her on the couch and nudged her with her shoulder.

"Not really." Jessie shrugged and forced a smile again. "But what do you do? Keep putting one foot in front of the other just like Papa taught us."

Papa taught us. She touched the pendant hidden under her shirt.

Tears stung her eyes. She missed Papa, his insights, his spirituality, his toughness, his teasing, his smile. If she was honest with herself, she was ticked at him for leaving her. Which was selfish and immature, but there you were. Jessie wanted to prove to everybody, especially a particular elite Navy SEAL demolitions expert who had joined them last week, that she wasn't selfish or immature. Maybe she was, and she was in no way someone Senior Petty Officer Zander Povey would be interested in. And good heavens why was she caring about that when the world was falling down around her and she was expected to save it.

"You've got this, beautiful sis." Maddie put her arm around her and hugged her. "Papa made you the keeper because of how incredible you are." Jessie didn't know if it was simply Maddie being insightful or if her worries were showing on her face. "And you've got all of us backing you up." She gestured around the room.

Looking around at her accomplished family members Jessie realized many of them were sneaking glances at her, even as they conversed with each other. Shelly sitting on Thor's lap. Aiden and Melene snuggled close. Her parents, aunt and uncle, Kelsey's mom Lori, and Granny Vance teasing with the little Mo as they played chutes and ladders at the table. Chandler, Kylee, Esther, and Reed cleaning up the kitchen.

Any one of her incredible siblings or cousins should've been made the keeper and final line of defense for the weapon before her. Aiden was a Navy SEAL for crying out loud. Esther was a lawyer for the Air Force and excelled at everything she did. Greer could wrestle a mountain lion with his bare hands. Her big brother Colton was as serious and impressive as any man she knew. Maddie was like Black Widow and protected children and families throughout the world taking out human traffickers and drug lords.

Why on earth was she the "chosen one" as hilarious Thor had teased her about to make her smile when she was stressed? She appreciated Thor and his humor but she didn't want to be chosen. She wanted to be the happy peacemaker and keep everybody smiling and do her part to guard the secret. She sure as heck didn't want to be the one to fire that weapon when the time came. She had trouble killing spiders or snakes. She second-guessed if all of God's creatures shouldn't be allowed to live, even if they were creepy.

"I'm going to go outside and get some fresh air," she whispered to Maddie.

"I'll come with you," Maddie said, standing, grabbing her hands, and tugging her to her feet.

"Sorry, sis, I just ... want to be alone. Can you cover for me?"

Maddie nodded and whispered, "Make sure one of the SEALs

is watching you."

An elite SEAL team had invaded their valley a couple weeks ago in a Blackhawk helicopter. They'd been assigned to retrieve the Delta weapon and take it to Area 51. They'd brought Maddie's Braden with them and Braden had begged their EOD, his friend Zander Povey, to trust him that Admiral Davidson Delta and his family were the only people who could protect the weapon and use it unselfishly.

The SEALs had disobeyed orders and joined the Deltas. It was a huge blessing to them, but Jessie couldn't help but wonder if the SEALs were questioning their decision now that Papa was gone and Jessie was the appointed leader. No. She wasn't the leader. Her dad and uncle had seamlessly taken over that role and Papa's many other responsibilities together. She was certain they'd been trained just as she had. They'd included her in decisions, correspondence, and information just like Papa used to. Of course keeping her name out of the conversations with anyone but family. As the keeper and executor of the weapon she had to know and be part of everything. No matter if she'd rather go work with adorable children learning how to form their r's and s's with their tongue's movement and placement in their mouth.

The SEALs had been patrolling the Delta's valley during and since the wedding. Reed, Esther's fiancé, was the Sheriff and his men had also been invaluable and trustworthy. They'd guarded outside the cave and the mountains during the wedding, but were now home with their families or getting some much needed rest and downtime. The Sheriff's department also had to keep patrolling Summit Valley so the deputies and Reed were working overtime. Great guys. Men they all knew and trusted who had their backs and could keep a secret, even from their wives or friends.

Jessie nodded to Maddie that she would make sure one of the SEALs was close by but she knew they'd follow her as soon as she exited the house. They all seemed extra diligent around her and she felt like Chief Petty Officer Zander Povey was always watching her. Zander was the epitome of tall, dark, and handsome with a quick smile that made his entire cheeks crinkle in the most appealing way. His dark eyes seemed to glint with humor. Jessie had fantasized about getting to know him since the first moment she'd laid eyes on him. He'd climbed out of the Blackhawk helicopter holding an A.R. like he was born to be a military hero. She'd been holding aloft an 84-pound .50 caliber machine gun, pointing it right at him as he'd seemed the natural leader to her.

He'd been focused on Papa as her grandfather strode confidently to the five men, the four-man SEAL team and Povey as their EOD expert, brought along to blow the cave door and to make executive decisions. On that crisp, terrifying morning, afraid she'd have to gun down American heroes to save her Papa and protect the secret, Zander Povey's dark gaze had zeroed in on her. It had been brief, but she'd seen appreciation and longing brighten his deep-brown eyes before he'd focused back on Papa.

She shook her head. She was going nuts. Officer Povey, as she needed to think of him, appreciated and respected her family but lately she worried that he'd eyed her with concern not interest. She could glance around this room again and see the same concern in her family members eyes as well. They didn't think she was capable of being the Secret Keeper. *Well, join the club*, she thought snidely.

"I have a question," Maddie called loudly to the group, walking away from Jessie and toward Thor and Shelly all snuggled in a chair not big enough for Jessie.

Jessie edged toward the laundry room, her shoes and jacket, and hopefully a quiet exit.

"Is Thor or Aiden the biggest simp?" Maddie demanded to know.

Jessie actually smiled as Thor roared his protest. Her male cousins liked to call any man a "simp" who tried too hard to capture a woman's attention. Thor and Aiden were both tough and awesome but they'd do anything for Shelly and Melene. Jessie thought it was cute to see all the strong and impressive men in her family so gone over their loves. Her sisters and Esther's men were the same—so tough but "simps" for the women they loved.

Aiden called out. "He might be the biggest simp, but it's because he's so ugly. Give the guy a break, he had to pull out all the stops to get Shelly with a face like that."

Jessie made it to the laundry room as the room exploded with laughter, and Shelly and Thor's rebuttals floated behind her. She slipped on her shoes and grabbed her jacket. She quietly opened the door and rushed through the dark garage. She dodged dark shadows in the garage that she knew by heart—Papa's truck, Razor, dirt bike, and Harley.

Her foot caught on something and she sprawled forward, but caught herself before hitting the concrete. She looked back and saw the outline of Papa's mountain bike. It must've somehow got knocked off the wall where it always hung, and in the craziness of the past two days nobody had stopped to lift it up.

Tears sprang to her eyes looking at that mountain bike on the garage floor. Out of place. Never to be picked up and ridden by Papa again.

Everything felt out of place right now. Even inanimate objects were missing Papa.

Especially her. She was out of place and missing Papa. Unfortunately, nobody could pick her up and put her back where she was supposed to be. Papa would argue that she was exactly where she was supposed to be. "Well it's dang sure not where I want to be," she shot back at the empty garage.

She waited. No response. Quiet. She was alone. No Papa. Just emptiness and her pain. Tears pricked her eyes. She blinked to stop them from forming. She was sick and tired of crying. Grasping for something positive, she thought about Papa on that mountain bike.

She and Papa had loved to go explore the gorgeous mountains surrounding their homes, using deer tracks on their rides together. He'd always claimed she was fearless. Not anymore. She felt like she had so many fears without him here to teach her and smile at her and encourage her.

The rest of her family would be even more concerned if they knew how lost she felt without Papa. Her parents would probably feel hurt that she didn't trust and turn to them as she had with Papa. The rest of the family seemed heartbroken, but it was natural for them to step up and keep going. They'd all sworn and were focused on protecting the secret and protecting her as the sole keeper of the weapon. Jessie had no clue how everyone else seemed able to go on with life when she felt devastated, empty, and scared. Really scared.

What was coming? Who was coming? She didn't know, but

she knew it was going to be intense. The mercenaries, Frederick's soldiers, and even America's best, their own military special ops, would be assigned to go after the secret. They'd be looking to manipulate and force her to give them the weapon. She shivered.

She picked up the mountain bike and hung it on the pegs on the wall. Touching it, she whispered, "Love you, Papa."

Forcing her legs into motion she went out the side door and embraced the sting of the crisp fall night. Lights danced on the lake from the boathouse, the moon, and Greer's house across the way. She slowly walked along the grass, hopeful Maddie would stop anyone from coming after her.

A shadow moved from behind the pavilion where Papa had held so many parties for the family and the entire valley. She could easily picture him at the barbecue grill or dishing meat out of his prized smokers. He loved everyone and welcomed everyone and some greedy, despicable mercenaries had shot him in the chest and stomach to steal the Delta weapon and make themselves millions of dollars. Anger hit her then, red and hot. She welcomed it. The anger felt a lot better than the sorrow.

The shadow lifted a hand to her, thankfully not speaking to her. She recognized Petty Officer Manual Leandro and wondered where the rest of the SEALs were. All watching her and feeling bad for her? Or maybe not. They were ultra-tough and experienced warriors who'd probably seen many violent deaths, and administered even more. She was certain they all knew how devastating and huge the loss of Papa was, but they probably didn't waste time on simple emotions like sorrow and grief. She couldn't understand or relate to them if that was the case, but envy came to mind. She wished somebody would teach her how to eradicate the hurtful emotions so she could be tough and be the Secret Keeper the entire world needed right now. It was so heavy she felt her shoulders round.

She plodded along the thick grass, Papa would've cut it by now but nobody else had time now for such trivial pursuits as cutting grass. Not that Papa had been focused on trivial things, ever, but he'd worked harder than anybody and kept up on everything.

Right now it was more than enough keeping the secret safe and trying to feed and clean up after the crowd now gathered in her parents, uncle and aunt, and Papa's house. Thor, Colt, Alivia, and Greer also had beautiful homes nearby and had offered to have the SEALs or any of the other family members stay with them. Maddie and Braden were staying with Colt as he and Bailey weren't married yet, but the other three were newlyweds and nobody wanted to interrupt any alone time they might have together in their homes.

The dock stretched out into the calm, peaceful lake. Jessie walked to the end of it, laid down on her back on the smooth wood planks, and stared up at the stars and the half-moon in the navy-blue sky.

"Papa? Are you up there?" she asked.

Immediately she felt silly. Of course he was up there. She wished she could see him and Granny together. That would ease the pain a lot. Was that really asking too much? Just to see them and know they were happy. If she couldn't even have that miracle happen how could she be expected to spiritually know when she should fire the weapon? She wasn't spiritual enough to be the Secret Keeper.

She closed her eyes and prayed for faith, wondering where her formerly-unshakable faith had gone. She was the Secret Keeper and the Lord would be watching over her and Papa was her Guardian Angel now. She knew Papa and Granny were together. She didn't need some miracle of seeing them even if she longed for it. Papa had known he was dying and had amazed her with the faith he'd had. He'd been excited to be with Granny and of course his parents and two brothers that had already passed. He'd been excited to see the Savior. He'd been full of faith and not even seemed to question how or when he was going to die, or do anything to try and prevent it.

Hot tears stung her eyes and trailed down the sides of her cheeks, wetting the hair at her temples. It was hard to close her eyes and not see that evil man turn and shoot Papa right above the bullet-proof jacket, then the other, unexpected shot from the trees hitting him above his hip. Jessie had been in those trees seconds before. The man must've been up on a tree branch, and somehow she'd missed seeing him, and stopping him.

She hated the memory of Papa hitting the ground, blood seeping from his wounds. She hated that picture so much.

She'd gotten to him first, pressing her palms into the wounds until Thor had ripped off his t-shirt and offered it. Papa's eyes had opened, filled with pain but he ignored it like the tough, experienced military man he'd been. He'd focused on her and whispered, "My girl. It's your time. I'm so proud of you, and now I'll be your guardian angel."

She blew out a breath and squeezed her eyes tight, but all she could see were his blue eyes focused on her, so proud, unquestioning, thinking she was the answer to the Delta secret's future and believing she could rise up and do whatever was required of her.

If only she believed that.

Footsteps on the dock yanked her to her feet. She saw black for a second going from lying down to upright so quickly. She responded like she'd been trained, knife out of her pocket and open, ready to fight, cussing herself for not carrying her favorite 9mm Smith & Wesson that was small and easy to conceal.

Her gaze cleared and she focused in on the beautiful deep-brown eyes of one Senior Petty Officer Zander Povey, EOD. Braden had told her and Maddie about all of his friend's extra training stints and accomplishments. Zander was highly-decorated and impressive. Jessie wished she could only focus on the benefit of having him and the other SEALs here and simply be grateful they'd given up their lives and careers and some of them their families to join in this battle.

She didn't focus on any of that. She reacted like a girly-girl and felt her stomach do a little flip as she met his dark gaze.

He walked slowly toward her, an A.R. strapped to his back, pistol on his hip, and she could only imagine the knives and other weapons concealed in his cargo-type pants. The strap of the A.R. across his chest and the t-shirt that fit him perfectly emphasized his well-built chest and arms.

He was impressive. And she needed to control her girlish reactions to him. This wasn't a man who would be drawn to a twenty-three year old girl fresh out of college, well almost finished with the master's program that was going to benefit many children. Ever her choice of career wasn't tough and impressive like his.

Zander had to be at least thirty to have the ranking and experience he did. But wait ... Braden was only twenty-eight and they'd both joined as eighteen year olds and done their basic training together. Twenty-eight was only five years older than her. This man seemed to have a lifetime of knowledge in experience in those eyes and those hardened pectoral and bicep muscles. She shivered just looking at those arms and wondering what it would feel like to touch one of those muscles.

Sheesh, she needed to get a grip. She was acting like a moony teenager, not the responsible granddaughter of the famed Admiral Davidson Delta and current Secret Keeper of the most sought-after weapon in the world and the only thing preventing nuclear warfare from exploding worldwide.

"Are you okay?" Zander, or Officer Povey as she should think of him as, asked in a husky but soft voice that seemed to penetrate through her.

He stopped a couple of feet away, studying her. Was he doubting her ability to be the Secret Keeper, or was he offering his support?

"I don't know," she answered honestly. "Everything's pretty heavy right now."

"I bet." He offered a grim, understanding smile. She appreciated that smile. She wished he'd offer a hug.

She rolled her eyes at herself, closed and pocketed her knife, and turned to look out at the water before she did anything stupid like try to touch him. Just one touch on that smooth, rounded bicep? No. Stop it. He would think she was insane if she trailed her fingers along his arm then cupped the bicep muscle and appreciated each striation. Goodness she needed to focus. But it was actually a very nice distraction to be worried about his arm muscles and not death and dying.

They stood there in silence for a few beats, her studying the water. She could feel him studying her. She wondered if he'd say something about being sorry for her loss. They'd told Pastor Sam to spread the word through Summit Valley that the Delta family appreciated their prayers and love, but wanted privacy at this time. They were planning a small graveside service Sunday afternoon for family only and would have a large memorial service soon. So luckily she hadn't had to endure friends from school, church, or the valley stopping by to offer condolences. She'd tried to keep up with the messages on her phone but her response most of the time was simply "loving" the message with an easy-to-click heart.

She could feel something like nervousness radiating off of Officer Povey. That made no sense. This man had traveled the world and set and placed the explosives on doors or buildings elite SEAL, Army Ranger, or Delta teams needed to get through. Bullets probably rained around him in situations she couldn't even imagine. What could he be nervous for right now? In the past day and a half everything had been as quiet as it could be with Papa's loss. Maybe the storm was gathering to take them out, and he could feel it with his long experience.

Risking a sidelong glance at him, she saw he was still studying her. He looked away quickly and the silence and tense feeling between them grew. She should head back to the house to get away from this uncomfortable, and at the same time, stimulating interaction. But she wanted to see why he'd approached her and hear what he wanted to say. Was he going to declare his allegiance like her family had to her as Secret Keeper? That seemed laughable. If her family, who knew how diligently Papa had trained her, were concerned, this guy was probably wondering how to lobby for a new keeper. He was probably trying to figure out how to keep her safe and keep her from messing up the free world.

"I wanted to say ..." He began then paused.

Jessie looked at him again and her pulse quickened. With the moonlight glinting off the smooth planes of his face and his dark, wavy hair he was so handsome she wanted to run her fingers over his expressive lips, along his strong jawline and then twist them into his hair, tug his head close, and ...

Goodness sakes, she was doing it again. Immature girl with a crush on the experienced, hot military guy who was completely out of her league. Stupid emotional reaction that she needed to stop.

He met her gaze and everything around them disappeared. Her body felt hot all over and she found herself edging closer to him. He reached out and his fingertips grazed her cheek, setting off so much warmth in her chest that she feared she'd explode. The touch was simple yet it gave her so much—acceptance, longing, desire.

His eyes widened and he quickly pulled his hand back and flexed it into a fist then relaxed it. A muscle ticked in his jaw. He looked out at the peaceful lake and said quickly, "I just wanted to say that death sucks and crap happens, but it's all inevitable and part of the plan."

What was he saying? Crap happens? How insensitive was that?

"Your grandfather was one of the best men out there, so I'm pretty sure the devil didn't get his soul. Right?"

Devil getting his soul? Heck no, the devil better stay far away from her Papa. She glared at him. How dare he joke about Papa's death and soul like this. She'd wondered earlier if these elite military men were calloused to death and dying. Apparently she'd been right. And far from wanting to become calloused herself as she'd thought, she wanted to hit him.

Officer Povey gave a hollow laugh and then pushed a hand through his thick hair. "Sorry this isn't coming out right, that's kind of a joke with Captain Hendrickson and I." He drew in a breath. "I just want you to know that we're all on your team, we're all standing by your side right now. We're all hoping you can buck up, put the death behind you, and focus on the mission."

She blinked at him. "Excuse me?"

He looked back at her, but he was focused on the top of her head as if afraid to meet her eyes again. "That's how you'll get through it. That's how we do it. Focus on the mission. Don't let the emotion affect you. Joke about it and, you know, someday soon the bullet will get one of us."

Her eyes and mouth both widened. What kind of sadistic, awful jargon was this? She'd been wanting someone to help her get through, but not like this. Forget Papa, push away all emotion, focus on the mission. And the bullet coming to get one of us was a joke? She'd take a bullet for any of her family members but she couldn't handle anyone else dying. She wanted it all to stop.

"But not you." He finally met her eyes and gave her that smile of his that she'd found herself looking for over the past two days. She'd thought before that it made his cheeks crinkle so irresistibly and made her feel like they were sharing some inside joke. She still liked his smile, but she didn't like his jokes much right now. He probably should keep them inside.

"Not you." His smile fled and he said it softly, his voice and his gaze suddenly turned to a a caress. The frustration disappeared like somebody had waved a wand and she instantly wanted him to hold her.

He'd told her to not let the emotion affect her, but he was affecting her and making her feel like she on an emotional roller coaster—upset at him one moment, wanting to have him touch her the next.

She didn't need this complication right now. Her emotions were a big enough mess already.

"We'll protect you." His eyes swept over. "I'll protect you. You're the focus of my mission now."

The moment stretched between them and electricity seemed to arc through the air. This man would protect her. She was his personal mission. He'd never, ever desert her no matter who came after them.

She was feeling that deeply and deciding despite his weird humor attempts she was drawn inexplicably to Zander Povey. Maybe Papa was orchestrating from heaven. Making sure she was taken care of and protected. Her family would all step up and take this single-minded protection of her role that Zander was offering, but they all had a significant other to worry about now and Jessie didn't want to take any of them from the beautiful people they'd found and relationships they'd developed.

As she was wondering how to respond to his declared allegiance, he shifted his weight and then declared with an almost smart-aleck smile, something Thor would happily wear on his face. "It's all you now, Jessica Delta. You're the man, or um ... woman, and ..." His grin grew. "You got this."

"I've got this?" She felt like she had whiplash. From beautifully declaring he'd protect her to telling her she was the man and she had this. She didn't know if she should laugh at him, hug him really tight, or slug him. His rambling, callous, comfort, encouragement, allegiance, declarations, or whatever he thought this was, made her want to cry, laugh, kiss him, pummel him, and ticked her off and made her long for him alternately. Was it just that her emotions were completely out of control at the moment or was it that this impressive man might be ultra-accomplished, but he was also a scattered, goof ball? Could she possibly make him nervous or maybe the military stud wasn't an accomplished ladies' man?

He kept smiling at her. Was he encouraging her or placating her?

She stepped up closer and poked him in the chest. It was as hard as it looked and she might've jammed her index finger, but she didn't give him the courtesy of knowing that. Instead she unleashed all the angst and frustration building inside of her. "Was that your idea of a pep talk?" she asked him, narrowing her eyes at him.

He shrugged. "If it worked."

"No! It absolutely didn't work. Crap happens? The bullet's going to get one of us? Declaring that you'll protect me and then saying 'I'm the man'. My Papa died yesterday and the devil did not get his soul!"

His face tightened but he didn't back up. He might be an elite weapon but she was going to shove him off this dock if he didn't watch what he was saying and stop toying with her raw emotions.

"You might be immune to death and be able to joke about it," her voice escalated, "and put it behind you and focus on the mission, but I am not one of your soldiers Officer Povey. I am a woman. I have a heart." She was thinking she should stop talking now so he and his SEALs didn't realize the truth. She was far too emotional, she really didn't have control of herself or want to complete this mission. Maybe they'd walk away, or worse take the weapon and put it in Area 51 like they were supposed to in the first place. They'd all given up a lot staying here and supporting Papa.

But now Papa was gone.

"I don't even care," she found herself screaming at him. He stared at her with his dark eyes wide and every muscle tense.

"I don't care what you think about me," she yelled. "I don't care if you leave. I don't care if I lose your 'elite support'." She made quote marks with her fingers. "I will protect the stupid weapon and kill Frederick because that's what Papa trained me for and what I have to step up and do. I'll do it for Papa and in his honor, but I'm not going to try to joke about it or not think about him or just move on like 'all is well'."

He was staring at her now as if she was unstable. She was. Could anybody blame her? She was a twenty-three year old graduate student with emotions and needs. Yes she was a Delta and had been trained and molded for a time such as this but she wanted to go crawl in bed and have a good cry. She really needed Officer Povey to just say he'd support her and give her a hug. Was that too much to ask? Yes it was. This man wasn't the hugging type. He was the let's focus on the war and the mission and not let emotion creep into it. Good for him. That wasn't her.

"Argh!" she yelled at him. "You don't understand. Of course you don't Mr. Macho Brave Tough and Untouchable."

He opened his mouth to say something but she overrode him. "Don't worry about it. Nobody understands. I certainly don't expect you to be the exception."

She pushed past him and up the dock and for the house. Tears streamed down her face and she was humiliated and hoping she hadn't already messed up her fabled assignment by losing the support of the SEALs who everybody looked at as a gift from heaven.

She was going to fail at protecting the weapon, or firing it at the right moment. Papa had claimed she'd "know" the exact moment. Yeah right. She didn't know anything right now.

Crazily enough she was more upset about Zander looking at her like she was unstable and wishing their first private conversation had gone vastly different. She wished he had lived up to her unrealistic expectations from the looks and smiles he'd given her before tonight. She'd built him up to be perfectly tough but also perfectly understanding. A man like that didn't exist. Not outside her family at least.

At the moment, the disappointment of her idealistic dreams of Zander being smashed hurt almost as much as the pain of losing Papa. And that ticked her off even more.

Chapter Two

Zander pushed his hand through his hair and watched the woman he couldn't get out of his head run up the dock and across the grass. From the moment he'd seen the small, dark-haired beauty with the impossibly-blue eyes hefting a .50 caliber machine gun that most men would have trouble lifting, and pointing it at him with no fear, but somehow compassion, in her eyes, he'd lost his heart and his head.

Finally after almost two weeks of being here in Colorado at the Delta's valley he'd thought he'd gotten his chance to flirt with her, talk to her, help her with the heavy burden she was carrying and somehow show her how attractive and impressive she was.

Nope. He'd gotten so nervous being around the beautiful sweetheart that he'd fumbled his words, tried to give her a "pep talk" as she'd termed it that probably came out all rambling, disturbing, and weird.

Instead of offering her a hug like he was dying to do, he'd ticked her off. He'd made her yell at him and then run away. He'd messed this one up. Badly.

His gaze followed her progression across the sweeping lawn. She avoided the crowd in her grandfather's house and ran into her parent's back door, slamming it shut. Pushing out a breath, he trudged off the dock and across the grass.

"Well, that went nicely," Captain Zeke Hendrickson said, stepping out of the shadows of the pavilion.

He nodded. "Right? She'll probably be asking me to sneak away and make out by tomorrow night."

"That's exactly what I was thinking. There is a woman who is gone over my buddy Demo. How do you keep them at bay with all those sweetly impressive lines?" Zeke grinned, enjoying mocking him. "Do you practice in the mirror at night?"

"I do. And yes it's rough to keep the women from attacking me. I mean the good looks, the impressive bio, the charm that just oozes from me." At least he could joke with Zeke. Sadly his attempts to joke with Jessie Delta had come across flat, weird, and offensive. He'd never been so nervous and uncertain of himself. When he focused on her blue eyes the world seemed to settle and he thought he could conquer the world with her by his side but then he'd start spouting crap that he'd meant to be helpful or inspiring but had the opposite effect.

"Seriously man, I'm sorry you messed that up so bad." Any of his other friends would've slapped him on the shoulder but he'd never seen "Cap" initiate physical contact, unless it was to tackle somebody or start a wrestling match. "I've seen you looking at her when you think no one is looking," Zeke continued, upping his humiliation of messing up with his dream woman.

"Can you blame me?" He pushed his hand through his thick hair. He needed a hair cut but it was like the sloping grass of the Delta's beautiful valley that needed to be mowed. Who had time for stuff like that right now?

"Nope." Zeke pumped his eyebrows. "She's not only beautiful, but it's a great combination, the sweet but tough thing she's got going on. Sensual and innocent. That's as irresistible as anything I've seen in a long while."

Zander's thoughts exactly. Jessie Delta was so beautiful he got nervous looking at her, so sweet you could feel it radiate from her, yet she'd been trained to fight. Though she was small, every line of her body was strong, appealing, and yes, sensual. He didn't appreciate Zeke noticing that.

She seemed like the perfect woman, facing a crazy obstacle that no twenty-three year old woman should have to face. She'd lost her beloved grandfather and now the youngest Delta was the one assigned to protect the secret weapon that only she knew the capabilities of.

Zander and his SEAL buddies had sworn allegiance to Admiral Delta and to keeping the weapon out of King Frederick's blood-stained hands. They'd had to pretend they were dead, luckily Zander had been able to get a message to his family that he was on a mission and to keep it quiet that he'd contacted them and was in fact alive. Manuel "Wolf", Kyle "Preach", and Braden had been able to do the same for their families so that was a load off. Zeke "Cap" and Van "Chaos" didn't have families.

They all knew they'd probably kissed their hard-earned military careers goodbye and would most likely be stripped of rank, court martialed, and thrown in prison when they resurfaced from the dead.

But it had been the right thing to do. Zander and each of them knew it. Zander had his friend Braden Moyle to thank for opening his eyes, and luckily the rest of the SEALs either trusted him implicitly or had felt the rightness of this mission themselves.

How to show Jessie that they'd transferred their allegiance from Admiral Delta to her? Zander wasn't questioning that, despite how she was obviously struggling. Would the other men?

"If I didn't hate human touch, maybe I'd go after Jessica Delta myself," Zeke said.

Zander felt a rush of gratitude that Zeke did shy away from touching anyone and a man could get laid out flat for forgetting that and initiating contact. Zander did not want to be in competition with the ultra-handsome and impressive captain. Nobody knew why Zeke was so adverse to anyone touching him. They were just careful not to. And they didn't ask.

"Hey, um, what do you think of assigning me as Jessica Delta's personal bodyguard?" The idea came to him as he spouted out other stupid stuff tonight. That was the one thing he said that he'd liked, she was the mission now and he'd protect her. Yes, he'd messed up tonight, but he felt he could help her with this emotionally challenging time as well as keep her safe no matter who came after her. There was the slightly-selfish thought of wanting to get to know her, be close to her, and hold her when she needed a shoulder to cry on. But he convinced himself it was a small part of the equation. And if he was her bodyguard he'd have to be in control of himself and not get romantically involved until the mission was over.

Zeke chuckled. "I think that's a pretty smart way to keep her safe, and to maybe get to know her better and get her to fall for an impressive guy who has no clue how to talk to beautiful women."

"Will I mess it all up?" he asked.

"Maybe." Zeke laughed. "I'll claim it's my idea so you don't look like a groveling slap to her parents and family."

"That'd be perfect." Zander's pulse skyrocketed at the thought of round-the-clock protection of Jessica Delta. "Yes, I like that a lot."

"Okay. I'll setup a time for us to chat with Joseph, Holly, and Jessie, and work out the details. I like this. From what Colton explained to me Jessie is the only person on earth now who can access and fire the weapon. If we keep her safe that's every bit as important as keeping unfriendlies away from the cave. Let's do it."

"Thanks Cap. I'd hug you but ..."

"I'd have to shoot you."

"There is that."

Zander patted him on the arm affectionately, and dodged a fist aimed for his jaw. He chuckled and jogged away. Luckily he heard Zeke laughing behind him. That was good. He'd risked his friend coming after him and pummeling him for touching him so casually. So weird how Zeke couldn't handle anyone touching him, but Zeke was great, always teasing and keeping things light but more importantly an incredible leader as well as a soldier who never failed at an assignment and excelled at marksmanship.

His thoughts returned to Jessie. He'd upset her. He hoped he could make that right. But if he was assigned to protect her, he'd get to stay close by. Really close by. He loved the way this was going and hoped Jessie didn't balk at the assignment. He also hoped her mom and dad would allow it.

Every one of the Deltas was ultra-protective of Jessie and that protectiveness had nothing to do with her being the Secret Keeper as they called it. Zander was playing with fire hoping to get close to her, in so many ways. Even though this assignment would probably the most important one of his career, and the end of his career, he couldn't get thoughts of Jessie and getting closer to her out of his mind. When he'd touched her jaw earlier he'd thought he'd found heaven. When he looked in her eyes he was lost, and found.

Now to talk her into being interested in him or maybe he should keep his mouth shut and just kiss her and see how that went. After the mission was completed.

Right now he had to focus on the mission of keeping her safe from whatever King Frederick sent their way next. Mercenaries, troops of armed soldiers, elite special ops forces.

Hooyah.

Chapter Three

It was late Friday afternoon and Jessie had been sent to her room to rest. By her mother. Like a child. She didn't need rest, she needed to figure out if Admiral Seamons was on their side or not and look through that zip drive Papa's coder Thomas had decoded again and see what more information she could glean. The last time she'd had a serious talk with Papa he'd been concerned if the zip drive's information was accurate or valuable. He'd sent the bank account information on to a very trusted associate in the IRS. The man had looked into seizing it but the account numbers weren't accurate.

During that same conversation Papa had looked deeply into her eyes and assured her, "Jessica ... I prayed long and hard to *not* make you the Secret Keeper. Colton or Aiden would willingly take this burden and they'd do a fabulous job."

Exactly. They'd do a fabulous job. She wouldn't.

Papa had continued. "Because I adore you so much I can hardly stand to give you this heavy burden. But I know, I know down deep, and have known for years actually, that you are the Secret Keeper and you are the only one who could be humble, conscientious, and at the same time, strong enough to take this responsibility, and use the weapon at the exact time it is needed. It is a spiritual responsibility unlike anything you'll ever know. But I've trained you and the good Lord will direct you when the time is right."

No pressure. The good Lord would direct her to kill a man. Papa had quoted a scripture she'd never heard, Psalm 37:9-10 "For evildoers will be cut off, But those who wait for the Lord, they will inherit the land. Yet a little while and the wicked man will be no more; And you will look carefully for his place and he will not be there." Papa had explained that she was the avenging angel and she had to make the wicked man no more so the good people in Banida, Poland, and Germany could inherit their land once more and many people throughout the world could be protected. King Frederick would not stop, and if the United Nations wouldn't step up and stop him soon, it would be time to use the weapon.

She pushed off her bed and paced her room. Annoyed with her mom and Colton for ganging up on her and insisting she take a break and upset at herself for taking it simply to avoid an argument.

The peacemaker in her didn't want to die no matter if she needed to. Die? No, fight to keep working and not rest. Not die. She was too focused on Papa dying. No matter if she didn't want to rest she was tired from the stress and she hadn't slept well last night. She'd mulled over the intense but awkward conversation with Officer Povey until far too late. He drew her in, and completely frustrated her.

"Jessie?" her dad rapped on her bedroom door.

She hurried across the room to yank the door open. "Hey. Everything okay?" Finally, they needed her again.

"Can you come down to the living area?" His blue eyes studied her thoughtfully. Her dad was protective of her like any dad would be, but he also trusted her. He trusted her because he'd seen how diligent Papa had trained her, and had been right there helping her excel.

She could shoot a bull's eye through a target with a pistol, rifle, shotgun, A.R., or .50 caliber machine gun. She could take down a man twice her size in hand-to-hand combat. She could track, navigate, strategize, or decode. Papa had made sure she excelled in every area. She'd always thought it was because her favorite person in the world loved spending time with her, or because he wanted to make sure she was safe because she was smaller physically than anyone in the family.

Nope. He'd been training her meticulously ... to be Secret Keeper. The very name weighed so heavy on her she wanted to puke.

She focused on her dad. What was going on that her "rest" had been interrupted. Her mom wouldn't like that. And why was he looking at her as if she'd been scheming something?

"Captain Hendrickson and Officer Povey have an idea they think you'll be interested to hear."

Officer Povey. Zander. She put a hand to her abdomen and hoped her dad didn't see how even the man's name affected her. She'd managed to stay away from him since last night on the dock. Almost an entire day. Nobody would let her take a stint of protecting the cave. She supposed the reasoning made sense if a mercenary somehow got through the resistance and to the cave they'd need her to open it. She touched the hidden pendant. It was smart to keep her safe and in their little valley where there was so much protection and many eyes watching out for her. Including Zander. Even though he hadn't gotten close enough to talk with her again she'd felt his gaze on her. And it made her hot clear through every time.

She'd spent the morning training with Colt and Bailey and then she'd worked with her dad and Uncle Keith to respond to condolences from Papa's vast network of military and political friends and associates, cross-referencing with Papa's notes about who had been at Olivet Seamon's party with King Frederick, who's names were listed on the zip drive Admiral Seamons had given to Braden and Maddie, and who Papa trusted from his experiences. The three of them tried to sort out who was on their side or not. It was tough not knowing if the zip drive was accurate or not.

In their correspondence her dad and uncle didn't talk about the Delta weapon to anyone. Interestingly enough, even Admiral Gusbane, who'd sent Zander and the four-man SEAL team to obtain the weapon, didn't ask. So far another special ops team hadn't come after the weapon but who knew how long they had?

They wanted to could keep the Delta weapon from being general knowledge with the military, the government, and especially the public. It seemed King Frederick was doing the same. Though he apparently had a fifteen million dollar reward out for the weapon, he didn't seem to want to shout to the world what he was after. It made sense as someone else stealing it before him would put a cramp in his plans of shooting his nuclear weapons at America while he hid in an unknown location.

Jessie lived every hour in fear that it would be the moment she'd know she had to go use the weapon. At the same time she wished it was over, King Frederick was gone, the world could have a moment of peace, and she could go back to finishing her master's in speech pathology. What a different life she was living right now. Nobody at school had any clue what she was trained to do or what family emergency had taken her out of the program earlier this fall.

"Are you going to tell me what it is?" She cocked her head at her dad.

"They haven't told me. They asked if they could meet with me, you, and your mom."

"Oh." Nerves made her stomach feel twitchy. She wanted to check her makeup and put on some lip gloss, but that was the girly reaction to Zander that she couldn't afford to indulge. Not now. Maybe not ever. An elite special ops demolition expert really wasn't a great fit for a speech pathologist.

What was a great fit? She hardly knew Zander but the thought of him being with any other woman made her body tighten and made her want to fight any woman who'd dare look twice at him. She was sure a whole slew of women had. He was irresistible. When he wasn't telling her that "crap happened".

"Okay."

Her dad stepped back as she walked out of the door. He followed her through the upstairs hallway and down the stairs. She smoothed out her features and tried to look relaxed and nonplussed as she left the entryway and entered the main living area.

Zander and Captain Hendrickson both stood from the couch as they entered. Zander's gaze zeroed in on her with all the power of deep-brown eyes, long lashes, and a connection that she needed to ignore.

Jessie pulled her gaze from him with a concerted, and she thought heroic effort, nodded to Captain Hendrickson, and walked over to sit by her mom on the opposite couch. Her mom quirked an eyebrow at her, her gaze full of questions and a little bit of mischief and matchmaking. Jessie wanted to beg her to not get any ideas. An elite special ops man like Zander Povey, who thought she should just callously get over Papa's death, wasn't the guy Jessie should be falling for.

Her dad came and sat by her mom. The two men settled back down and Jessie wondered if she'd ever noticed how glorious it was to watch a man sit on a couch. Zander's leg muscles flexed as he settled onto the couch and his fit, tall body uncoiled against the cushions but somehow he looked poised to jump and fight against bad guys at any moment.

"What's going on Captain?" her dad asked. He wasn't snippy or annoyed but he didn't have time to waste. Nobody but Jessie really did. Everybody else had assignments different hours of the night and day and had to make sure to fit in sleep and eating and time with their significant other and other family members during those breaks. All she had to do was train, try to help correspond and keep people from coming after the weapon, and stay safe.

"As I've spoken with different Delta family members I've become more convinced that keeping Jessica safe and away from the weapon is the most foolproof plan to keep Frederick from obtaining it. Am I correct to assume that only you can access the cave and remove the weapon?" He looked to Jessie, his grayish-blue eyes looking only for a confirmation.

"Yes," she admitted.

Her mom put her arm around her. Jessie knew it was both a show of support and a mother terrified of the responsibility and danger surrounding her youngest child. Her mom had been surrounded by the Delta secret most of her married life and trained her children right along with her husband, but she was still struggling with Jessie being the one to have to take over the responsibility and danger of wielding the weapon.

Jessie appreciated and loved her mom. She was still a little perturbed from being forced to go "rest" earlier and she didn't want to look weak in front of either of these men. Especially Senior Petty Officer Zander Povey, EOD. But typical Jessie peace maker she didn't shrug her mom's arm off.

She did boldly meet Zander's gaze and the room seemed to get warm. Very warm. Jessie swallowed hard and hoped no one else saw or felt the connection that sprang between them. She needed to remember the different phrases he'd said that had made her mad last night but unfortunately she was remembering his fingertips grazing her chin and him telling her he would protect her and she was his mission. His mission to protect, or to hold and kiss?

"I fear as soon as Admiral Delta's graveside service is over, or maybe we don't even have that long," the captain continued, yanking her concentration away from Zander, "we're going to face unprecedented attacks from Frederick's soldiers, armed mercenaries, and probably our own military."

The room felt suddenly chilly. It was a gorgeous, and warm for their Colorado mountains, late-September day outside. The maple, cottonwood, and birch trees ringing their beautiful lake were turning orange, yellow, and red. It was a picture perfect scene as the green pine trees stood straight and tall amidst all that color and the lake and sky were a calm, crystal blue. Was their valley going to be shattered by attacks and war?

"I agree," her dad said. "We don't have the layer of protection of my dad any longer. I think his reputation and connections held at least the American military back who might want to seek the secret for the military or personal gain. Plus the anonymity we had for so many years is disappearing. Secrets are hard to keep once they start gaining momentum and the weapon is something every military man would like to have for himself or his troops and the politicians would love the power of it."

Everybody nodded. It was unnerving to think of the secret weapon being talked about and leaked around military and political circles. They might not have entire troops coming after it as no leader would want it to be common knowledge or risk losing it to another branch of the military if they broadcast it, but enough people knew about it now that they were on a slippery slope of exposure, danger, and attacks they hadn't previously seen.

"I feel even Frederick and his people had a fear of my father's power and status," her dad continued. "I've wondered if the man who kidnapped Kelsey and Mo didn't have the assignment to secure the weapon and kill Papa as well."

It made sense. Frederick would want the well-known and widely-respected Admiral Delta out of the picture. It was doubtful he knew that all the Deltas were trained like they were. And he had succeeded in killing Papa. Jessie wrapped her arms around her stomach and her mom tugged her closer.

"Which brings me back to the idea Officer Povey and I had." The captain looked at Zander and something passed between them. Jessie wondered whose idea it was. It almost seemed like Zander wanted to present it, but he felt Captain Hendrickson sharing it would be received better. Why?

"If we can keep Jessica safe," Hendrickson said. "We can keep Frederick from the secret. No matter what happens to any of the rest of us."

That was an awful thought. Would they all be laying down their lives to keep these soldiers from getting to Jessie? She shivered, not sure she could live with that. Papa had laid down his life for them. She'd wondered if she'd have to do the same but it was far worse to think about those she loved being killed and her hiding out and staying safe.

Her parents both nodded. Her mom pulled her arm back but stayed pressed into her side.

"Jessica," Hendrickson said very seriously. "Even if Povey had blown the safe door, which I have complete confidence he could've done, Admiral Delta designed it so only you, and the key I assume you keep on your person," the key around her neck seemed to burn against her skin and she barely kept herself from touching it, "are the only ways to access and either use or remove the weapon. Correct?"

Everybody was staring at her. She should respond but Jessie had a sudden unexpected and terrifying thought. What if Hendrickson was a fraud? What if his men were? What if they'd come here at Admiral Gusbane or Seamons' instructions to get the weapon, no matter what, and when they'd seen all the firepower and resistance from the Deltas they'd changed their game plan?

"Maddie?" her mom questioned.

"Just a moment," she requested. She'd heard about Braden's gift to discern what someone's intentions were and she thought that was incredible. When these men had shown up in the Black-hawk and Zander had told the story of Braden confronting him and begging him not to take the Delta weapon. Zander had said that Braden had reminded him that he "knew him". Braden had seen Zander's goodness.

Maddie looked from Captain Hendrickson to Zander. He met her gaze with his deep-brown eyes steady and true. She said a prayer in her heart, asking to see clearly. Everyone else in the room disappeared as she and Zander locked gazes. He was impressive. He was loyal. He'd meant it, to his steadfast core, when he'd said he'd protect her last night. He'd protect her from everyone, even his friend the SEAL captain sitting next to him.

She felt a pulse of warmth as the truth shot through her. She could trust Zander.

Her dad shifted next to her and took her attention from Zander. She wanted to keep focusing on Zander but now was definitely not the time for that. She looked at the captain. His gaze was guarded, shut off. His blue eyes were cool, almost a bluish gray and she couldn't read him.

"Maddie?" her mom asked again.

"I can't answer Captain Hendrickson's question right now," she said softly, studying Hendrickson for his reaction.

He cocked an eyebrow at her and she thought he'd make fun of her but he simply said, "What do you need to be able to answer the question?"

She thought about it, and she knew she couldn't get through to Captain Hendrickson's intentions but she knew who could, and his reaction and assessment would answer the question for her. "Braden."

"You want to know if you can trust me?" Hendrickson asked.

"It's not a matter of want, Captain. I need to know if I can trust you."

"I can respect that." He nodded to her and pulled a walkie-talkie off his belt. None of the SEALs had their cell phones as they'd blown them up in the Blackhawk to support the story of them being "lost". Papa had given them each an RT29 walkie-talkie. The preferred military walkie-talkie had excellent transmit signals and the ability to receive weak signals at extreme distances. Hendrickson pushed the button and spoke into it. "We need Moyle at his future in-law's house."

"Copy," a male voice said, she wasn't sure which of the SEALs it was.

Hendrickson clipped the walkie-talkie back on and turned back to her. The silence felt tight and Jessie was certain she'd offended him. These men had given up everything to transfer to the Deltas' side and now she was questioning his loyalties.

She let her gaze trail back to Zander. He was much easier to look at. Those deep-brown eyes were really intriguing. His gaze was steady on her, not condemning, not even questioning. She appreciated that. After his offensive words last night she wasn't sure what to think of him, but she could admit she liked looking at him. She liked a lot about him.

"Jessica." Captain Hendrickson pulled her gaze away from Zander. She wasn't sure what to think of him, but at the moment she was annoyed at him interrupting her staring. "I have no issue with you sending for Braden to 'read' me. I'm a very closed off person and don't let many people close."

That was kind of him to reassure her he wasn't offended.

"Many people, Cap? How about none?" Zander had the nerve to laugh at the captain.

Hendrickson elbowed him.

Her dad smiled. "My nephews have had brawls and wrestling matches on the carpet if you two want to have a go."

"Don't you dare encourage that," her mom threatened. "I just got that new lamp and you haven't had to redo the sheetrock and paint for almost two weeks."

Zander and Hendrickson both laughed at that. Jessie even found herself smiling. She was glad Hendrickson could relax a little bit.

"Why don't you let people close?" she asked him. It was intriguing and sad. She had all of her family close to her heart and many friends from grade school up through graduate school who still kept in touch. Before she'd left school she was hiking, biking, or going to lunch or dinner with different friends and dates most days of the week.

The laughter disappeared. "If I let people close then I'd be more likely to answer a question like that, wouldn't I?" He arched an eyebrow.

"If you want me to trust you, answer your questions, and consider whatever proposal you have, maybe you should give a little bit and try to open up," she threw back at him.

"Ooh," Zander teased. "She got you there, Cap." He winked at her, as if they were in cahoots together. Jessie felt warm all over. She wanted to be in ... something with him.

No, that was the girlie girl in her trying to get out. She was a responsible keeper of the biggest secret of the century. She couldn't indulge girlish fantasies. Not now. Maybe never.

Hendrickson actually cracked a smile.

Jessie gave him a sassy look that Maddie would've been proud of. "Oh, you actually possess a sense of humor."

Zander laughed loud at that one. She really, really liked him. Was that wrong? Probably with the situation they were in at the moment. Maybe someday, when the weapon was secure. She doubted that day would ever come. Maybe she should let herself get to know Zander. Tell him off for trying to tell her that "crap happens" and she should bury her pain and emotions to get through. Maybe he'd been trying to help or look tough or something last night. She wanted to give him another chance, see if they had anything in common, and see if he was as appealing as he seemed right now, or a let-down and source of frustration as he'd been last night.

"Maddie," her mom cautioned.

Jessie looked at her mom, and then she burst out laughing. She looked back at Zander. "I know I'm out of line when she calls me 'Maddie' by mistake."

"Oh, shoot I did," her mom said.

Her dad chuckled at that. "Jessie's right. Don't tell Maddie."

Zander shared a conspiratorial look with her. "Maddie's the sassy one?"

"Oh for sure. I'm the angel and the favorite." She put her hands under her chin and blinked rapidly.

Everybody laughed at that.

She'd been Papa's favorite. Everybody knew it, and though they might tease her about it, her parents, uncle and aunt, cousins, and siblings all looked at her just as Papa had—like she was an angel peacemaker who could do no wrong. She'd flourished in her role as the happy, bright light in the family, the one everybody wanted to hug and do something nice for. Because they loved seeing her smile and she had usually done something nice for them first.

The memories were filled with sunshine, fun, loving smiles ... it felt like a different lifetime. Like watching Rapunzel on

Tangled run and twirling through the flowers, so sweet and adorable and did she see that men with big knives and Flynn himself were going to hurt her soon—emotionally, physically, and spiritually. Was Zander her hero? A very different hero from Flynn as he definitely wasn't a thief but a devoted, tough, special ops soldier.

She locked eyes on him as the laughter settled.

Suddenly Hendrickson leaned forward, stealing her focus from Zander, again. "Jessie. If I wasn't committed to the Deltas, why would I have given up my military career to be here?"

She eyed him and asked the question that might upset him more. "Did you give it up?"

He shrugged. "I would assume so. Unless this all plays out like a Disney movie, we save the world, and everything is forgiven in the end." He smirked. "I'm not planning on that."

"I understand what you're saying. I'm not trying to accuse you of having a track phone in your backpack with only Admiral Gusbane's number programmed in it."

"That would stink," Zander said, giving his friend a look as if to make sure he wasn't corresponding with Gusbane. No. He trusted his friend. It was more a look of, sorry she's questioning you.

"I'm just saying I have to trust you completely. Until I do I can't answer your question, or agree to whatever plan you and Officer Povey have concocted." She congratulated herself on not calling him Zander out loud. "And I'm assuming it's a fabulous plan, because you are some of the most highly-trained people in our military. Correct?"

"We are," Hendrickson agreed. There was nothing cocky

about his words, just factual. He tilted his head toward Zander. "Do you trust Officer Povey completely?"

The room went too still again. Jessie focused in on Zander, and as she was coming to see was a troubling thing, she got lost completely in his dark eyes. She nodded and admitted, "I do."

Zander's quick smile curved his lips and made his cheeks crinkle.

"Whoa," her mom whistled and said in a low tone, "That's an irresistible smile."

"Did you just ..." Her dad broke off and shook his head.

Jessie could only agree but she wasn't about to voice it. "You see where Maddie gets her sass," she said to Zander instead.

"Maddie ... I mean, Jessie," her mom sounded exasperated. "You watch it, little girl."

Jessie laughed but she didn't like being called "little girl" by her mom in front of these men. She needed them to respect her, and she had no desire for Zander to look at her as a little girl.

The front door opened and closed and rapid footsteps came. Braden walked into the room, his gaze quickly sweeping around. He was a handsome blond with teal-blue eyes. Jessie had flirted with him last June when he'd come to their valley and attempted to hike to the secret, having no idea what he was messing with. She'd always been impressed with him, and thought he was the perfect fit for her sister Maddie. He loved Maddie unconditionally and had helped her to see that her Savior loved her too and she could be a warrior and still be righteous and filled with light from on high.

"You need me?" Braden asked.

"Yes," Hendrickson said evenly. He stood and faced Braden.

"Jessie has a request of you. She needs you to 'read' me and tell her if I can be trusted and if I'm a hundred percent loyal to the Deltas and to protecting the weapon as per Admiral Delta's instructions."

Braden looked to Jessie. He didn't know her well, but he knew she was deeply spiritual and trusted in heaven above. She had to be or she'd never know what the right time was to use the weapon or not. If only it was done and they didn't have to go through all of this. She'd played tennis in high school and had absolutely loathed warmups. Once she was in the game she could settle, focus, and succeed but warmups just made her nervous. She was definitely nervous in this warmup phase they were in, waiting to be attacked, or waiting for her to feel prompted to use the weapon as Papa was so certain she would be.

"You didn't trust what you saw in Captain Hendrickson's eyes?" he asked.

"It wasn't that I didn't trust him," she said slowly, "But he admitted that he's closed off and doesn't let anyone get close. That's more what I felt. He was choosing to shut me out. It scared me that maybe he's hiding more than just his desire to be this tough military guy that nobody can touch emotionally or spiritually."

Braden nodded to her, but Captain Hendrickson's jaw tightened. The captain looked over at Zander and muttered, "I hope this is worth it."

"It is," Zander said evenly. He looked at Jessie and his dark gaze was warm and liquid. "I promise it is worth it."

Jessie wasn't sure if he was talking to her or his captain.

"Okay." Captain Hendrickson literally gritted his teeth. She heard it. What was his deal? Was he scared of Braden seeing that he was double-crossing them or was he scared of Braden seeing him?

The captain stood straight and tall and faced Braden as if he was facing a Naval Discharge Review Board or maybe worse than that, as if he were facing a firing squad. No. This man wouldn't be afraid of dozens of rifles pointed his way. He'd probably call out "Hooyah" and face death with his grayish-blue eyes cool and still being unable to reveal any emotion to anyone, even the fear of dying. She was relieved he wasn't the man she was drawn to. The poor girl who fell in love with him.

Braden stared at the captain for a few seconds then said softly and respectfully, "Captain Hendrickson doesn't want any of us to see what he's feeling. He's very good at hiding his feelings. I respect that, but it's hard to know what he's truly about with how expert he is at hiding behind a mask of toughness and profes- sionalism."

Jessie couldn't live with that. This was life or death, the end of the world if King Frederick had his way. "Captain Hendrickson might need to open up a little bit so we don't lose the weapon to Frederick and have nuclear weapons obliterate America as we know it."

Zander looked at her, and his gaze was full of respect. Maybe he didn't see her as a little girl but as a woman who could hold her own, even with tough Navy SEALs. She'd show him she could hold her own with him. She could. In many ways. Ways she shouldn't be thinking about right now.

"Do you want me to listen to you and Zander's proposal or not?" Jessie realized her mistake instantly. If she corrected to

Officer Povey now it would probably highlight her slip of the tongue even more.

Captain Hendrickson turned to her. His eyebrow lifted but it wasn't mocking. It looked like her slip of the tongue made him happy. "I do want you to listen, and agree," he said. "I'll try to let down my guard so Braden can 'read' me." He turned back to Braden and muttered. "I thought your gift made it so you could read anybody."

"Not anybody. Most people let their guard down at one point or another, especially when emotions are high. You don't."

"Dang straight I don't. I've worked for years to not let people see what I'm truly feeling."

"Yet you want me to trust you," Jessie pointed out, even though the captain was focused on Braden not her. She wasn't trying to be snide but she couldn't trust him if neither she nor Braden could get a glimpse of what was going on inside, of what his intentions and goals and allegiances were.

"I need you to trust me," Captain Hendrickson admitted quietly, almost humbly, changing want to need like she'd done earlier. She didn't know the guy could be humble. "Okay, let's get this over with." He faced Braden and as they looked on both men stood straight and stared at each other for several long beats.

Jessie felt like the staring contest or examination of Captain Hendrickson's closed-off heart would never end. She felt almost bad for putting Hendrickson through this. It obviously was hard for him, but she couldn't let her tendencies to be the peace maker and try to keep everybody happy rule her life in these extreme circumstances. Those tendencies could be strengths in regular life, but in her role as Secret Keeper and their current unstable situation, trust, loyalty, and a team that was going to fight to keep Frederick away from the weapon were what she needed to focus on.

She let her gaze slide to Zander and dang if his dark eyes weren't focused on her. She blew out a breath. It wasn't easy to focus on serious issues when Zander had a slight smile on his appealing lips. Why was he smiling at a time like this? As she studied him she realized. He was smiling for her. To help her relax and know that he was on her team, Captain Hendrickson was good, and it would all work out.

It would all work out? She usually had oodles of faith. Some in her church groups at college had expressed envy that their faith didn't come as easy and wasn't as strong.

Not right now. Faith was in short supply when you felt like the entire evil sector of the world was breathing down your neck and possibly twisting those who should be on your side to betray and backstab you for the old filthy lucre.

Wow. Filthy lucre? Really?

Braden nodded to Captain Hendrickson and the captain's shoulders relaxed slightly. Had he passed? Braden patted the man on the shoulder. Captain Hendrickson immediately stiffened and murmured, "Don't touch me."

The tension in the room amped up as Braden raised questioning eyebrows at him but lifted his hand away.

"Braden is only trying to help," her dad said softly but with a voice of steel. "I don't appreciate you being short with him for reading your intentions."

Maybe the captain wasn't on their team if he could so easily snarl at Braden.

Zander stood and strode to Captain Hendrickson's side.

"Zeke isn't trying to be short with him. It's common knowledge with his team. Nobody touches the captain. He's very adverse to human touch."

This guy just got colder and colder.

"I apologize," Captain Hendrickson said stiffly. "I don't like to draw attention to my issues. It's a holdover from ... childhood."

The room felt stuffy and sad. Captain Hendrickson studied a mirror on the wall above the couch Jessie sat on her with her parents. Braden looked like he wanted to reach out to the captain again but thought better of it. Zander begged her with those deep-brown eyes of his to not judge the captain too harshly. It was illuminating and brave of Hendrickson to admit that his issues stemmed from childhood. Compassion filled Jessie. She'd seen some cases of abuse in her work of speech pathology with some of the downtown schools in Denver. It infuriated her and broke her heart. How anyone could hurt an innocent child was beyond her.

"So." Captain Hendrickson squared his shoulders and focused back on Braden. "What's the verdict Lieutenant Moyle? Am I loyal to the Deltas or do I have evil intent?"

Everyone focused on Braden. Jessie had gained a lot of compassion for Captain Hendrickson, but she still needed to have her concerns resolved and the SEAL's loyalty affirmed. Or she wasn't agreeing to any plan. No matter how appealing EOD Zander Povey was to her.

Find *Devastated* on Amazon.

About the Author

Cami is a part-time author, part-time exercise consultant, part-time housekeeper, full-time wife, and overtime mother of four adorable boys. Sleep and relaxation are fond memories. She's never been happier.

Join Cami's VIP list to find out about special deals, giveaways and new releases and receive a free copy of *Rescued by Love: Park City Firefighter Romance* by clicking here.

cami@camichecketts.com

www.camichecketts.com

Also by Cami Checketts

Delta Family Romances

Deceived

Abandoned

Committed

Betrayed

Devoted

Compromised

Endangered

Accepted

Returned

Devastated

Famous Friends Romances

Loving the Firefighter

Loving the Athlete

Loving the Rancher

Loving the Coach

Loving the Contractor

Loving the Sheriff

Loving the Entertainer

The Hidden Kingdom Romances

Royal Secrets

How to Design Love

How to Switch a Groom

How to Lose a Fiance

Billionaire Boss Romance

Her Dream Date Boss

Her Prince Charming Boss

Hawk Brothers Romance

The Determined Groom

The Stealth Warrior

Her Billionaire Boss Fake Fiance

Risking it All

Navy Seal Romance

The Protective Warrior

The Captivating Warrior

The Stealth Warrior

The Tough Warrior

Texas Titan Romance

The Fearless Groom

The Trustworthy Groom

The Beastly Groom

The Irresistible Groom

The Determined Groom

The Devoted Groom

Billionaire Beach Romance

Counterfeit Date

Snow Valley

Full Court Devotion: Christmas in Snow Valley

A Touch of Love: Summer in Snow Valley

Running from the Cowboy: Spring in Snow Valley

Light in Your Eyes: Winter in Snow Valley

Romancing the Singer: Return to Snow Valley

Fighting for Love: Return to Snow Valley

Other Books by Cami

Seeking Mr. Debonair: Jane Austen Pact

Seeking Mr. Dependable: Jane Austen Pact

Saving Sycamore Bay

Oh, Come On, Be Faithful

Protect This

Blog This

Redeem This

The Broken Path

Dead Running

Dying to Run

Fourth of July

Love & Loss

Love & Lies

Five Free Books

Christmas Makeover:

Chelsea Jamison has been infatuated with Drew Stirling longer than she's loved playing basketball, high-top sneakers, and the Knicks. Unfortunately, all Drew sees is the kid who kicked his trash in the high school free throw contest and not the girl whose heart breaks into a fast dribble when he's near.

Drew makes an unexpected visit home to Echo Ridge and their friendship picks up where they left off as they scheme to make a teenaged boy's Christmas dreams come true. When Chelsea realizes she's fallen for her best friend, she wonders if there is any hope of a relationship with Drew or if she's stuck in buddy-status for life.

Last of the Gentlemen:

Despite the hardships she's faced, Emma Turner is determined to make a good life for her three children. Working nights and struggling through life doesn't leave much time for romance, which is just fine as far as Emma is concerned. But when her son's good-looking lacrosse coach takes an interest in her children, Emma has to fight off the smolder in her stomach and banish her daydreams. This schoolgirl crush needs to end before she embarrasses her son and herself. If only she could tell that to her heart.

My Best Man's Wedding:

Jessica Porter made a vow to marry her best guy friend, Josh, when they turned thirty. When Josh calls with the news that he's coming home to Echo Ridge for his wedding, Jessica is determined to break up the happy couple and take her rightful place as his bride. Gentry Trine, a coworker, agrees to pretend to be her fiancé to stir up feelings of jealousy. However, Jessica didn't realize fake fiancés could kiss like champions, and make a girl smile nonstop. Can she figure out which is the right man for her before she loses them both?

Change of Plans:

Kaitlyn knows who she's destined to spend her life with, until superstar Axel Olsen turns her dreams upside down.

Kaitlyn Johanson is chosen by heartthrob, nationally-acclaimed lacrosse player, Axel Olsen, for a dream date. She didn't know a man touching her hand could feel like heaven, but she awkwardly blacks out then admits to him that she's in a relationship.

Kaitlyn comes home to Echo Ridge hoping to rekindle her relationship with her high school boyfriend, Mason. She never expects Axel to show up in her hometown, hosting a lacrosse camp with Mason and his stepdad.

When Axel steals her attention and possibly her heart from the man she is supposed to marry, she has to decide if she'll take a risk on new love or give old love a second chance.

Counterfeit Date:

Mason Turner only has eyes for Lolly Honeymiller. She's vivacious and hilarious and unfortunately thinks of him as her best friend's ex. Lolly's friends cook up a scheme: pretending Lolly is making him over for a special date with his dream girl. The more time he and Lolly spend together, the harder it is to keep his feelings a secret.

Lolly offers to help Mason Turner prepare for a date with his dream girl. Through makeovers, shopping, and practice kissing, she tries to keep her distance but finds herself falling for a man she can never have. As the date approaches, both wonder if they can keep things fake or if the farce will implode and shred both of their hearts.

Download your free copy here.